A TIME TO CELEBRATE ~ Book Review

I couldn't put this book down! It is more than a book … it's a
rescue story … it's a survival manual … it's a road to find life and
healing. Spiritual truth is written throughout this captivating
novel. You will see yourself in some facet of this story through
Cindy Wilson's unique writing style. This talented author
captures reality in a way that is more like painting a masterpiece
of God's redemption story in full and living color. We all find
ourselves in places we never would have expected, desired,
or thought were possible. Cindy Wilson uses scripture and a
powerful plot in a way that shows He can take any situation
and turn it into His glory. He alone can transform broken lives
and put the pieces back together in a way that will show the
perfection and beauty of God's unfailing love and His unending
mercy and grace. Many lives will experience transformation as
they embrace the faith found in *A Time to Celebrate*."

Brenda Peitzman
www.sanctuaryrevival.com

A Time
To Celebrate

Cindy Jean Wilson

WestBow
PRESS
A DIVISION OF THOMAS NELSON

WestBow Press books may be ordered through booksellers or by contacting:

WestBow Press
A Division of Thomas Nelson
1663 Liberty Drive
Bloomington, IN 47403
www.westbowpress.com
1-(866) 928-1240

This is a work of fiction. Names, characters, places, and incidents are products of the author's imagination or are used fictitiously.

ISBN: 978-1-4497-5306-1 (sc)
ISBN: 978-1-4497-5305-4 (hc)
ISBN: 978-1-4497-5307-8 (e)

Library of Congress Control Number: 2012909171

Printed in the United States of America

WestBow Press rev. date: 05/29/2012

Charming Jake and dependable Lisa want to inspire;
but in a shocking twist, they lose precious Angela
and experience unimaginable heartbreak—
before sovereign circumstances transform
their willing hearts into a lighthouse of hope.

Contents

Acknowledgments

To my wise and kind husband, Doug, who believed I was capable of completing a second intriguing story ~ and offered countless hours of help with my chores, in addition to tasty meals when I worked late many evenings;

To cherished friends and family who interceded on my behalf as I painted another novel with words;

To treasured mentors for inspiring me with godly insight that I might have missed without their input (and couldn't keep to myself) including Charles Stanley, Paul Bawden, Dave Tooker, Vic Ransom, Andy Richardson, and others;

To Brenda Peitzman, Belinda Dunn, Susie Shock, and Julie Webb Kelley who offered creative ideas and support as I raced toward the finish line;

To several delightful authors who encouraged me to continue writing when everything inside me shouted, "Quit!"

Thank you from the bottom of my heart!

Chapter 1

Celebration

WHILE FILMING A NEWS promo about sky diving for KMOL TV-Albuquerque, charming reporter Jake Clark could hardly resist the obvious temptation. He fiddled with his tawny hair and scratched his forehead as they waited. Equipment was set up, cameras were in place ... yet all attention diverted to the celebrity jumper abruptly lured to the side of a hangar by an emergency phone call. A frown on the renowned star's face, his brows peaked at attention, and increasingly dejected posture indicated the conversation was grave. "No go!" he finally yelled to the pilot.

In a split second the gig was over.

Murmurings among crewmembers broke the hushed atmosphere as someone uttered a string of profanity. A cameraman reeled back in disgust.

"Wait guys! I can do this segment myself, the whole megillah. Anybody bring a battery powered microphone?" Jake asked confidently. His face beamed with excitement looking at Joe Garcia, an experienced production manager for the station.

"What do we have to lose?" Joe said in a matter of seconds. "We've already wasted time and money out here for a non-event."

Sizzling New Mexico sun beat down while the enthusiastic fledgling reporter struggled to buckle a slippery parachute firmly around his lean abdomen. Trying to convince his boss to consider new options was becoming an increasingly fun challenge. *Wonder what Lisa will think?*

"Sure you know what you're doing?" Joe asked, his dark eyes flinching.

Jake winked.

"Been up several times," he said. This was the plane his father flew on occasion. No big deal. Jake had even maneuvered the controls once. Getting a pilot's license would be next on his bucket list.

Circles up to ten thousand feet took a matter of minutes. The thrill increased with the altitude. Anything good involves risk.

His fiancée would be amused at his bravery.

Just before the Cessna 182 came into full view, with cameras ready to roll, Joe squinted. Perhaps he was a bit uneasy about his decision. A shadow emerged from the open door, dropping through the sky in an initial free-fall, a few hundred feet in mere seconds. Jake stretched his arm trying to grab something—surely not to wave. With hushed breath, station co-workers watched his chute tangle.

Gasps of disbelief followed.

The film crew rushed frantically to the brush-covered edge of the airport where the self-confident jumper lay unconscious. When they reached his side, he miraculously started breathing. He rolled over and opened his eyes.

"Hope you got that on camera!" Jake said groggily.

"Next time," Joe said with a smirk.

Jake grimaced as the shiny rescue drove up, sirens blaring. "Maybe this wasn't a good day to learn how to jump," he said. Several were ready to strangle him with the twisted cords—once medics untangled his parachute—including Joe who was fuming under his breath.

"Can someone grab my water bottle when you pack up? And don't forget my favorite Yankees cap," was Jake's final request before being hauled off with the trail of a siren echoing behind.

At the hospital, Lisa scowled seeing her fiancé bandaged and ready to go home. "How did this happen?" she asked. "Thought you were filming a special report at the airport? You're a journalist, Jake, not the object of breaking news!" she ranted without taking a breath. "Will you be more careful in the future? How can we inspire the world if you're dead?"

Though she never knew what to expect from him, one thing was certain: Jake was always up to something.

* * *

Voted most popular in his senior class at Apache High School, Jacob Theodore Clark had dated cheerleaders, all-star athletes, and most of the cute chicks. "Accepting *this award* in no way means I have eyes for anyone but you," he said—smiling at his current flame, at a school party after the awards ceremony.

Everyone laughed.

The lead in numerous plays cozied up to actresses and musicians. Life was one continual party. Impulsive, with few cares in the world, his assistance to anyone in need provided an endless supply of pleasure. "Eat, drink, and be merry!" was his mantra.

No day excluded affectionate interactions with his adoring classmates. "We love you!" they shouted in unison, as the charmer walked across the stage to receive his diploma. Dried-but-still-gorgeous corsages, ticket stubs, signed programs and score cards, joined other heartfelt gifts in memory boxes to be treasured forever.

"Save your heart for me, Jake," one friend wrote in his yearbook.

"Yeah, sure," he said.

The bumper sticker on his prized Honda read: *God made girls...for guys to enjoy!*

Following graduation from high school, Jake took off alone for a weeklong trek to establish his independence. Similar adventures added intrigue during the remaining summer months. His Honda finally breathed its last breath while climbing a steep pass through the Sierras. "There'll be other females to take your place," Jake said sadly, climbing into a stranger's truck. Within a week, he showed off in a shiny red Camaro before beginning Journalism classes at the University of Arizona.

The summer before his senior year in college at the U of A, an internship of a lifetime became reality. "I'm an intern for KMOL," Jake shouted, rushing through the door of his parents' home. "My dream is coming true!" In between bites of dinner he discussed responsibilities to gather and report news, the professional wardrobe he needed to procure—for visibility in front of cameras—and the pay he would receive someday as an experienced journalist.

"Wealth will grow wings and fly from you," his father warned. "Don't fix your eyes on it, or cater to it. Be rich on the inside, Jake. Nobody can take that away from you."

"You'll do great," his mother agreed.

His first day on the set at KMOL TV-Albuquerque as an intern had been chaotic, with adrenalin bursting from his scalp to his toes. Jake tapped his foot waiting for station manager, Mike Hintz, to finish a phone call and show him around. Watching live action at a TV station increased his desire to be involved in this business of reporting news.

"Sorry for the interruption," Mike said.

Brianna Smyth flashed a big smile and welcomed Jake before running off to follow a story. Most of the morning was spent with anchor Paul Esse who explained usual tasks, did research, and showed him the news desk. Enlightened with tips of the trade, Jake went on a shoot with Paul and cameraman Hector Lopez. The van was abuzz with the breaking news of a solar-powered aircraft attempting to set a record for the unmanned flight.

By Friday, he had a handle on news reporting.

Jake casually locked his car and strolled across the parking lot—deep in thought about going out with Brianna to do a story on a hot movie being shot in the area. He smiled at a female getting out of her car. Then he glanced again.

It couldn't be.

"Lisa? ... Lisa Stewart?"

As a child, Lisa lived next door to the Clark Family on Brookshire Lane. She played hide-n-seek numerous times with Jake. Older and wiser, she offered tidbits of insight into life—always with a cute smile. He was taken with her maturity; three years seemed monumental. Stealing kisses from her became his pastime.

If only his sister Abby had left them alone.

At first, Jake didn't mind a younger sibling trailing his moves; but during adolescence it turned into more scrutiny than he wanted. It was one thing to escape the watchful eye of your mother but Abby's interrogation escalated during his teenage years. She seemed suspicious. Connecting her with his friends was the only answer. With little sis distracted, he pursued more personal interests.

Watching Lisa walk through the KMOL parking lot, Jake's fascination with her incredible figure intensified. "Wow! Oh, Jesus … Thank you," he said. "I've always been in love with this girl." He hurried over to talk. Years of separation deepened the childhood infatuation into mutually strong feelings.

"Do you remember trying to kiss me through the fence?" Lisa asked.

"No, I was too little." He chuckled, knowing it was true; that wasn't the first affectionate gesture he made back then.

"Your sister told me you were determined to win all the girls' hearts," Lisa said.

"Well, there's only one female that matters now." He proceeded to kiss the top of her chestnut locks, her forehead, and her nose. Lisa giggled. "I don't see a future with either Brenda or Hilary," he said, sealing his fate in her heart. "I'm certain you're the one for me."

Lisa provided dependability and stability.

Jake amused with his wit.

In front of college friends, the fall of his senior year, he bent on one knee and handed her a little blue box. "You can't be serious," she said blushing. Then Lisa whispered in his ear, "Why are you doing this—with them here? Is this why you wanted me to come to Arizona?"

Ignoring his girlfriend's uncomfortable predicament and cry for privacy, he insisted she open it. Her breath quickened and her hands shook as she peeked inside the Tiffany box. A scream pierced the air when a fat bug popped out and slid down her black sleeveless tank top.

"Jacob!"

He fell on the ground laughing so hard his face turned red. Embarrassed, Lisa smiled at the crowd watching his antics, then laughed when he tickled her slender body. "Just wanna have a little fun with you," he said, pulling her down on top of him. Her long designer skirt barely covered her legs and one of her delicately strapped sandals left a mark on his khaki Dockers. Jake didn't seem to care.

"If you weren't so much fun, I'd have nothing to do with you," she said under her breath.

The next visit proved more worthwhile for the blossoming relationship with two meaningful talks under the moonlight during an event filled weekend. Jake impressed with his charming personality, captivating her attention and filling Lisa with joy.

Christmas together back in Albuquerque was even better. Looking adorable in an emerald sweater with jeans, he couldn't take his eyes off her. Her brown eyes glistened in the festive candlelight while colorful blinking lights mesmerized the couple.

Waiting for her parents to return home on Christmas Eve, Jake pulled a gift from under Lisa's tree. "Do you think it would matter if you opened this now?"

"Not until everyone gets here," she said.

"Why not?" he asked. "You prefer private moments with me. You might even want to wear this tonight. It's your favorite color."

Convinced Jake was being sincere, Lisa pushed red and green tissue paper aside and pulled a journal from the bottom of the bag. "You prankster!" She shrugged and then opened it. The inside was cut out, and a diamond ring sparkled from the middle.

Jake held his hands together like he was begging. "Please, Lisa. Will you marry me?" His blue eyes looked deep into hers as he waited for a reply.

He winked.

"You stole my heart years ago," she finally said. "If you promise to take care of it forever—yes, I'll marry you." He hugged her affectionately and they were still kissing when the Stewart family arrived home.

"Look what Jake gave me," Lisa said, beaming as she flashed the dazzling ring on her finger. Sparkling diamonds covered the band with a brilliant carat mount surrounded by smaller jewels on top. "Even though he's still up to his old tricks, I decided to marry him."

After their hearty congratulations died down and presents were opened, Jake pulled her aside and reached for his phone. "We need to make arrangements with the *all-time-best-party-planner* to welcome you into my family over the holidays."

Hearing the wonderful news delighted his parents, Holly and Adam Clark.

"I think you've made a good choice," his father said. "Lisa is lovely and dependable. She'll make a great wife."

Friends and relatives recounted similar experiences with the couple. Jake provided gusto with his fun-loving ways, usually offering warmth and encouragement, but Lisa could be counted on to provide insight and stability.

"We want to make a difference in this world," Jake announced at their engagement party. Lisa agreed wholeheartedly. Being together forever was certainly proof of providence at work.

The "fireworks" cake was a hit with sparklers singeing Jake's hand when he sliced a piece, popping the balloon hidden inside. Laughter from friends muffled his response but he seemed to enjoy the surprise. "Life is starting off with a bang for you two lovebirds," Peter Johnson said, happy for his best friend Jake.

Together Jake and Lisa were like a huge stadium with enough electricity to light up the entire town.

*   *   *

Reconnecting with former neighbors was fun for both families.

Lisa's brother Jason, his wife Brenda, and daughters Christie (5) and Chelsea (2) came with Pete and Mary Stewart to a cookout at the Clark Ranch. Jake's parents were caring hosts who exuded warmth and sincerity. "We've been changed from the inside out," Adam explained while grilling scrumptious ingredients for fajitas. "Didn't realize it's been so long since we moved here. We'll give you a fly-by of our property when we finish eating."

"Pete's job evolved from setting up computer programming to being an IT and fixing problems. I'm still just a librarian," Mary said glumly. She glimpsed the laughing lovebirds. "It's hard to imagine Jake turning into such a fine young man after all those pranks."

"Well, your firstborn's transformed from a cute little dolly into one of the most beautiful creatures! There's no one on earth like her. She exudes qualities of femininity that guys search for in their quest for companionship. Fortunately the wolves didn't eat her alive before I found her down at the station," Jake said, as everyone laughed. "God protected her for me."

"You're the best guy I've met," Lisa said quietly.

"What about me?" Jason asked.

"There's something different about your whole family," Mary said. "Must be the fresh air out here." The former neighbors bonded closer than ever, sharing theories about life and communicating beyond their usual superficial level of conversation.

Watching baby sheep jump in the field—playful as friends—was the highlight of the evening. Christie and Chelsea chased them until they were out of breath. "Would you like to hold one?" Adam asked. Munching corn out of tiny hands was a great reward for the lambs.

Lisa climbed on Jake's back for a ride back to the jeep. They ended up taking the long way around the darkened red barn—arriving a bit later than the rest. Stars twinkled in the glorious indigo sky, winking to light a pathway for two lonely souls longing to find a purpose in the dark world.

An unexpected call from Tina Parker surprised Jake while brushing his teeth later that week. "I think about you night and day, Sweet Baby," she whispered. "Are you absolutely positive this Lisa's the right girl for you?" He was at a loss for words. When he didn't answer, she continued. "How often do you think about me?"

He rubbed his chin and cleared his throat. "Tina, you dumped me for a South American soccer player. What happened to him?"

"He doesn't compare to you, Jake … No one tempts me like you do! Think about all our climbs through the gorge, all the waves we've caught, each sunrise we watched together at the edge of the canyon. The time we fell asleep on the dock while we were fishing—what you promised during that night made me feel so special. Did you mean it? Give me another chance to prove my love. I miss you, Tarzan."

After hanging up, the sick feeling in his gut lingered but he decided to let her go for good. Valentine stickers on his car window early the next morning convinced him it wasn't her final attempt.

Time would tell.

An extravagant dinner at the Melting Pot captivated Lisa with surprisingly deep conversation and unexpected romantic gestures.

The atmosphere was bathed in rich candlelight; melodious Hungarian ballads hummed in the background. Platters of tasty morsels bent on appealing to hungry patrons filled the menu. Choices were difficult. Good thing Jake was impulsive. Aromatic creations were then delicately dipped in oil before touching lips, causing her sensations to explode with desire. In the corner a couple kissed recklessly, oblivious to other guests dining nearby.

Strong legs stretched under the table right beside hers; his hand reached for a napkin on his lap, brushing past her thigh tentatively. "You mean the world to me, darling. I'm lucky to finally have you in my life."

Lisa sighed.

"Your eyes sparkle in the candlelight," she said.

"If you only knew the burning passion fueling them, I could do a hundred flips; I'm so in love with you."

"It'll be wonderful when we're married."

Again, his eyes roved to the peach shirt gently clinging to her ample chest. His fingers pressed more firmly against her thigh, turning his body as he spoke. She longed to touch him but that would appear inappropriate. Nice girls don't.

"You're wearing my ring. We're soul mates. What more could convince you of my love?"

"Can we go to the car?" she whispered … glancing around shyly.

"Sure."

They left the mystique of romance in *The Melting Pot*, eager for greener fields of destiny. Jake hurriedly opened the door. "Never thought you'd ask," he said, settling in for some sugar. Flickers of moonlight peeked in the windows. Her tresses of burnished chestnut smelled like tropical coconut. "Ummm, mama!!! Good enough to eat."

"I'm not dessert!"

"That's what you think." The scent of chocolate on her breath was heavenly! He caressed her face, then her neck.

She trembled.

Her pulse quickened as his hand moved slowly down her shoulder, teasing for a minute. His right hand pulled at her waist. "Can I have this dance, my love?" He pulled her tighter. His lips pressed hers softly.

"We need to go slower."

"I'll never brag about you like other guys."

"Jake, that's not what I meant."

"I'm not asking you to part with your purity. You've no idea where other girls have tried to take me—but finally I've found someone to passionately connect with on the deepest level possible. I've waited since childhood to have you sit on my lap, Lise: for trysts on the beach, moments of delight, and chilly evenings in front of a fire."

For a brief instance it felt so tantalizing she forgot. Lisa immersed herself in his embrace, his warm hands pulsating on her body, his fingers dancing along her skin.

She reached for his hand, intent to keep her treasure locked until August.

"Listen to the music of my soul."

"Daddy always said to sign a contract before giving goods away. Why buy a cow if the milk is free?"

"Please run away with me," Jake begged.

"What about our families?"

"Who cares about them? We have each other."

"You're so impulsive, Jake. What about being a reporter for KMOL? How will we explain this to our parents, family, and friends? Traditions are important. We need pictures, wedding cake, and napkins to mark the date."

"We'll stop at Target."

Lisa straightened her clothes as she readjusted herself in the seat. "You naughty boy! Look what you do to me."

"And I was so close to victory! You can't punish me more than that."

He started the ignition, deciding to restrain himself—for this night, anyway.

*   *   *

Jake's mother arranged a special lunch for Lisa's birthday, on July 30, at *Grounds for Celebration*. A creatively wrapped surprise inside rainbow foil, with wisps of glittery ribbon, waited on the table. Munching cranberry chicken salads, the two females re-established their friendship with delightful conversation. Following tantalizing snickers cheesecake slices, Holly handed the present to her soon-to-be-daughter. Tucked inside the foil was a burgundy leather Bible imprinted with ... Lisa Stewart Clark. "This is to celebrate your life, Lisa."

"Oooohh! Thank you so much, Mrs. Clark."

"Did you know scripture is a love letter written to you by God Himself? It's fresh and new every morning. I hope you enjoy reading it."

"You've made my birthday so happy," Lisa answered. "Jake's lucky to have you for a mother." She glanced at her watch and clutched the gift. "I need to get back to the station. Thanks again." They hugged before parting.

Only God knew what the future would hold but both said private prayers.

Wedding planning took precedence as Lisa tried to accommodate Jake's list of friends joining treasured family members in a joyful celebration. Each day he added more.

"This is the last one, I promise," he kept saying sweetly.

The big day approached as she scrambled to get ready. August 21st was earlier than wise planners recommended; but Jake refused to wait until later in the fall or winter.

"Why am I relegated to live on the edge with tension while you de-stress while golfing and hiking trails looking for adventure? Help me," she begged.

"Program administrators don't need help," he said. "I'm the guy who shows up in a tuxedo and dances. Hold on, Lise! I'm going to turn your world into a fairytale."

Chasing breaking news stories—with thrilling jaunts and action galore in front of cameras—was right up Jake's alley. Lucky for this lovable guy who ignored problems, doom and gloom would surely come but he would now have a soul mate by his side to guard him.

Sunshine streamed through the Honda Pilot windshield as Adam raced toward Grace Fellowship Church where his only son Jake and former neighbor Lisa would soon be married. "Get us to the church on time ... ," he crooned in his dreamy baritone voice. Holly smiled, fiddling with her hair for the tenth time.

"You look awesome, Sugarplum, and the pictures will be delightful!"

"Here we are in a new chapter of our lives," she said. "Are you ready?"

The next hour was a blur of excitement.

"Oh, by the way, bro … ," Abby teased, passing Jake in the hall. "Tina Parker called and says she misses you dreadfully. Does Lisa know about her yet?"

"I'll get you back."

Members of the wedding party rushed to finish dressing while guests poured into the increasingly crowded foyer, eager to witness one of the most talked about ceremonies for months. The stunning stained glass windows in the lobby captured many eyes, and conversations, sunshine radiating through the rich hues with extraordinary delight. A welcoming tapestry on the wall extended hope for those who read the motto.

Soon everyone was in their proper place.

Holly nudged Adam who hummed with the background music.

When Jake's best man Peter Johnson escorted sister Abby down the aisle, she giggled and almost tripped. She clutched his arm tighter.

"You still like him, don't you?" Jake whispered when Abby reached the front.

She blushed.

Ivory candles scattered around the sanctuary created a dreamy atmosphere. Sapphire accents sparkled brighter than stars. Lisa's ivory lace gown softly draped her body like a filigree snowflake; her porcelain face was translucent next to dark tresses, held back with a diamond tiara. A bouquet of rainbow roses complemented multi-colored bridesmaid dresses.

"You're so beautiful to me … ," played in the background.

"The vows you promise aren't meant to entertain, Jacob and Lisa, but to remind you how precious marriage really is," Phil Davis said. "Remember that God is listening. Make this relationship your priority. Every day, for the rest of your life, give your spouse a reason to stay married to you—and let these moments carry you thru difficulties and challenges life will throw your way."

Lisa's face glistened as her betrothed pledged his love. She listened intently. Her fiancé's presence always made people pay attention. Hand in hand, the radiant couple exchanged rings. A small note rested on the table where a white unity candle observed the solemn proceedings. After lighting the wick together, Jake reached over and offered it to Lisa, whispering in her ear.

She smiled, tucking it in her bouquet of multi-colored daisies.

Following three dramatic kisses, the couple turned to face guests and the minister said, "May I present the newest husband and wife, Mr. and Mrs. Jacob Theodore Clark." Cheers arose as they walked briskly off the platform. Jake suddenly stopped, sitting on the steps with a smile. He waited; then pointed. Lisa pulled the note and quietly read—as Jake motioned for his wedding party to join them.

The crowd watched eagerly.

"I have only one thing to say," he said. "Let the party begin!" Nods, winks, and laughter followed.

An unexpected compliment for Lisa began the reception festivities, no surprise as friends and family looked over to see Jake holding a microphone.

"To understand and be understood—that is my goal! The finest possessions are worthless without sweet relationships. My adorable wife has been a vital asset in my life for as long as I can remember." He elaborated on their childhood years as neighbors and then co-workers at the TV station, offering bits of information that made Lisa blush. She was obviously in love with a fun-loving guy who enjoyed sharing detailed news-worthy highlights.

Throwing the bouquet over her shoulder involved a traditional pose just for the camera. As soon as flashes ceased, Lisa twisted and lobed it to Abby ... as her husband suggested.

"Hooray!!!" the crowd yelled in surprise.

Moments later, cameras were ready to continue.

Slipping a lacy garter off her thigh, Jake's hand strayed higher. Lisa stepped back almost falling. Laughter filled the room. After catching his bride mid-air, he again reached for her leg. This time he pulled a dainty gold bracelet with engraved heart from his pocket and clasped it around her ankle. The guests cheered, prompting Jake to bend down and pretend to kiss her foot.

Lisa chuckled.

"Our son usually shows good common sense," his father said, finally getting a chance to talk. "We're especially happy with his choice for a wife. Welcome to our family, Honey."

Words of encouragement from other relatives, friends, and co-workers followed.

Peter Johnson divulged humorous clips about Jake's childhood and encouraged Lisa to forgive and forget as much as she could. "You're going to Disneyland every day with Superman. That will make the tough stuff more enjoyable."

A closing prayer from the minister preceded cutting the cake.

"May this marriage be filled with joyful surprises and tears that deepen and enrich your character as the years pass. My prayer is that you both will praise God on your golden wedding anniversary because of a meaningful journey together."

"We're going to make a difference in this dark world," Jake promised.

"If a miracle will convince people, why not be one?" Adam challenged them.

An elaborate honeymoon to Namibia, a hidden jewel off the beaten path in South Africa was fortunately private. Adventure began where the road ended. Lisa had Jake's exclusive attention—until he bantered with natives about gossip that fascinated him. A dozen ethnic groups including nomads intermingled. One toothless elderly sage spoke loud in a language no one understood. A small boy sitting on the sand stirred it with a twig.

Weather was a major topic of conversation.

Intense sun caused Himba Tribe women to cover skin with protective cream made from ash, animal fat, herbs and ochre causing their bodies to glow. One afternoon, Jake pretended to rub sap on Lisa's face while she slept. She woke in a panic. "Think how beautiful you'll be when we get back home," he teased.

She didn't appreciate his joke.

The skeleton coast provided views of hundreds of shipwrecks with an odor to match the debris. An ever changing air system produced harsh conditions that impacted many pirates' destinies. Captains of ships never knew where they were along the rocky shoreline and ran aground. Jake was fascinated. Whalebones, carcasses, and mummified remains reeked where the wilderness safari guide demanded they stop for a picnic lunch.

"Phew! Let's get out of here," Lisa said.

Sibiu had another plan. He ordered food for the trio.

"Imagine rebuilding your life piece by piece," Jake said, as they choked down dry bread, beef jerky and withered vegetables—or whatever the items consisted of. "What a diet those pirates had."

A festival brightened their mood considerably when natives danced down sand dunes in ethnic costume. A young lady with skinny limbs pulled Jake into the circle and the astute guide wrapped his arms around Lisa, chanting in her ear. Partners changed as they moved in different directions but Sibiu stayed attentive to Lisa.

She could no longer see Jake and became miserable—with heat and stench growing—and wished the drums would stop and swaying would end. Lisa fumbled her steps and sat down, insisting she was too tired to continue.

Her escort went for a drink.

By the time he returned, almost everyone had dispersed including Jake. "Your man eating in hut," Sibiu explained. "He skis on dunes when finished."

To avoid more time with an unwanted admirer, Lisa was eager to join her husband.

Sand skiing captivated Jake. "It's much easier than snow!" he said, shooting down like a demon. "A little dance to shake the sand off and you go back up for another thrill ride. Come on, Lise."

"This sand is from hades," Lisa said, increasingly disgusted with the new outdoor sport.

Swallowing a mouthful of sand after falling a third time convinced her to discontinue the strange diversion. She observed from a hammock underneath a primitive stall, with burlap pulled back over poles, as Jake perfected his skills. Sipping a reddish concoction with a hint of berry soothed her dry throat.

Sibiu watched from a distance.

"Intricate braids are woven in hair of females—before bathing in smoke over herbs" Jake informed his bride at dinner. "I'm going to have a local woman set you up for this cleansing ritual tonight, unless you'd rather splash in the crocodile infested water to get clean."

"None of that is going to happen," Lisa said with animation, emphatically shaking her head. "Tourists from everywhere come to glimpse the sun going down. Can we just watch a beautiful sunset and go to sleep early? It's been a long day."

Jake obliged reluctantly.

Lisa was intrigued by exotic animals and mesmerized by her husband's desire for thrills. Lush rivers, despite elusive rain, were influenced by mist and dew ... somehow protecting endangered species. A zebra drank from the edge. Elephant rides, trips down snake-infested rivers on a raft, and hunting game from a makeshift tower were secondary to sleeping in the 50 foot high tree house where glowing eyes lit up the surrounding landscape.

Monkeys jumped on chairs as they dined.

Walking over a swinging bridge to the rustic outdoor bathroom— sometimes in the middle of the night with eerie caws, yowls, and scratching noises—provided more excitement than Lisa enjoyed.

Souvenirs included an ivory necklace, shrunken-head doll, and authentic drum. Jake purchased a safari hat for his father and a colorful picture made from interesting seeds for his mother.

A rare sighting of a baby elephant on the way to the airport was a highlight.

Returning home where friends eagerly waited to hear the adventurous report, Jake continued celebrating. "You should have seen her eyes that first night," he said smiling. "Never knew Lisa could scream that loud—when the crazy pole fell down. Almost made me deaf! I still have scars on my arm from her fingernails."

"And God knows she would never have been sitting on my lap in the boat, if it wasn't for that crocodile." He bragged how his work as a loving spouse began in earnest trying to calm and comfort his beautiful wife. His friends laughed hilariously.

Lisa tried unsuccessfully to tell her side of the story.

Back at the station, rumors flew as different accounts of the vacation surfaced. *A favorite journalist has much to say about life while reporting. Few hold him responsible for speaking the truth when he shares interesting personal tidbits now and then,* the local paper reported.

Fellow newscasters and commentators reiterated the current findings, giving their own personal slant. His charm kept viewers coming back for more. But at night, there were disturbing comments and questions Jake refused to answer.

"We need privacy in our lives, Jake. You can't reveal everything! I suppose you wouldn't have a problem revealing intimate details about our bedroom—if someone should be curious. We have an agreement about workplace information. Keep your word."

"Chill out, sweetie. You're putting too much attention on trivial issues. Focus on what's essential."

"You're missing the point. Maybe I should find another place to work," Lisa said.

"Better get to work sorting through this stuff we both dragged in. Maybe we should have left it with our mothers for safekeeping."

He looked suspiciously at the growing heap of discards, mostly his belongings. "Where in the world are you gonna put that?" He picked up her prized Thanksgiving turkey, spiffy in a colorful tuxedo with rainbow feathers sticking out. "Looks like he needs a haircut."

"Gobble will entertain from the foyer every Thanksgiving."

"Do you have an Easter Bunny?"

"I have something better!" She had a basket of them, he discovered later. Her cherished possessions provided some sort of soothing balm for her nesting. He understood some had emotional baggage but others were worthless. He could help her detach from priceless heirlooms and discover the world of interesting people.

"You are absolutely not keeping that sign!" Lisa said—pointing to a '*Guys, just kiss the girls*' poster from Jake's bedroom. "How long have you had that?"

"Some of your competitors seemed to enjoy it."

"It's childish. You should have thrown that out in middle school."

"You're the immature one, Lisa. You keep harping at me like I'm doing something wrong while I'm involved with real folks just trying to have a good time. Why do you think I have so many friends?"

"Because you want them to do your chores. Abby told me you got your best friends to do homework for you. You're self-indulgent, Jake."

"Why not indulge me with a nice juicy steak? I'm starving."

* * *

Being happily married became a challenging venture for this extravert husband and his accommodating wife—but that secret was zealously guarded. "A necessity in our business," Jake said. "We impact people wherever we go."

Blowing a kiss her way before beginning newscasts continued with regularity but no longer conveyed his former passion. It was just a formality. Sometimes Lisa was nowhere in sight.

"Ready to go, Babe?" he said, hurrying past her door before rushing down the hall after a new intern. Twenty minutes later he finished a private and in-depth debriefing, upbeat and smiling. "You're finally ready? What took so long, Lise?"

"You seem to be in a bad mood," he said flipping stations on the drive home. The music blocked her response. He slapped her knee. "Oh, well. Guess you have your reasons."

"Take me away to a better place … ," Jake hummed to himself.

Tropical isles with sultry sun-tanned women ready to share secrets were whispering in his ear.

Chapter 2
Cottage Of Hope

FLICKERS OF SUNLIGHT THROUGH beveled-edge windows cast prisms on the kitchen walls. Lisa watched with delight, sipping peppermint tea before Jake woke up. Comfy aloe infused slippers energized the bottom of her feet. It was going to be a glorious day! Judging from the way things were starting, one could only guess how it might end.

"Morning my love," her husband said, coming over to kiss the shimmering chestnut hair. "Still a bit wet from your shower?"

"Guess I should have waited till we finished working in the garden," she said. "Do you want a hearty breakfast before we exert ourselves outside—or eat some oatmeal now and devour a delicious brunch after we complete our chores?"

"You chose. Whatever you want."

"I'm here to please you, Jake."

"Then let's go back to bed."

"Not this morning."

The garden was finished in no time and the happy couple returned to their kitchen to share chef duties.

Relishing final crumbs from their feast, Jake burped. "Sorry."

"Maybe we ate too much. Are we going to celebrate our anniversary this evening?" Lisa asked.

"My chariot will be waiting."

Memories of their wedding ceremony captured her thoughts all afternoon. While she dressed in his favorite yellow sundress, Jake peeked in with a bouquet of flowers he picked from the yard.

"For my darling wife with all my love."

"Awe ... they're beautiful, sweetheart but you probably should have left them growing in the garden. They'll be dead in a couple of days."

"Every good deed doesn't go unpunished."

"I love you, anyway."

"Are you aware how much hostility my house once held?" Jake asked Lisa at dinner. "Emotional conflict, constant bickering, and intense resentment were inhabitants that wouldn't leave. We just pretended to have it together. Following Dad's terrible accident, changes began stirring in our home."

"We're not going to act that way. We know better."

"That's what I love about you most, Lise. Hey, remember my Gram and Gramp Armstrong's 50th anniversary extravaganza last summer? We're all love birds with special events close together. Glad they have a solid relationship. Just a minute, I'm gonna call them."

"Congratulations! We married exactly 50 years apart, Grandpa ... Yes, I know. We just wanted to say hello. Love you, too."

Jake took pride in his ability to meet people easily and build stable friendships. Weekends often resembled a fraternity party. "The perfect opportunity to interact with others—hopefully giving us chances to share our faith," he said boldly.

Somehow he sensed Lisa didn't have similar feelings but he would work on that. Reading magazines was a time waster but he held his tongue.

Occasional barbecues and get-togethers with family, checking out hot restaurants, even hob-knobbing with celebrities offered moments of fun for the couple. Mostly he talked; she laughed.

Jokes filled the awkward silence between fights.

"You've got to see this!" Jake said, rushing inside after finishing trash duties. He grabbed Lisa's hand and pulled her toward the door. Her struggle only made him more insistent.

"Oooohh!"

"Told you so."

Neither could take their eyes off flaming crimson with bursts of peach, tangerine, and ochre shouting from glorious maple, beech, and oaks. Jake put his arm around his wife as leaves danced like a magic carpet on their way to a peaceful siesta on terra firma. Picturesque mountains lay beyond with dreams unimaginable from such a distance. Only as they got closer would they spot mountain goats and wilderness critters surviving in the natural elements.

"We're gonna have an awesome life, Lise. Trust me!"

Before she could answer he darted into the house to fetch his camera. "I have plans when we finish," Jake said.

A ringing phone interrupted the couple entwined on a chair. "Bummer!" Jake said reaching over. Only a minor distraction, before they resumed a rare magical moment.

"Are we going to church tomorrow?" she asked, getting into bed.

"Been a lot going on this week and Monday will be busy ... think I'll just relax. I can't keep putting in fifteen hour days. On second thought, can't miss that game between the Bears and Vikings."

When Lisa returned alone from Grace Fellowship on Sunday, Jake showed her stats for the entire football season. His picks were highlighted.

"Great news!" she said, with a smirk. "Here's something more important." She handed him a pamphlet with scenes, themes, and events for all 13 chapters in Hebrews. "We need to read this by next Sunday for a new sermon series."

"I already know about the Israelites."

She dropped it in his lap. He wadded it up and threw it toward the waste basket.

"I've had it with you," she screamed at the top of her lungs. "Everything's a lark! "I don't mean a thing to you anymore."

"Says who?"

"You ... by your actions. I don't want to be a side show in your circus, Jake"

"I have no comments for clowns right now," he said getting up quickly, before slamming his glass on the kitchen counter. "By the way, stop by makeup in the morning. They can fix you up ... your lipstick smeared."

In the beginning, worshiping together at Grace Fellowship was poignant, a religious high on Sunday mornings. Hundreds of parishioners entered the beautiful lobby to greet acquaintances, inspired by glimpses of heaven through exquisite stained glass windows centered in front of the looming sanctuary—*a modern day Noah's Ark with embellishments minus the animals,* Jake told everyone. Flickers of sunlight hinted of the eternal beauty longing to be seen when days were cloudy.

Responding with enthusiasm during praise time brought mutual joy.

Jake was animated while singing and often during the sermon. "Gets to me, like an arrow in my heart, Lise!"

Wandering thoughts soon captured his attention instead.

Within months, church attendance became a place to interact with other attendees. Jake arrived early to greet the congregation and assist with usher duties when he could fit it in his schedule, usually leaving his wife sitting alone for most of the service.

"Maybe we should have visited the little country chapel down the road before we started coming here," Lisa said.

"Why would we do that?"

"Less people would guarantee closer relationships."

"I'm comfortable where we are."

She didn't know how to put her thoughts into words. There was so much missing. "Standing on a stage performing is not bonding, Jake. You hardly know anybody beyond their name," she said.

"Know what they do. That's important."

"Like a real man ... but what about spiritual things? Is it a sham for everybody? It feels like we're pretending to know God."

"Get on your knees woman," he said joking.

Being in close proximity day and night offered little respite for soft spoken Lisa. *No one would understand her increasing frustration with marriage ideals that seemed a fleeting mirage.* Lisa stayed in her production position at the station until she became pregnant—good timing because their relationship endured intense public scrutiny and her changing physique revealed insecurities no longer able to be hidden.

"Thank heaven for such a peaceful change." She sighed each morning after Jake left for work, drinking peppermint tea on the veranda until the sun heightened. She rearranged chairs, bought purple pillows, and cross stitched a delightful infant design for the nursery.

Home became her refuge.

With a new being growing within her abdomen to focus on, the pressure to present a good image subsided. She could take strolls to a neighborhood park unobserved and spend precious time daydreaming in her yard. Something called to her from outside and she longed to spend time listening and observing.

Working in the garden invigorated Lisa with a passion for living. Cool earth between her fingers, fresh air and sunshine, nature renewing the universe—all celebrated creation. Each tiny change in a plant or whiff of a fragrance gave her reason to smile. She remembered back to childhood when her own mother cherished the serenity and joy of nature. Next door, Jake's mother spent endless hours gardening. "Creating delightful showcases of God's handiwork," Holly said.

Speaking of Him, over a month had passed since they last worshipped together. Morning sickness kept Lisa away initially; other weeks Jake gave convincing reasons why it wouldn't work for him.

"What about this Sunday?" she asked over dinner.

"God isn't a dictator who demands certain behavior," Jake explained. "He loves us just the way we are."

"But I'm starting to feel like a visitor."

A ringing telephone interrupted the conversation.

Preoccupied with staying fit for meeting occasional dignitaries, many evenings excluded spending time with his wife. It didn't appear she wanted to join him anyway. Her body was changing dramatically and his attempts to help better her image were usually rejected.

"You never have time for me anymore," Lisa complained.

"Just can't give it tonight. We can talk later," he said, attempting to deepen the relationship before falling asleep.

*　　*　　*

The beautiful stained glass windows, and homey *Welcome Friends* tapestry on the wall, beckoned when Jake and Lisa entered Grace Fellowship. "Glad to see you, neighbor," Pastor Davis said. "We've missed you."

Hearing him speak was good for their souls.

"God knows what His plan is; give Him time to reveal it. He's busy putting details in place. Is 64:4 says, *For since the world began, no ear has heard, and no eye has seen a God like you, who works for those who wait for him! (NLT)* You'll be surprised at what you miss rushing ahead of Him, maybe fouling up His intended joy for your life. Things might end in ashes, my friend, not what they could have been."

Driving home from church, Lisa had questions. "Is having a desire sinful?"

"Nope! Remember what you showed me last month in Psalm 37:4? God tells us to delight Him and we'll receive the desires of our heart. He'll withhold nothing from us."

"But He wants to make us the kind of person He intends for us to be."

"Can something be both a need and desire?"

"I suppose," she said.

"Then I need to have my desires met this afternoon before the football game."

"What about my need to plan a great Thanksgiving?"

"The holidays are just around the corner!" Holly said, in a conversation with Lisa that evening. "Do you have plans yet?" She invited them over for turkey dinner with all the trimmings. "You don't need to bring a thing, sweetie, except your handsome husband."

"Thanks for the invite. I'm sure we can make it."

Lisa was preoccupied preparing for a baby anyway. An extravaganza at her in-laws was a delightful way to celebrate.

"Some of our friends think we should take pictures together since I might not make it until Christmas," Lisa said. She pulled in her tummy.

"Our first grandchild will be the new focal point for our family," Holly said. "This is a wonderful time. By January, a precious newborn will be the center of attention in real life!"

"Hurry Jake, you need to be in this picture," Lisa said.

"When you hear the beep, we have five seconds to smile."

Beep.

"Now for just one more," he said.

Laughter filled the room as Jake reset his Minolta …

"Remember that afternoon when Jake's tires screeched in the driveway and he rushed in the back door announcing he was a new reporter for KMOL?" Holly asked Adam. "Abby heard the commotion and walked in the kitchen."

"That's a great graduation present—I'm sure your fiancée is delighted," Holly said, mimicking her daughter.

"So Jake jumped up," Adam said, trying to sound like his son, "Oh no, I forgot to tell Lisa!"

They all had a good laugh.

"Guess I wasn't significant even back then," Lisa said seriously.

"Fine-tuning my responsibilities as a reporter requires diligence," Jake said. "I have no intention being anything but fantastic at this job. As soon as possible, I hope to become the station's top anchor. For the moment, as many shoots as I can manage with Hector Lopez are priorities. Nothing else matters."

"What a difference a few lights make," Adam said.

Wonderful news was reason to celebrate when Jake took over the evening anchor position unexpectedly—adding a significant raise and increased clothing allowance—just in time. Lisa no longer contributed any income and increased financial responsibilities for new baby expenses whittled their meager savings. Only problem for the new father, it would involve considerable time away from home.

"Are you going to tell her?" Lisa overheard a friend ask Jake.

"Not if I can help it," was his reply. Background noise at the restaurant muffled most of the conversation.

Jake chatted nonstop on his cellphone while driving home. "If it's not a friend who needs me, it's someone from the station who requires immediate attention," he muttered to himself between calls.

An icy silence filled the air walking into their home.

Lisa waited 'til bedtime to confront her husband.

"What was that about at the *Serendipity*?" Without waiting for an answer she continued, "More important—you weren't planning to tell me? Your excuses are becoming a game you seem to enjoy. Doesn't your God require honesty, openness, and transparency? Why in the world would anyone keep a secret from his wife on purpose?"

Her mind conjured up more options than she cared to acknowledge. "This is a two-way relationship, Jake."

"You can't expect intimate moments when you're doing all the talking."

Lisa had no intention to listen.

She slammed the bathroom door, taking as long as she could to brush her teeth and wash her face, before climbing into bed with a sleeping husband. Fortunately, the comforter created a barrier down the middle.

Jake found a note taped to the front door—before he headed to the station early.

> The value of any promise is based on the character of a person who promised it. Does the person have integrity to keep their word?
> *A word fitly spoken is like apples of gold in settings of silver.*
> Prov. 25:11

Lisa slept late and woke startled. Was that a contraction she felt? The baby surely wouldn't come a month early; they were often born later than the expected due date. She dressed cautiously and decided a bit of nausea was probably the reason. Oatmeal might help.

A note on the kitchen table caught her eye.

> *How painful are honest words! But what do your arguments prove?* Job 6:25 Have a meeting with Brianna Smyth tonight.
> Don't wait up for me!

She attempted to contact Jake but the station said he was out filming. He didn't return calls. She tried again unsuccessfully.

Her uneasiness continued.

Darkening cumulous clouds dimmed the afternoon sunlight. Lisa watched an approaching storm. Streaks of lightning zigzagged through the sky; intense thunder ripped through the neighborhood. Pelting rain increased rapidly from staccato to thuds of marble sized hail. Cloud to ground lightning cast eerie shadows on the walls.

An object hit the side of the house … maybe a bird.

She opened her Bible but an electrical failure prevented reading words of wisdom. Just as well. Jake had no interest in learning the truth. Lighting a candle, she speculated on what happens to restless souls trying to keep the party going. It was frustrating dealing with an immature mate. He was a chameleon—sincere in his intentions to please one minute; then switching back to irresponsibility. His promise to turn over a new leaf was getting boring.

I don't know what to do with this guy.

Jake thrived being around people, especially as the center of attention. His career advancement suited him perfectly. Rushing from hotbeds of breaking news to strategizing with producers left little time for behind-the-scene preps and crew updates. His mind was filled with exciting events and people who tickled his fancy, especially when he trekked around the globe. He seldom remembered Lisa and the need to phone home.

He preferred leaving messages. It was much simpler.

"Only have a second between segments. Just want you to know I'm thinking about you," he said in a new message. Lisa was miles away. Getting embroiled in another discussion about his days on the road wasted precious time. No recourse for his job responsibilities whether she understood or not.

"Ready to take on a harem in Ankara?" his boss asked.

"Is that before or after my trek to Winnipeg?"

With much accomplished during a brief visit to Nairobi, he returned eager to unwind and share on a more personal level with Lisa. Memories of their honeymoon reappeared in his dreams while he was away. A newfound desire to get re-acquainted griped his mind somewhere over the Atlantic.

Magazines were scattered everywhere when he arrived home. Obviously her week had been much different.

"Anybody home?" he called from the front door.

"Hello stranger," she said from the kitchen. "I'm almost finished."

Preoccupied with making dinner, she barely looked up. Jake took her in his arms and planted a kiss on her lips anyway. "I have more to divulge but only if you have time in your life for me."

Colorful tales of Africa unfolded as the couple ate. Two stuffed toy monkeys watched from their home on a chair—a present for an unborn baby.

"Do you remember our first night under the stars on that safari?" Lisa asked.

Laughter mingled with story after story.

"My mom enjoyed the jungle so much; we were transported into the exotic world of an African safari in our family room," Jake said. "The tropical retreat with palm trees, ivory, and wild animals took us to realms unknown while a hand-painted bombé chest, realistic lion, and miniature elephant urged people to touch them."

"I remember," Lisa said. "Her love of nature also greeted guests with colorful wildflowers and shimmering gold in your living room."

"Oh, I forgot to give you something," Jake said, jumping from the chair to grab his bag in the foyer.

"Ivory earrings to match my necklace," Lisa said, paper dropping on the floor. Her eyes misted. "I've been here alone, thinking you didn't care anymore. Was I ever wrong?"

That wasn't the only thing left in the kitchen as they hurried away.

*   *   *

"Get your glam ready, Lise. We have a Chamber of Commerce soirée next week," Jake said.

"I can't! Look how huge I am—nothing fits and I'm certainly in no shape to shop. Besides, paying precious money for something I'll wear only once is a waste. We need to spend our money more wisely."

"You'll be pregnant again."

"True, but who knows what season that'll involve."

"You love these events—it's your chance to connect with people you hardly see anymore."

"Not this year, Jake. Everybody knows I'm having a baby. It won't be a surprise if I'm a no-show." Much as she respected the glamorous aspects Jake's career offered, making a comfortable and happy home life was more imperative right now. Time would be at a premium after the baby arrived. If she shrewdly conserved energy and mastered each day wisely, routines could be established for the whole family to follow eventually. Jake had no idea the effort necessary for Lisa to create a castle where he could relax.

She had essential work to accomplish.

Lisa organized a new peppermint pink nursery with infant necessities while the Chamber soirée delighted debonair businessmen and their attractive wives—who were joyfully involved in civic affairs. There's a season for everything.

Lisa imagined the scenario would probably be boring.

Oblivious to his wife, Jake spent extra time getting to know Mrs. Austin, a college friend of Tina Parker. She and her husband, the former mayor, sat next to Jake. As the lively platinum blonde chatted with her attentive audience of one, her husband droned on about his effectiveness in politics to an older couple on his left. Her emerald satin gown matched her eyes, plunging daringly at the neckline—a heart locket rested on her bare décolleté. She touched it occasionally.

"From a former boyfriend?" Jake asked.

"Hah haaah haaaah," she laughed. "How did you know?"

"The pensive look in your eyes."

"Never know how things might turn out with our choices," she said, brushing back a wisp of hair tumbling from a silver clasp.

"Nice to feel significant to someone."

"I've had several admirers!" Kiki said, leaning over his arm to whisper. "At the moment, it's pretty lonely." Her fragrance was heavenly and the hint of almond in her hair made him want to move closer.

Their hushed conversation ended when the band struck up the first song. "Care to dance?" Jake asked. "Will your husband mind?"

"Nope. He's too busy making a good impression with strangers."

Several hours later, when the music ended and partygoers were leaving, Jake and his new friend said goodbye.

Mr. Austin was still exchanging business cards with soirée attendees.

"Just called to say how nice it was to meet you," Kiki said minutes later on Jake's mobile phone. "If you can help with the Christmas Santa program, we'd love to have you volunteer."

A package waited forlornly on the steps when Lisa returned home from Christmas shopping after her OB appointment on Monday. As she opened a box postmarked from Zimbabwe foam peanuts spilled on the floor. The inner box held a metallic pouch, encasing a cut-glass holder. Resting inside on a red satin pillow lay a sparkling diamond bracelet, "A unique, one-of a-kind gift from DeBeers—for a princess!" the card read.

"That's not the only package, Jake said coming up behind her. There'll be another."

"What's in that one?" Lisa begged to know.

"An oil painting of Victoria Falls," he said—unable to keep the secret. "It was so beautiful; I want to see it again every day. The spray goes in the air a thousand feet and is visible fifty miles away. Sometimes the falls are shrouded in mist. When the moon's full, a *moonbow* replaces the normal rainbow prisms in the spray. Someday we're going back together, Lise, and gonna walk to the bottom of the First Gorge and climb the rocky face. You'll be in awe. The whole thing is twice as high as Niagara Falls."

"Sounds like your trips are more fun than work."

"I was made for this career … By the way, don't wait up tonight. I'll probably be late again," Jake said.

An uneventful afternoon turned into an exciting production for KMOL's favorite evening anchor. Lisa's water had broken. Animated while reading his script, Jake miscued teleprompter lead-ins but no one seemed upset. Ratings would soar for days hearing childbirth news and seeing pictures of his offspring. The world was ready for Baby Clark.

He rushed to the hospital before midnight.

"Amazing!" he said, holding his newborn daughter for the first time. "Did you get photos from several different angles?" he asked a nurse.

Lisa smiled contentedly; relieved the act of birthing was finally over. She sipped some water watching the new daddy meet and greet his sweet little bundle dressed in pink. Tiny fingers grasped Jake's pinkie.

"Awe … a precious princess!" Jake said hugging her tighter.

"She knows how wonderful her father will be," the proud mother said.

Pictures of newborn Angela Marie Clark were broadcast on the early morning news by Paul Esse but Jake was in his own world. "Wonder how they come out with their marvelous body systems intact, plus long lashes to impress the boys," he said to Lisa.

"I'm going to protect you, my precious darling. No one will ever lay a finger on you," he said to Angela.

She captured his heart from their first moment together.

Daddy's Girl became known around the entire viewing audience— and not one day passed without a fascinating comment or new photo.

His statement, "You should have seen this adorable girl try to shake her head *yes*," brought oodles of delight.

Jake's parents rushed over to enjoy grand parenting and were next in line to pour their love on this greatly loved creature. "I can't wait to read you a story," Holly said. She gave Angie kisses, until Adam gently pulled her away. His rich baritone voice sang every children's song he knew before it was time to leave. "Pampa and Mimi will come back tomorrow," Holly said reluctantly leaving.

Lisa was in her own world.

* * *

Tinsel town was shining when Jake pulled up. He grabbed a Santa suit from his trunk and strode to the entry. Kiki Austin met him, giving an overview before showing him a dressing room. "Thanks so much for taking over for Henry. You'll be a more charming Santa. I'll be back in a minute."

Dressed as cute as a button and ready for hundreds of memorable pictures—to be treasured for decades—Jake perched on the chair.

His eyes sparkled.

"Happy holidays, stranger." Peter Johnson said, urging his toddler to climb on Santa's lap. Throngs of shoppers lined up behind them. Didn't matter to the performer; Jake had nothing better to do.

Christmas comes only once a year!

As the last candy cane was handed out, Mrs. Austin approached. "Great job, Jake. You should have heard the comments."

"My gift!"

She gave him a kiss.

After the display lights were turned off, she asked, "Can I sit on your lap Santa?" Jake motioned for her to come. She did.

"Do you have a wish this Christmas?"

"Wish I had more time to reveal details about my lonely life—you're such an encourager." He hugged her. In the midst of twinkling lights, holiday sounds, and excited shoppers, isolated hearts cried out for a connection from somebody who cared.

"Maybe we can chat over coffee tomorrow when we're finished," Jake said.

"I'd like that. Are you gonna tell your wife?"

"She's busy with the baby. I don't want to bother her."

Laughing, they snuggled for a minute before closing up. "Don't be a bad girl, Kiki. I'll have to spank you." He gently patted her behind before she could get away.

"You have so much to offer, Jake. I'm glad I met you."

A lover of people, Jake had a new favorite and she filled his world with joy. He wanted to take Angela everywhere. The tiny girl was photographed in more settings than, *Where's Waldo?* Sometimes his requests were out of line. "A three month old somehow misses most of the intended effects at the zoo," Lisa said.

"Gotta do a segment on babies having fun," he joked.

"I don't see how a seven month old baby can really enjoy a circus."

Before her first birthday, she had seen sights and done things few other children experience. Angie's preferred activity became hiking with her father in an electric blue padded back pack—traipsing around the hilly countryside on rocky trails.

Angie's first year passed quickly.

The Festival of Trees was a perfect place to highlight the family man's cherished wife and daughter. Dressed in a red velvet frock with tiny green holly applique, a shiny red bow in her fluffy golden hair, Angela looked like a Christmas angel. Lisa stood by proudly. This was her daughter's time to embrace the world publicly. Occasional pictures would no longer suffice.

She won new hearts!

Jake wore his Santa suit for a Christmas Eve news report to everyone's delight. A tiny girl wrapped in a stocking was the biggest thrill. Viewers called in overwhelmed—expressing appreciation for his adding such holiday joy.

Presents flooded the mailroom.

"Knew it would be a hit," Jake told his co-workers.

"Maybe I'll dress like an elf next year," Lisa said.

Her time to shine was at the Lion's Club Sweetheart Ball. Dazzling in red satin for the Valentine affair, she openly displayed affection for Jake—happy to be important in his world for a change. He surprised her with a beautiful ruby necklace and earrings, to compliment the broche holding her chestnut curls piled high on her head.

Reaching for her hand all evening made Lisa glow.

"My glamorous wife is my best friend—Stay away guys; she's all mine," he said beginning his speech. "I've traveled the world and found none finer."

"That was sweet," Lisa said later.

"Glad I picked you. Settling down with my sweetheart for a lifetime has finally come true."

Eating chocolate in front of the fireplace at home, Lisa snuggled in his arms. Kisses of another kind waited. He stroked her hair, face, and neck, before reaching to unbutton her shirt. Hungry for extra sugar, the evening turned more enchanting. Jake tenderly catered to his wife.

"Doesn't get more marvelous than this!"

They talked about goals, dreams, and desires long into the night.

Bright sunshine filled the morning.

Laughter between daddy and daughter was contagious. The toddler sprinted after Jake wherever he went; together, they tumbled in the grass. A butterfly intrigued the father/daughter duo temporarily, before they jumped up again ready for another toss of the disc.

Pulling weeds in the garden, Lisa watched.

"Angie's too young to play Frisbee," she insisted.

Happy for the interest Jake took in their daughter, Lisa wanted someone to listen to her concerns. "Nothing you do is for me personally anymore. I feel left out. It's all about Angela." The second pregnancy was difficult and taking care of a toddler zapped her strength. "Either you ignore me purposely or you miss deeper stuff unintentionally. Do you think God wants us to express our needs? Reveal hurtful parts of our day? Or is life just one happy party with superficial actions that stay on the surface?"

"Why all the questions?"

"You have meaningful interactions at work but I'm home alone."

"Invite a neighbor over."

"I have questions about spiritual things. We hardly go to church anymore or even talk about God. Can we pray together for a few minutes, Jake?"

"I'm late for a meeting but we'll talk when I get home." He kissed the top of her head and brushed past on his way to the car.

*   *   *

Jake's mother had always been elated seeing tender shoots of green pushing through the earth. "Glorious blooms appear overnight—as if they are magic," she told little Lisa, who watched through the fence as a child. Now grown, Lisa followed her example pulling weeds around hearty plants. The best part of gardening came when produce could actually be consumed. Fresh green beans were delicious.

Her mind wandered to futile tasks and people who engage in worthless issues.

Why were people so intrigued by the crusades? Radical Middle Age schemers plundered and conquered in the name of conviction. Lisa's father berated Christians because of such actions. Whenever religion came up, Pete Stewart became agitated and extoled the virtues of peaceful methods for handling conflict. He demeaned those who clutched religious tenants in the spirit of personal advancement.

Most of the time, Lisa's parents forbade spiritual discussion, viewing it as a waste of time.

Jake's family was different. After Adam's accident, religious topics became significant for the Clark family—at least Holly, Adam, and Abby.

Jake didn't participate in spiritual discussions. He preferred to see, touch, and feel stuff on the surface ... never deeper—ignoring what was meaningful for what he could hold in his hand. "I'm in control of my own life," he boasted. His current struggles and dismissal of scripture with endless excuses were increasingly frustrating for Lisa. Maybe he didn't know better, or maybe he was making a deliberate choice to harbor sin.

Had she missed the warning signals?

She picked dirt from under her nails—waiting for Jake to come home. He was late again. Soaking in bubbles loosened grime and energized her spirits. She lathered thick froth over her body. The fragrance diminished slowly as the clock ticked.

Angie was sound asleep.

A beautiful bouquet of crimson roses celebrated on the kitchen table when she went down to eat—long after the Chicken Florentine had cooled. Jake was seated at the table waiting. "Darling, I forgot about our anniversary," he said convincingly. "I'll make it up to you. We can eat at the Melting Pot this weekend."

He handed her an envelope.

Before she could open it, he pulled her on his lap. "You're much too serious for such a wonderful occasion."

"I'm tired, Jake."

"Dance with me before we go to bed?" he asked.

They did but only in her dreams.

To please his wife, Jake attended church on Sunday.

"Hello," he said, greeting everyone with a big smile. He enjoyed additional time in the lobby chatting with friends, only slipping in next to Lisa as the minister began the sermon.

"Every adventure has a milestone moment when we realize the significance of a precise point in our journey. Perhaps the first day of school was poignant; or something vital was learned in a phone call from a trusted friend; or maybe your boss hinted of a job possibility relocating to another part of the world."

"Where is your starting point in spiritual matters?" Phil Davis asked the Grace Fellowship congregation. "We just finished singing … *You alone are my heart's desire and I long to worship you.* What do those words mean to you? Attending church isn't what gives us favor with God. Giving generously, or serving with our time, isn't what adds joy to our maker's heart. His delight comes in having a personal relationship with us. That begins with salvation—the moment God forgives sin in response to our belief about why Jesus came to this earth. We can't feel, touch, or see what He accomplished at Calvary but everything changes when our name is written in the book of life."

"What do you struggle with? Don't get discouraged by circumstances. Look beyond what you can see. Defeat is guaranteed when we leave God out of the picture. Is your faith stronger today than it was yesterday? The only way to know how much faith you have is to encounter trials. Jesus heart was broken for his disciples when they failed to learn who He really was. They panicked in storms—even though He awoke in the boat and instantly calmed the waves. Sometimes the darkness of despair is overwhelming and blinds our eyes. This is too much, we believe."

"When we learn to trust, He can begin to use us."

A heated argument driving home caused Lisa to throw her notes out the window.

*   *   *

A tiny Christmas stocking joined others on the fireplace mantle. "Dat is for somebody else," Angela told Pampa and Mimi. "She's coming with valentines."

"Who is this calico one for?" Adam said pointing to the next one.

"Me!!!"

Holly and Adam adored this precious grandchild and poured love into her life. Reading stories to their granddaughter was always followed by songs. "Sing some more, Pampa," she begged. Her favorite was Twinkle, Twinkle Little Star—wiggling her tiny fingers in the air as high as she could reach for the entire chorus, repeated again and again.

"The birdies in the treetop sing their songs … ," was always followed by lots of bird sounds—and running in circles flapping wings.

Her enthusiasm for life was contagious. Tumbling on the floor in somersaults brought both grandparents down to her level. Adam tried to stand on his head. Holly held his legs up.

Angie cried whenever they left.

While Jake was on a trip to Australia, a towheaded pixie with beautiful eyelashes joined the family on January 16th. The newborn was named Elizabeth Joy Clark. Her personality was peaceful for the first three days in the hospital.

Big sister Angie was delighted to meet her. She tried to wrap Lizzie in a dolly blanket before attempting to pick her up. "Shhhh honey," she said, trying to comfort her baby sister.

Their personalities were entirely different.

When he returned, Jake was preoccupied having fun with his firstborn. The fussy infant irritated his sense of joy. Maybe when Lizzie got older, he would enjoy her more.

Watching Adam and Holly interact with grandkids brought joy. Lizzie had fallen asleep while Pampa was singing. Angie was all smiles sitting in her adored grandma's lap. "Her attention span is incredible for a two year old," Holly said.

Angie pulled on her arm, trying to get some attention. "Tell it one more time, Mimi."

"Just once more," Lisa said. "Then it's time for bed."

"A princess was in the garden swinging on a little piece of wood, tied with golden cords from a beautiful oak tree ... when she eyed a beautifully decorated pink cake on an engraved silver platter. Tempted to have a taste, she placed her feet firmly on the ground hoping she wouldn't fall ... as blue birds watched gleefully from a branch. Finishing her cake ... she brushed the crumbs off her mouth before ...

Chapter 3
Angels

DRESSED IN MATCHING WHITE sundresses, a photographer rearranged Elizabeth and Angela in cute poses, capturing their adorable expressions. Lisa looked on tenderly as Jake tried to make them laugh. "Hey there, my dumplings. When we finish, we're going to the Botanical Gardens to make Mommy happy. She's forgotten how to smile.

They have wonderful flowers you can smell, Lisa!!!"

Angie held her sister in a charming hold, dropping her arms lower as time progressed. Lizzie was happy, for a change. Wonderful news for the eager parents. Pictures meant everything.

"What other backgrounds do you have," Jake said curiously. Daisies in a meadow caught his eye.

"Yeah, I like that one," Lisa said.

Photos of his angels would impress grandparents. If only he could get pictures of his wife—looking pretty sweet herself in a new maize frock, ruffles gently creeping down her chest. Her painted nails and delicate gold bracelet complemented her attire.

The photographer had similar ideas.

Before they were finished, Lizzie was wailing.

"We'll be back in three months. Maybe summer will be easier," Lisa said scooping up the baby as Angie climbed excitedly into her father's arms.

"Let's make mommy smile now."

With kids secure in car seats, Lisa relaxed as she buckled her seatbelt.

"Having children sure brings joy, doesn't it?" Jake said getting in the car.

The delightful afternoon together was better than imagined.

Arriving home with sleeping daughters after an eventful afternoon, Lisa purred like a kitten and peace filled her soul.

"Thanks for the enjoyable outing, Jake. It was fun."

A lavender and peach background filled the sky with glory. Deep indigo clouds filtered through—breaking intense tangerine with rose highlights, to flood delicate pastels with majesty. "This is the most beautiful sunset I've seen. Can I grab a camera before we carry kids, inside?" Jake said.

Comfortable in his home life, Jake settled in for the long term.

His wife focused on building a strong, stable family. Pleasing her husband, taking good care of the girls, organizing a refreshing and orderly home; he was proud of her. *Lisa's criticism has merit, I guess.* She's concerned about imposing values and preferences on a sometimes wandering mate—but always regarding him with respect in public.

He endeavored to become the prince she believed he could be.

Slipping through Macy's lingerie department, he found surprises that would delight both Lisa … and himself! He purchased enticing lacey underwear with tiny filigree hearts, blush intimates, a silky red nightie, and other fascinating necessities any girl would die for. His mind could hardly focus on traffic.

Armed with a bouquet of orchids and box of Ghirardelli truffles, he arrived home late. Old fashioned courtesy still fascinated his wife. Thank goodness the girls were already sleeping.

Lisa was impressed.

"You look ravishing!" he said, coaxing her to try on more of the negligée. She blushed against the backdrop of a candle burning on the dresser.

He could tell by the look in her eye that she wanted more. Not willing to let a perfect opportunity pass unnoticed, he reached his hands to grasp her waist and the thrill tingled every ounce of his flesh. Gently stroking her skin, he became increasingly passionate about the object of his affection.

Lisa sighed in his arms.

"Hooray! Daddy got sparkles," Angie said with glee. She rushed into the house eager to show the world.

"Is she too young to hold those?" Lisa asked. "I don't want her to get hurt."

"Don't spoil her fun. I'll watch her closely."

When it got dark enough outside, Jake lit a match and Angie held her sparkler out. "We're practicing for tomorrow. Follow me Mommy. We're a parade." Lisa tried to keep up but the tiny toddler changed course several times. Jake laughed harder.

"Catch me, mommy," she shouted again.

The 4th of July began with a bang—a surprise only Jake knew about or Lisa would surely have prevented it—and they hurried to where the parade was scheduled to begin. Riding with her daddy, the honored Master of Ceremonies, Angie wore an adorable red, white, and blue sundress made by her mother. She proudly waved a flag through down town Albuquerque in a shiny red corvette convertible. Jake beamed beside her, obviously a sidekick to his famous daughter who stole the spotlight.

"Are you going to speak after the parade?" the mayor asked Angela.

"No, I'm going on a picnic."

With watermelon dripping from her mouth, the fireworks began. "Oooohh. Daddy, did you see that?" she asked … again and again. When Jake failed to answer, she turned to him with sticky hands and held his chin higher.

"Ready for the roller coaster?" he asked before heading home.

"No way, Jake," Lisa insisted. "She's tired and needs a bath."

Waving to Mommy in the parking lot was the last thing Angie saw before falling asleep. "Don't be angry. She begged me," Jake said in the car.

Lisa's growing disgust was obvious.

"You're spoiling a wonderful day! Get out of your bad mood, Mrs. Grouch, before Angie wakes up and discovers this isn't a dream."

"Zip it, Jake."

"Maybe the bratwurst isn't agreeing with you. Should we stop for some ginger ale?"

She plugged her ears and shut her eyes.

"We have so much, Lise. God intended great joy for families like ours."

Lisa gave him an earful about immaturity and lack of reasonable planning. Somehow it always came back to his indiscretions. No matter what he did, his character was open to criticism … by Lisa, the public, and by God.

Jake decided to include his family in an upcoming trip to the East Coast. They could fit in a wonderful weekend at the beach before heading to the Big Apple. A change would do everyone some good.

Celebrating their anniversary in style would redirect a flailing relationship and they could return home rejuvenated and ready to pursue living with gusto.

*   *   *

On a glorious Thursday in August, Jake peeked at sleeping Lisa before kissing her on the cheek. It had been a difficult night with Libby restless—possibly an ear infection from their flight to Virginia Beach. Maybe they shouldn't have come along for his work assignment; but Lisa had been so grouchy lately. "A different view might do everybody some good," he said when booking the tickets. He stretched eager for a chance to fish before they woke up.

He tiptoed across the room, pulled clothes on in the darkness, and opened the door.

Faint light emerged down the beach as he spotted a perfect place to cast his line. His feet made impressions on the smooth sand covered only with a few tracks early in the morning. A fishing boat barely caught his eye. Next time!

"Brrrr … Should have grabbed some coffee," he said to a passing jogger.

The crisp night air held while warmth from a sunrise tried to break through. Tinges of mauve mingled with shades of gray—a delight for anyone up this early. He set his gear on the wet sand. "Glad the tide is moving out so I can have this private space for myself." A bite on his line brought him back to reality. "Good catch, for the first one!" he said, dropping the slippery devil into a pail. By the time a cheerful sun peeked its head, Jake already caught five fish.

"Daddy … ," Angie called out, running across the inviting sand.

He turned to see his precious firstborn headed straight toward him. Lisa followed closely behind, holding the baby. She struggled to keep up with Angela. "It's fine. I'll keep an eye on her," he said without thinking.

They connected with a huge warm hug!

"Did you get a fish?" she asked with big eyes.

Before he could answer, Angie knocked the pail over trying to see what was inside. "Oooohh … sorry," she said, bursting into tears. Jake picked her up pronto; and after a few seconds, she patted his back. He squeezed her tight. "I'll help you get more, Daddy. I Promise." Together they put the fish back in the pail.

Lisa smiled and Jake greeted her with a kiss.

"What a dramatic way to begin the day," she said. "Hope you can find a grill to cook these on." She reached for one of the shells sprinkled on the shore, washed up with the evening tide. Fishing boats ambitiously ambled in the waves out on the horizon. "You're not planning …"

"Glad to see you're outside with the kids this morning. It's gonna be a beautiful day," he said.

A surprise wave splashed on her feet. She jumped back. "Now I see why you don't have shoes on." Jake was too busy catching another fish to answer. "Oh no, not again! Your pail just got washed out to sea," Lisa said. She tried to grab the handle and almost dropped Lizzie. "Angie, can you help daddy catch his fish one more time?"

The silence was deafening.

Time stood still.

Nobody saw it coming.

Aghast at what was happening, Jake sprinted to the end of the sand bar. Her face was in the water. Turning Angie over, he thumped her tiny chest. Again and again he tried to rouse her. In a panic, he picked her up and pounded her limp little back. Lisa ran over and stared.

"Do something!"

Nothing much mattered anymore. They never should have come. More waves splashed on the sandbar as the tide ebbed farther and farther out—but nothing could take away that one rogue wave. All the news in the world would never be this terrible. No story could ever be this wretched. If a million people felt horror at the moment when what was truly significant was obliterated before their eyes; expressing those deepest feelings would be impossible.

Kindly strangers rushed to help.

A siren screamed in the distance.

Jake was on his knees but nothing was happening. Seagulls swooped down for a closer look. Dolphins popped their noses in the air, jumping playfully nearby. A vender with wares began his rounds.

"Why God? ... Why?"

As rescue personal covered the body, Jake tugged on a responder's shirt. "Isn't there something else you can do?"

"We've done all we can, sir."

With equipment packed, rescue team members waited for the coroner to arrive. Bystanders gathered. Jake paced. Surely God would never allow such a tragedy. Lisa rocked Lizzie, squinting her eyes from the bright sun. Someone offered coffee but there were no takers.

Watching the hearse pull up, Jake turned away and walked to the hotel.

"I saw her playing happily in the sand," one woman said later in the lobby. Others tried to cheer Lisa. She smiled, clutching Lizzie tighter—waiting for Jake to load their suitcases in a taxi. Someone handed her Angela's rainbow beach towel left on the sand bar.

Rain started as they drove to the airport.

Obviously the sky was crying, too.

"Hey Dad," Jake said on his cell phone in the cab. The next words were muffled. Another call resulted in a brief conversation. "If you want to," he told someone. Not one word was spoken to each other. Just before boarding the emergency flight home, the loud speaker drowned out a call from his mother. Jake's phone rang again after taking their seats. "Yeah ... OK ... in a couple hours."

Lisa had no interest in the conversations anyway.

Turning pages of a magazine faster than they could be read passed a few minutes for Jake. He twisted an empty bottle of water after finishing it. "Want another?" the flight attendant asked, while walking by.

"Nope ... but you can have this one."

Lisa cuddled sleeping Lizzie—finally content after a miserable climb to altitude.

Didn't matter where she was at the moment. Her head hurt. She couldn't wait to return home from … *a vacation to hades*, hopefully never to be visited again. How soon will I wake up from this terrible nightmare? The minutes stretched into hours.

An exquisite sunset off the wing entertained most passengers. Layers of rose and azure danced amidst a background of tangerine. Jake was too busy fiddling. Lisa turned away before she could start weeping.

On August 24th Adam sang, "The Lord loaned us an angel to come live with us below … and when he said I want her back, we had to let her go …" His voice creaked in the middle. Misty eyes filled most of the seats. A sniffle or two joined a sob, focused on a little white coffin draped with delightful, rainbow-colored daisies. The whole church joined in on, "Jesus loves me this I know."

Jake's tattered bunny *Happy* and favorite book "Corduroy" sat in the corner of Angela's casket.

"Angela was only here for 2 ½ years, but she made an impact on our lives," the minister said. "She leaves behind a wonderful family and baby sister Elizabeth who is just learning to crawl and talk. I'm sure Lizzie would have enjoyed spending more time with her precious big sister, who left this earth much too early."

Cousins Christie (8) and Chelsea (5) hosted an outdoor party, excited to pass out festive reminders. Warmth from a sunny end-of-summer day cheered guests. Jake cracked jokes about circus tricks he and Angie had enjoyed months earlier.

Watching the sky, full of rainbow colored balloons, Lisa brushed back a tear.

It all ended so quickly.

"Where are *Benji* Bear and 'The Country Bunny' book?" Jake asked his sister Abby about her favorite childhood toys. "Throw them away now."

Struggling to make sense of the past month, Jake and Lisa headed down the street toward Grace Fellowship. Arriving late, they avoided conversation and stares.

Phil Davis was preaching about pain having a purpose. "Be open to the methods God chooses to change your hearts and minds; might be thru someone we don't even know; may even be through an enemy. He does things out-of-the-blue in unique ways because we are His precious children. When He gets left out, we become preoccupied with selfish priorities; blurred vision results."

Lisa took notes but didn't hear one thing.

Jake was busy surveying the quarterly calendar for upcoming activities. An all-male hunting trip in November sounded like a wonderful adventure to check out. Male-bonding was something he had previously avoided. Maybe now was the time to change course. He took note of the organizer and determined to hunt him down

Before praying, Rev. Davis closed with, "Your difficulties, battles, and heartaches unite for one conclusion—the glory of God. Like David, we have two choices: bolt or confront the giant."

*   *   *

Finding her Bible under the bed, while fall cleaning, was a surprise and Lisa dusted it off. Maybe she would never understand as much as her in-laws but reading these insightful words calmed her soul and often gave hope. *Life hasn't been exactly what I envisioned but my husband does provide for me. I could have worse problems.* My mother used to say, "Being thankful for what you have is important."

It was a little unsettling talking to a supreme being after no contact for a while. She hadn't meant to ignore him. *Had he heard her prayers? Maybe he had forgotten all about her.*

"Could God be angry at us?" she wondered.

"There's so much that confuses me about scripture," Lisa confided to her mother later.

"Perhaps you're placing too much weight on spiritual stuff. Religion's a crutch for weak individuals who lack strength in living," Mary Stewart told her daughter. "Get in touch with yourself in more realistic ways, Lisa. Find a yoga class; take up a new hobby; spend time in your garden—hug a tree if you need bonding."

"Then why do you attend church, Mom?"

"Holidays include special traditions at First Methodist. Remember the children singing wonderful carols? Christmas and Easter wouldn't be the same without greeting other parishioners. Where else do you wear new clothes? That's as far as we take this religious stuff, however."

"Don't forget the great mother's day sermons you forced us to listen to," Lisa said.

"And flowered bookmarks; those are precious mementos. Thanks sweetie."

The following week Lisa's parents, Pete and Mary Stewart, died in a tragic head on collision returning home from a weekend in the Rockies. Hungry deer were using the same highway and caused a Ford F-150 to lose control. A sliver of moon cried overhead while rescue personnel cleared splattered asphalt of debris.

A deputy from the local Sheriff's office knocked on Lisa's door to tell her the breaking news.

Chapter 4

Secret Garden

SUNSET FUNERAL HOME, SEQUESTERED between a formerly beautiful city park now haven for skateboarders and a small aging business district filled with Spanish speaking shops, was chosen for services. An eerie premonition filled Lisa's heart driving up. Rubbish from a recent neighborhood festival littered the street.

Jake dropped her off at the front before parking.

Her heart pounded while struggling to open the creaky door, in the drizzle. A friendly gentleman inside noticed. "Hi, come on in," he said. "I'm Rev. Pine—the others just stepped out for a minute."

"I'm Lisa."

"Oh … the daughter. Glad to meet you again. And this must be your brother," he said, watching a male enter the lobby.

"That's my …"

"Hi there," he said reaching his hand out to Jake. "Glad we have a chance to talk before the onlookers arrive." He motioned for them to follow him. Scrunched in a corner of the visitation room were two black caskets. Lisa gasped. Jake reached for her hand.

Rev. Pine pulled a chair around abruptly. "Any questions before I go over the order of the service?"

"Will someone give us directions tomorrow?" Lisa asked.

"You bet. We're here for you."

"My brother Jason and his wife Brenda are flying in from Wyoming later this evening. Problems with flight connections delayed their arrival. They hope to make it here before we leave tonight," she said.

"Just need approval from one of you for final details."

"It sounds fine," Lisa said minutes later, eager to find a restroom.

Before parting, they met the family of Harold Jones in the next room.

Pouring rain continued throughout the night leaving a soggy mess for morning services. As family and friends gathered, the electricity flickered briefly—but fortunately came back on. Adam and Holly sat behind Lisa and Jake, reaching out to comfort before the minister began. An organist played music from her past.

Most of the chairs remained empty.

"Harold and Mary Jones died in a tragic collision, heading home from a vacation in the mountains. A family of deer was using the same highway," Rev. Pine said. "They've gone to life's resting place, free from worry and pain. Too bad Harold, err … Pete and Mary couldn't have enjoyed this earth longer," he said, looking at the program while clearing his throat.

Jake struggled to restrain his laughter. "The stupid minister doesn't even know their names," he whispered.

Her mind plummeted back to events and conversations from the past that would never be understood. Lisa managed to keep her sadness in check. She had subconsciously built barriers to keep most of the unsettling childhood emotional upheaval from leaching into her current thought patterns.

After a luncheon with baloney sandwiches, carrot sticks, and chips, she cordially thanked guests before escaping tormenting emotions hidden not far below the surface. From what she knew about her parents' atheistic beliefs, they had gone to hell. Years of hostility toward Pete Stewart's father resulted from his grandfather's arrogant spiritual devoutness—with no regard for loving his children who he beat routinely while intoxicated. The sin was perpetuated by his son.

Mary Stewart was sexually abused by leaders of a local church who befriended her needy family under the context of helping them become better individuals. Nothing anyone could say would undo hatred she harbored for anyone who embraced an almighty god. It was too late to make a difference when Lisa learned the truth about Jesus.

A bitter fight ensued on the drive home.

"Slow down. I'm trying to understand what you're saying," Jake said. "You isolate scripture and use it for selfish purposes."

"The Bible says, 'Don't lean to your own understanding.' That's all you do."

"Think you're taking that out of context, Jake said. "What gets us in trouble is when you pressure me to act on your timetable."

"I'm not your enemy."

"You were meant for me ... and I was meant for you. Think you need some sleep, Lise."

A call from her own pastor's wife early Monday morning caught Lisa off guard. Fumbling with laundry, she accidentally knocked over the Tide. "I'm sorry to hear about your parents. We learned about the sad news and tried to phone last night," Brooke Davis said. "Are you doing okay?"

"It was a shock but that's what life seems to be throwing us."

"I miss seeing you on Sundays."

"Jake's pretty busy."

"Can I stop over for a few minutes? Made some pumpkin bars I know he'll enjoy. If you have some time to talk, I can stay 'till noon."

Lisa agreed and rushed to pick up after changing into a forest sweater and jeans. Lizzie was down for her morning nap. Laundry could wait until later in the afternoon. She brushed her hair and put a hint of lipstick on.

Sipping peppermint tea, she opened up. "Does God want us to express ourselves, our needs? Everyone wants to feel listened to; and believes her desires, discomfort, hurts are significant."

"He loves us more than we can comprehend and longs to talk intimately with us."

"Wish my husband was more like God," Lisa said.

"No doubt he'll be a wonderful work of art when our creator finishes crafting his delightful Jake Clark. Be patient, Lisa."

"But keeping secrets from your spouse purposely? No way can a sovereign almighty allow those violations, right? You have no idea what

I put up with, Brooke. It's dark in his world once you get off the merry-go-round."

"A two-way relationship requires honesty, openness, transparency—and a forgiving spirit."

"I know! But you have no idea how insensitive Jake gets. Doesn't he know I'll close up sooner or later?" Lisa confided. She would have continued but Brooke needed to run; and promised to come back on Friday.

With a door cracked open to communicate from her soul, Lisa had no intention to stop. Maybe she needed to use force to get her husband to talk. Sure he usually became furious and ran off—but after three months of ignoring the truth about death, it was becoming too difficult to continue evading the issue.

"I'm sick of your secrets," Lisa said to Jake on the phone, trying to communicate.

"Can't expect intimate moments if you do all talking," he said briskly. "Say what's on your mind because I have 30 seconds before I go live."

"Your hostility and refusal to talk about Angela are getting to me. Let's play a different game. This one is getting tedious."

"Now is not the time to talk, Lisa. You sound bored; we'll do something together tonight. Get a babysitter, if you can."

Lisa contacted grandparents who were available and excited to play with Lizzie.

A fun evening going up the Sandia Peak Aerial Tramway with Jake was long overdue. As they were transported to the 10,378 feet observation deck, breathtaking canyons and the Cibola National Forest offered a wonderful panoramic view at sunset. Desert skies produced brick red dancing with cranberry before melting into purple moats at higher altitudes—with luminous gold rays layering into pumpkin on the horizon.

"Ohhhh! It's beautiful!!!"

"No camera?" Jake asked.

"Sorry. Didn't even think about one tonight," she said.

"We'll be back again. Forgot how great this place has always been!"

Arm in arm they observed the splendor of New Mexico spread before their eyes. Time stood still as they blended their spirits with nature, in harmony for a change.

"Look. There's a bighorn on that ridge," Lisa said.

"Think I'm gonna do a special about this place. It's a must see for out-of-town folks but locals need to come here more often. If I add a promo about customers enjoying a relaxing dinner, even better. How does this sound, Lise … Escape the city and enjoy a unique dining experience atop Sandia Peak," he said in his professional tone. "Nowhere else can you dine two miles high and savor such delicious entrees."

A crowd gathered, intently listening to the local viewing area's favorite anchor.

"I saw that guy on TV," one woman said.

"He's a celebrity," another added.

"We've enjoyed everything about this experience," a man said, reaching his arm out to shake hands with Jake. "We would love to spend more time on this mountain. It was certainly worth the money."

"Don't forget Mt. Taylor, a dormant volcano over there dominating the western horizon," Jake said.

When the sightseers dispersed, the cooler air made Lisa shiver. Jake pulled her close. "You had a good idea, sweetheart. This was fun!"

As they waited for the tram to return, and dock at the High Finance, a few last sights caught their attention. "Isn't that where you used to take Angie hiking?" Lisa asked, pointing to the Sandia Foothills.

"Why spoil a perfect moment?" he said aggravated by her insensitivity.

Jake remained silent on their ride to the bottom.

Occasional time together breathed refreshing energy to the ragged relationship. With a painful Thanksgiving behind, they looked forward to spending quality time over Christmas.

Tradition was significant to Lisa who suddenly tasked herself with an urgent need to develop family history over the holidays. She invited Jason and Brenda to come with their girls—and Jake's parents joined them most meals. Several twists were incorporated including a Christmas Eve drama of the nativity in real-time with family members drawing characters and improvising in a play; and a Christmas afternoon family holiday bowl with everyone playing touch football.

"Next year we're adding a Christmas bazaar," Lisa said.

"Congrats, Captain," Jason added.

"You have this routine down," Jake said. "Feels like we've done this forever."

* * *

Preparing for Lizzie's first birthday took priority over attending the Chamber of Commerce Lover's Ball. Lisa contemplated each detail carefully. She struggled not to remember Angela's two wonderful parties. This one had to be completely different.

Center of attention on January 16th was a flaxen haired beauty dressed in purple-smocked-ruffles with a white pinafore. "Enjoy your cake, candle, and fun day Sweetie," Lisa said, as Jake snapped oodles of pictures. The safari-themed cake with mini African animals perched around a blue lake was inspiring. Lisa hoped it would somehow help reconnect emotionally with her husband.

Adam and Holly's gift was an adorable toy cocker spaniel with a red collar and leash that Lizzie immediately bonded with. She dragged Biscuit everywhere. "Dada," she said pointing. Everyone laughed.

"Sometimes I end up in the dog house," Jake said.

Forgetting about a planned meeting, he excused himself to meet a co-worker. He returned several hours later after his parents had gone home and Lizzie was asleep. His pillow and a blanket waited outside Lisa's locked bedroom door.

Sleeping on the sofa enabled him to avoid further confrontation until morning.

He was gone when she woke up.

Three weeks later Lisa was in a better mood.

"Our best babysitters are here so your wish is my command," Jake said. "Is the royal princess ready for the ball?"

"Don't think about fleeing to Florida for the winter, Mom and Dad."

"Grandparents sprinkle stardust over little grandchildren," Holly said picking Lizzie up in a tight squeeze. "I'm thankful to have this precious one in our lives. We need to spend more time with her."

Lovely in crimson satin with lace—"inside and out," Lisa informed Jake—upswept curls spilled down her neck. A hint of the amazing fragrance Amarige resulted in a passionate kiss to begin the evening.

"My valentine and I will return at the stroke of midnight," he said.

"Have fun!!!"

Lisa stepped her Peoni pumps into Jake's candy apple Hybrid Escape, fresh from the showroom floor. "Nice car, lover boy! Hey, what did your dad say when he saw your new toy?"

"He wanted to take it for a spin."

"Really?"

"Looks like you spent the remainder of my hard earned money on your snazzy attire. How much did those Jimmy Choo's set us back, Lise?"

"Ted Baker … got them on sale, I swear," she said.

"As long as they can dance the night away."

His hand on her shoulder sent chills up Lisa's spine. It had been months since he paid quality attention to her. Sharing an appetizer, their hands touched. The twinkling candlelight and heart confetti sprinkled around on tables reminded Lisa of their first date at the University of Arizona—Fall Fantasy it was called. Jake had whispered sweet nothings all evening. Now he only watched but his look was intense.

He winked.

As the band began playing, Jake stood and touched her arm. "May I please have this dance?" They swayed together in complete harmony for hours. "Amore, my darling …" He sang as they moved to the edge.

"I'm glad we came," she said.

"Ready for dessert, my little cherry?"

Melting eyes over a chocolate fondue fountain, she licked her lips. If only the night could go on and on. Everything was perfect again.

The sensation of bare skin, passionate embraces, and a pulsating touch took them back to their honeymoon for a brief respite. "You were meant for me … and I was meant for you," Jake said before falling asleep. A comfy pillow cradled his head as her perfume lingered in his nostrils.

He remembered years before.

"Lisa Stewart? What in the world are you doing here?"

"Hey, Jake! Almost didn't recognize you. It's been years since I last saw you; can't believe you're all grown up. I work at KMOL. Why are you here?"

"I haven't seen you around all week."

"Technical people are locked in their offices. We seldom see reporters and anchors," she said.

"Awesome!!! I'm interning for the summer and hope to see more of you."

Jake held the door open as Lisa walked through. His mind was focused on reporting news but his heart was beating wildly. He had a crush on quiet little Lisa when he was young—never imagining she would grow so beautiful. "You always did look at me with that seductive smile, like you knew something I didn't," he said when she passed him later in the day. "Hey, my 21st birthday is on Sunday. I'd love to spend it with you—and reconnect—if you're available."

"You know where I live. What time should I be ready?"

Driving up Brookshire Lane, Jake's thoughts raced. *So much has happened since we moved. I don't even feel like the same person.* He glanced at a squirrel racing across the lawn of his former home.

Lisa looked ravishing when she opened the door. He hugged her energetically, without thinking. It was a sweet reunion.

"Tell me more about what you do?" he asked after ordering dinner.

"I'm the promotion coordinator for KMOL creative services department. My job involves processing station logs, handling department bookkeeping, coordinating various projects, and performing administrative functions. I guess you could say I'm an extremely organized, efficient, and hardworking individual—who works well under pressure."

Jake stared in her eyes as she talked.

None of his old girlfriends had been anything like Lisa. Her personality was unique—soft-spoken but firm in her convictions. Something special sizzled under that veneer of stability and dependability. *If only she was interested in a flamboyant younger man who was capable of much productivity as he aged. If only she would give him a chance to prove his worth to her.*

"You'll never guess who I met," Jake told his mother. He didn't pause to hear an answer. "Lisa Stewart works at KMOL."

"I've been thinking about her," Holly answered, excited to hear the news. "I wonder how her family is doing. We lost contact after moving and I've been meaning to reconnect with our old neighbors for several years."

After their fourth date, Jake asked if Lisa wanted to get together with Adam and Holly. She agreed wholeheartedly. A day was chosen for a barbeque, bringing lovely 25-year-old Lisa Stewart to his parents' home. Driving onto the property, she took a deep breath. Fresh mown grass and "baaing" sheep greeted her.

"Are you okay?" he asked.

"Yes, just a little nervous. I remember being intimidated by your family when you lived next door—you all seemed so together and a step above the rest of us normal humans. In spite of that, I was fascinated and wanted to know you better."

He reached for her hand, pressing it to his chest. He would do everything he could to make this creature feel more at ease. She was the one who possessed depth of character his family had missed all those years.

* * *

A ringing alarm woke them both. "Hey sleepyhead, it's your turn to get coffee on. I'll check on Lizzie," Lisa said.

"How 'bout if you do both and I wait here?"

"What happened to the prince charming I was dancing with last night?"

"Cinderella left him at the ball."

"I'm driving your Escape to church this morning. Coming with me?" Lisa said. Reluctantly, Jake dressed and helped make a quick breakfast with croissants and strawberries before they headed to Grace Fellowship. It had been a while.

"Welcome, dear friends," the minister said. Everyone greeted them warmly. "We miss you when you're gone."

"He's to blame," Lisa said pointing.

"For everything," Jake joked.

In his message Phil Davis said, "We all want it ... don't get it ... give up. But that's not how God operates. He wants more for his beloved children. What gets us in trouble is when we demand our own way. Listen to people around you. Where do their interests lie? What do they talk about? What motivates them? How do they act in secret? We pursue everything in sight—wealth, gadgets, clothing, sports, relationships, but where does God fit in? Do you want a relationship with the Almighty or just get in the door of heaven?"

"How we develop a deeply personal connection to God is similar to our responses bonding with other people. After getting married couples often stop talking. It appears they have little interest wanting to know their mate more intimately or spending quality time together, and no longer enjoy or cherish each other. Instead they may question if they've made a terrible mistake."

"He has a point," Lisa said.

"Think you're taking that out of context."

"What do you want to be remembered for in ten years?"

"I don't want to argue anymore. Can we just live in peace?" Jake said.

Chapter 5
Trouble In Paradise

A DREARY FOG CLUNG to the air, rare for this region on a spring morning. Lizzie was immersed in Country Girl paper dolls Mimi purchased while on vacation. Lisa tiptoed away quietly, attempting to finish mega-cleaning and reload closets.

She sorted through a stack of pictures. "What's this about?" she said out loud.

Jake had his hands on an old girlfriend's waist, both with big smiles, apparently having fun. Then another with him in a sapphire convertible—filled with half-dressed females, one kissing him passionately on the check. Lisa recognized her from the KMOL Christmas party.

"What's the meaning of these pictures you hid in the closet?" she asked Jake cynically on the phone.

"Nothing."

"Do you like her?" Lisa inquired.

"No."

"Nobody acts like this, Jake. You're married."

"It's nothing Lise."

"How do you keep getting into these awkward positions? What is it about you?" Jake remained silent. His endless excuses didn't explain one thing anyway. Lisa hung up.

Jake called back.

"My treasured wife seems bent on disrespecting and shaming me for something I had no control over. Jealousy is rearing its ugly head. You have your own … shall we call it weaknesses? Just yesterday when we stopped at the stoplight, and the blonde chick waved, you said I could have her. Without warning, you divulged information about a hunk you communicated with online. I'm innocent until proven guilty, Lisa."

"I was just joking. There's no guy. Why did you keep those pictures?"

"They're my friends. The redhead is Brianna's cousin from Australia. She was excited to meet a real celebrity in the journalism world. I'll tell you more when I get home." Lisa could tell by the sound of his voice that he was lying. There was a note on the back of one picture he apparently had forgotten about.

"Just don't be late!" she warned.

"A Magnitude 6.3 earthquake rocked southern California today off the coast of Long Beach," Jake reported on the evening news. "Part of the Santa Cruz-Santa Catalina Ridge fault zone, this quake was felt throughout all 10 southern counties, and north into the Coast Range and San Joaquin Valley. Fortunately the shock occurred at 5:42 a.m., before most people left home for work; so streets were less crowded, reducing injuries and potential death. Efforts to coordinate emergency responders, utilities, and other agencies are ongoing. More details will be forthcoming as updates become available. Most authorities speculate aftershocks will continue for days and possibly weeks."

Lowering his information sheets, Jake breathed a sigh of relief.

"The most significant point for me personally is that my grandfather is safe. He has damage to his home but not his life." They cued up a Skype call Jake previously recorded.

"So what happened, Gramp?" Jake asked.

Grandpa Clark began talking.

His receding hairline slipped back farther than Jake remembered. Somehow he looked older. A clock ticked in the background. "Born and raised in Southern California, this isn't the first quake I've been through but they're all a bit unique. Some come in waves. Others shake. I was reading a newspaper in my front room when the earthquake started. It sounded like a train rushing by my house but the engine continued to churn. I tried to stand, but couldn't. Felt like I was being shaken on a tilt-a-whirl in my lazy boy. A couple pictures fell off walls and a shelf of books toppled. Some cracked plaster and a broken window are the only damage I can see—unless you count the gooey mess on my kitchen floor from something broken in the refrigerator."

"Looks like you have a cut on your cheek?" Jake said.

"No, just a scratch from doing yard work yesterday. It's hard enough to be alone without my beloved wife but these earthquakes and aftershocks are recurrent bad dreams. Think I'm ready to leave this troubled world and try my hand at paradise. I've been here long enough."

"Oh, no Gramp … Hang in there. Life is good! I'll try to visit next month. Take care of that sunshine for me."

"Bye."

Deep in thought about his grandfather's statements caused speculation for Jake after the broadcast. He hesitated commenting about his concerns to Lisa or his parents. Perhaps he was reading too much into something that wasn't a real issue. Spending Sunday morning at Grace Fellowship would be beneficial.

Lizzie was sick so Lisa was unable to join him. Her grouchiness was getting unbearable anyway so he left the two females to be miserable together for the day.

Pastor Davis spoke about having emotional, physical, and spiritual issues. "How do you go about solving yours? Some people are self-sufficient, attempting to solve problems on their own. Some expect others to intervene—and become resentful when they're incapable or don't appear to care. What's your downfall? What is the basis for your expectations?"

Jake determined to search scripture for possible answers.

Gramp Clark needed immediate direction.

He had little interest in spiritual things, he said on the phone. "I'm looking for the reward for all my hard work on this planet. Good things eventually happen to good people. You get what you deserve. Ever hear about the golden rule, Jake? A supreme being, if there was such a person, certainly would never allow upright people to suffer the worst kind of fate. Thoughts of my dear wife—languishing in a fiery pit of evil forever—are more than I can contemplate. She had a difficult enough last few years with her breast cancer. No, Becky's at peace in the ocean that she loved after I scattered her ashes from the lighthouse. Maybe the waves even brought her to back to paradise in her beloved Tahiti."

"What if you're wrong Gramp?" Jake asked.

"I'll never know."

Grandpa Clark simply didn't believe in accountability for a life hereafter.

However all this stuff about eternity in the Bible surely had some merit? What happened to Jesus on earth couldn't have been a hoax. It was too convincing.

By the time Jake finished a 10K hike north of town, his body was exhilarated and mind refreshed with new options for his career. He also met a friend on the trail that was fascinating to talk to and they spent the evening laughing together at a restaurant. The joy of being significant to a stranger was exciting.

He sang all the way home.

*   *   *

A potential trip to the Hoover Dam researching innovative power and wind generators would create a distinctive news story—and if he was lucky offer career incentives. Advancement potential was critical in journalism. He could add a follow up about the quake in California … and check on Gramp personally. Jake took the necessary initiative to make it happen.

With a few perks, his time would be well spent.

Before leaving, he copied his wedding vows and put them in an ornate bronze frame he purchased while on assignment in Calgary. Lisa would be impressed on their eighth anniversary.

On August 21, flanked by three dozen red roses in a crystal vase, Jake orchestrated the big reveal. "Happy anniversary, darling!!! Here's a gift straight from my heart," he said on air, making the presentation in front of viewers and co-workers. Lisa watched from home—alerted by a station intern.

"Thanks," she said when he called. "It seemed almost like a joke."

"You don't sound appreciative about making the evening news?"

"I want a real relationship, Jake. Do you honestly care about me?"

He paused for a minute. "Here you go again. Nothing I do is right. Might as well give up trying to please you."

"I want you to value me; cherish spending time with me and Lizzie."

"We're unable to have normal conversations," Jake said.

"Because there's so much hostility between us. I can discuss topics with other people in a rational, reasonable manner—and have no problem listening to their point of view, asking questions, and maybe even disagreeing. But I can't do that with you."

"Good to know since I'm working late tonight on a project with Brianna. She likes me, needs me, and enjoys talking to me. Really craves spending time with me to be honest! At lunch we even talked about our futures. Think over your critical spirit, Lise. Hope we're on better terms tomorrow."

She slammed the phone down.

At least she had Brooke.

Lisa shared her despair on an outing to the zoo while Lizzie and Brooke's son, Matthew, watched two tiny black bears climbing a tree. When mama tired of their fun, the cubs followed her to a basket of fruit set on steps to the cave. They playfully tossed the colorful lunch under her observant eye.

"It's bizarre we get along at all when our relationship is so shallow," Lisa said. "We enjoy activities together but there's a brick wall between us at deeper levels. When I try to communicate, he blows off everything I say."

"Words are powerful. Guard them carefully because they can be used for good or evil. They can inspire, encourage, bring laughter and joy … or crush, accuse, and provoke," Brooke said.

Lizzie needed a restroom.

A couple of hotdogs and juice, followed by an interactive farm area for kids, gave the two friends more time to talk.

"I try to protect Jake; be his helper on this journey—but it seems no one is there for me. Didn't realize as a child but my parents never took time to connect emotionally with either Jason or me. They were in their own worlds far from reality. Guess they had issues from the past that were too difficult to overcome. Unfortunately, none of that can be resolved anymore. Sometimes I wonder if the almighty even cares about us as individuals."

"He does ... in fact, God tells us to delight Him and we'll receive the desires of our heart in Psalm 37:4. He promises to withhold nothing from us. He wants us to be the person He created us to be—like a daring mountain lion or leaping gazelle overcoming hurdles."

"I can't get past the unmet desires of my heart," Lisa said, suddenly overcome with tears.

Brooke leaned closer. "Adjust your expectations. What you expect out of life, or out of a relationship, or from God, has a big impact on your experience of those things. Your outlook might not determine how life treats you but will definitely color things one way or another. Put on rose colored glasses and eventually everything will look pink. Expect the worst and you will experience problems. Expect the best and you will get it more often than not!"

"So the problem is really me, not Jake?"

"Allow Him to change you into a gorgeous silver platter with patina that shines in the dark world, as evidence of His grace and mercy—especially when it comes to those weaker or immature. Lead the way; don't incite a blaze of destruction to prove a point. He'll help you. You don't have to do anything alone."

Gentle rain sprinkled down as they found safety in their vehicles before parting. Lisa stayed behind pretending to answer her phone. She fiddled with the radio and Lizzie leaned back drowsy.

Patters turned into staccato.

After Brooke exited the lot, Lisa broke into tears. Pelting rain washed the windshield in unison. "It's hard but I will trust you to work in me and Jake until we're eventually the people we should be." A rainbow eclipsed the zoo as she drove away.

Peace would come but probably not from Jake.

An abandoned puppy, waiting at the door, whimpered when Lisa brought him into the house. She dried him with a towel as he rested his head in Lizzie's lap on the kitchen floor. "I wanted a real dog, Mommy."

"Well, we need to find if he belongs to someone else."

"Let's call him Cookie," Lizzie said. The powdered mutt with a tender disposition captured their heart strings from the beginning.

Lisa asked Jake to bring doggy food home—he added treats. The frisky pup climbed on his shoes, looking up with eyes widened. "Cookie wouldn't be so lonely if someone intended to keep him as their pet."

Trying to find an owner seemed unnecessary.

Jake took him out for potty training and could hardly get him back inside. A few tosses of a tennis ball and his paws were muddier. When Lizzie opened the door, Cookie zipped right in.

"He likes me daddy," the bright eyed child announced.

"I see that."

"Now you can see how fun his bath will be," Lisa said, handing Jake the old towel she used earlier.

Comfy in a bed made from a box, tucked in for the night, Cookie ended up in Lizzie's bed much to her delight. His droopy eyes told a sad tale.

"If you had to leave your family and wander in the world alone, how would you feel?" Lisa said to Jake. "Good thing we're here for him."

"I say this little guy keeps her entertained until we can find her a brother."

Lisa frowned.

A candlelit bedroom waited when the moon peeked its head. Her reflection in the mirror was already pleasant. "There's your red silk nightie; I'm curious how you'll look with that fresh red manicure. By the way, I need you to scratch my back." Jake said with a cheesy smile.

"Haven't seen you this frisky for months."

"Live in the moment, Mama."

"You're always up to something and seem to get your way, no matter what I say. How come you only listen when you're physically attracted? Maybe I need to learn how to negotiate," she said.

"Your lucky break was catching me that morning in May down at the station. After all those years of childhood longing, you got what you wanted. Now it's my turn."

Lisa smelled heavenly with her Jardin du Gardenia. "New perfume from an admirer?" He grabbed her as she tried to pass the bed. She apparently had something on her mind but his persuasive ways made her forget.

"Don't remember what you gave me for my birthday?" she said. "How am I supposed to use my perfume when I'm home alone all the time?"

"Guess a few more romantic interludes could be handy for both of us."

She settled willingly on his lap and leaned closer as his hands began caressing her skin. Jake was a romantic. He brushed her tresses back before fondling her neck. When she shivered, he gallantly coaxed her farther. Kisses kept her from talking. Withdrawing from this relationship was not a possibility. Her reception enticed him to advance in regions long ignored. She laughed. She sighed. She enjoyed him immensely.

"Jake … oh, Jake."

"Sweet dreams, darling. I have more surprises planned for tomorrow evening."

Chapter 6

Shadows

THE BLEAKNESS OF WINTER matched the bareness of her soul. Lisa struggled to keep anything down, snacking on crackers and peppermint to calm her nausea. "I never intended to get pregnant again." She glanced at the clock. Lizzie would wake soon.

Jake threw a quilt over her legs. "Why don't we go on a cruise and you can heave over the rails all day?"

"I'd rather be dead."

"Then who'd take care of Lizzie?"

Lisa had a better idea. "Would you rather watch her this morning or come with me?"

They all went together when Lizzie woke.

"A cup of ginger tea might help but could stimulate a miscarriage," their neighborhood pharmacist warned. In her quest for relief, Lisa heeded his potential side effects story and chose raspberry herbal tea instead. She also grabbed peach.

"Why not try them all?" Jake asked.

"My favorite remedy was a smoothie I concocted from mint and pineapple," the woman in line behind her said.

"I used pieces of citrus fruit in hot water," the cashier volunteered.

Even honey pops in the shape of bears couldn't get her to smile. Her husband tried a comic book. Flips on the grass outside flopped. Jake would have jumped over barrels of water but she stopped him.

"People are looking," Lisa said.

"Did you know nausea comes from nautical?" Jake said on the way home. "My mom told me about sailors reeking of vomit after upchucking on the high seas while crossing the Atlantic, trying to find relief in the New World."

"Too much information," she said struggling for control.

To make her feel better Jake mixed a ginger and raspberry smoothie—before suggesting she take a warm bath while listening to Andrea Bocelli. "I'll play a game with Lizzie," he offered.

"We don't have any games for kids," Lizzie announced.

"Then we'll go buy some."

Two hours later they owned six new ones including Candy land, Angry Birds Knock on Wood, and a Glow Crazy distance doodler. Leftover Reece's and Snickers wrappers fell under the table unnoticed. Jake threw leftover pepperoni pizza away with several unfinished cans of Pepsi.

Lisa never allowed children to drink soda.

*   *   *

"If we could see beyond today as God can see …" Holly said to Lisa "Take one day at a time." Her offer to help was priceless and her spirit was contagious. Having hope and stability at this precarious point in Lisa's life was crucial. Speculating on whether or not it was wise to conceive again would be for sages to debate long into the future. She didn't dare dig deeper for the truth bottled up years ago.

"Maybe you'll have a chance to be an angel of mercy for me someday," Holly said.

Her mother-in-law was a blessing.

Lisa's struggle wasn't with Jake—though refusal to accept responsibility for his actions and dislike of solving issues, forced his wife to bear unnecessary resentment. At risk was their unpredictable future that loomed out of control. "We have insurance," was his repetitive response but he missed the truth—as he did with all serious reality issues. Annoyed by his stance to intrigue and cajole others while ignoring the obvious, Lisa harbored feelings of suppressed emotion that gnawed away at her core. How could she remain safely anchored and down to earth? Little actual time or money was left to guard against calamity.

"My life's a jumbled puzzle," Lisa said.

"All of our lives are similar to puzzles. Some pieces are upside down. Others don't fit where you think they should go. The whole thing seems like a mess to you but to God your life looks like the finished picture on the cover of the box. He knows exactly where each piece fits and not one is ever missing."

"It's amazing how God can open your eyes to see what you're doing wrong through scripture, or the words of a friend."

"I'm a phone call away if you ever need me, Lisa."

Before Holly left, they went over plans for Lizzie's birthday party. They already agreed on a Strawberry Shortcake Party at one of Mimi's favorite shops. The invitations were adorable.

You are invited to celebrate:
A Strawberry Shortcake Tea Party
For Elizabeth's 6th Birthday
On Thursday, January 16th
From 10am-12:00pm
1234 Peppermint Lane
FYI: Please come in costume or wear a fancy dress.

Holly arranged details and prepared festivities with the shop owner. They would eat sandwiches cut in assorted shapes with petit shortcakes for dessert. Tea would be served in fancy china cups with cream, if preferred. A silver bowl would hold tiny pastel mints. The girls would learn how to curtsy, sit properly, and wave like a princess as they rode in a carriage.

"Thanks for caring about your granddaughter so much!" Lisa said.

"Don't think you're any less special," Holly said to her only daughter-in-law. "God sends robins to cheer you; and flowers to delight you. Anytime of the day, He loves to hear your voice ... so spend some time with Him. And Lisa, I'll help with spring cleaning after the party, if you need me."

"Your beautiful spirit makes me want to sing. Thanks Holly."

A sermon on Sunday was poignant for Lisa.

"Raise your hand if you know what you need right now," Pastor Phil asked the perplexed congregation. A few giggled. "Be specific with your requests. When you ask with wrong motives, it's not His fault what happens. Something's wrong with you. He hears our prayers but His answers are often different from what we imagined. Why? Because He knows what's better for my life than I do."

"Don't think so," Jake whispered. "What about free will?"

He insisted they leave early and hurried home.

*   *   *

Filming a special about New Mexico's twenty-two American Indian Tribal Nations, Jake worked long hours with Brianna Smyth. They documented details on five separate areas—unique languages, colorful dances, cultural traditions, ethnic arts & crafts, and feasts of food—bringing them together in a culmination ceremony with Chief Zagunta from the Susquash Indian Reservation. Ready for final lights, camera, and action—with adrenalin bursting from his scalp to toes—Jake tapped his foot waiting for station manager, Mike Hintz to arrive with the Chief.

"No show?" Brianna asked Jake after a thirty minute delay. Phone calls were made hurriedly.

A flutter of activity created a buzz.

"Wrong date was recorded," Joe Garcia said loudly. "Should have double-checked months ago, Jake. You botched this up big-time. There'll be no big promo with the Governor, either."

Anchor Paul Esse gloated from his desk, reading over newssheets about a high water rescue following local flooding—preparing to go on camera imminently with the latest news. "Dumb oaf, should be fired," he muttered about Jake.

"Couldn't be my mistake," Jake said. "Brianna's assistant must have mucked this up when she handled preliminary contacts." He rushed to the front desk for more information. Earth, sky, and water were out of sync with sun, moon, and stars. Nothing could be more humiliating. Today was no laughing matter.

Mike Hintz' personal admin glared at Jake.

"If you paid more attention to personal weaknesses and refrained from interfering in the business of others, you would have fewer problems," she said behind closed doors. Her curled lip and barbed tongue exuded growing animosity. "By the way, there's going to be a price to pay for your foolishness." Being confronted by Jake, in a back office with Mike Hintz on three occasions, turned ugly when Jake threatened to reveal the infidelity to Mike's wife.

"Maybe it would've been easier for you to play slots at the Route 66 Casino?" Joe said when Jake returned.

"We can eat grilled corn while Jake does the Buffalo dance," Paul said smirking.

Both anchors seethed with animosity toward the other.

"Our competitive edge," Jake called it.

"If you put two donkeys back to back in a circle, what do you think will happen?" Joe Garcia said. The camera crew chuckled. "Why don't we film a reality spectacle from our showroom floor?"

"There's always more to the story," Brianna said.

He decided to withhold telling Lisa about the fiasco. It would blow over. He could remedy the situation and pull off an even bigger bang with additional time—doing the job better than he first envisioned. Jake watched people come and go between segments but most action was the few seconds before *on-air* time.

"What a difference a few lights make," he thought.

The van was abuzz with breaking news about an ongoing Occupy Albuquerque demonstration downtown and KMOL needed video. Jake listened with interest as cameraman Hector Lopez laid out plans for action. Police were dispersing crowds with colored water—spraying bright yellow onto everything in sight. Seemed to be working.

"Cleaning that up will make another great story," Hector said.

"Reminds me when students demanded change in educational policies at the U of Arizona," Jake said.

Aahhh, for those good ole days!

Seemed like yesterday when he was going out with Brianna to do the story on a hot new movie, lovely Lisa got out of her car and caught him off guard. Maybe he needed family to support him in case things didn't settle down.

"Remember when Jake announced he had an internship at KMOL in Albuquerque for the summer?" Holly said. "The station manager confirmed he would start June 1st so I asked, Will we see you on television? He responded—*not unless I make a big mistake!*"

Laughter erupted.

"That was an opportunity to gain valuable insight into becoming a great anchor after I graduated," Jake said. "Little did we know how quickly I'd climb the corporate ladder?"

"Charm infused with skill goes far!" Adam said.

"Don't ignore what's at stake," Lisa said cautiously.

"I'm innocent until proven guilty. There'll be a showdown, if necessary," Jake assured them all.

School-bus-colored-water-bombs dispersed on fidgety demonstrators earlier were nothing like TV Station fireworks erupting on Monday. "We've offended the Chief and the Governor. You'll need to eat some crow, Jake. Make your amends and we'll see how we can resurrect this milestone event," Mike Hintz said.

Jake wasn't about to take the rap.

Mike couldn't understand his ranting and raving—face crimson, sweat dripping off his nose—but everyone in the studio heard the commotion.

Tiptoeing away, Brianna headed for the ladies room. "He's gonna come after me next," she said to Hector.

The confrontation spilled onto the airways.

"Come enjoy the Heart of New Mexico where our local yahoo will try to stab you," Paul said. "Just don't take a trip down Route 66 with him; never know where you'll end up. One of our curious journalists may be out hunting soon for the legendary Golden City of Cibola."

"Mike wants you to take a few days off for administrative leave," Joe Garcia told Jake at the end of the shift.

Everyone else had disappeared.

A phone call the following day informed Jake he was being demoted to morning anchor. He fumed trying to reach Mike. "They've taken the freakin phone off the hook," he said to Lisa, enraged.

Stoic and proud, the skirmish was revisited his first morning back.

"I refuse to accept this new honor as your morning anchor," he said to Mike Hintz. Jake normally pretended to comply, rather than make waves, but his dignity was at stake. It wasn't about money as

Lisa suggested. Impatient with administration, and intolerant when procedures striped joy from living, got the best of him. A different side emerged. Contempt for management flowed faster than floodwater from the Colorado River gorged the spectacular Grand Canyon.

Somehow this became uglier.

"Hey friend, you can always take a sunset stroll around the White Sands National Monument," Paul said smugly. "That's where retirees hang out."

"Mind your own business," Jake said, denying the gossip. "I filed a grievance and in the meantime need time for a vacation before my son's birth."

No time for that.

A little firecracker with red frizz and big blue eyes entered the world at 5:02 AM on the fourth of July. Almost a month early, Alexander Jacob Clark was eager to see why the world around him was shouting so energetically. Six year old Lizzie was ecstatic to have a brother.

"We need to get back to normal soon," Jake told Lisa.

To celebrate, he took Lizzie shopping to buy toys for his son. With a 1,000 piece LEGOLAND and remote controlled Ferrari for Alex, they bought a Nintendo DS Gaming System in poodle pink for Lizzie to play when Jake was working. Then she spotted a black Barbie suitcase with pink hearts.

"You're the best daddy ever," she said feeling special.

"Anything for my princess."

The new techno gadget greatly reduced Jake's stress. He got to be a whiz and mastered every level—determined to buy more advanced versions.

"Can you help me?" Lisa called.

"Busy in the bathroom," he answered.

When he wasn't preoccupied playing games ... traipsing around local hiking trails alone superseded twiddling this thumbs.

Being fired from the station was unexpected.

"This wasn't your only problem here at KMOL," Mike Hintz said, shifting papers in his hands before laying them on his desk. He lowered his glasses. Reaching for a paper clip, he twisted it rapidly.

Jake refused to answer. Complaints by management were unfounded. Jealousy kept co-workers from appreciating his true talents. Signing termination papers and gathering belongings was the embarrassing frosting.

"Try walking the Turquoise Trail and maybe you'll discover an abandoned mine where you can recover your treasures," Paul said in jest.

"Lisa and I were talking about going out there again. Thanks for the good idea," Jake said in reply. The rest was left to Paul's imagination. Jake muttered as he headed for the exit.

"Folks, sorry to inform you charming Jacob Clark has migrated to other pursuits in these adjacent hills. His new career is studying ancient rock carvings along the West Mesa," Paul announced at the beginning of his news segment.

"Can't believe an idiot is the last guy standing," Jake said to Lisa on the phone.

In a double punch, Jake's wallet loaded with cash and credit cards was stolen at Whole Foods enroute home. He had no idea who pickpocketed him, brushed by eager customers on both sides while pulling frozen shrimp from the cooler—but when he reached the checkout, it was gone.

The crutches Jake built his life on were being knocked out ... one at a time.

"Remember when Phil Davis inferred how laziness doesn't warrant action on God's part," Lisa reminded him. "If you want to eat, you need to work. There's always something you can do. Look around your neighborhood. Offer to cut someone's grass or paint a shed. Titus 3:14 says, *An undisciplined life is not pleasing to God, regardless.* What you do is up to you; but there will be consequences for your choices."

"Don't look at me that way," Jake said after lunch. "Your garden is so choked with weeds, nothing can grow."

"What are you teaching by your actions?" Lisa asked.

"Are we playing a new game—truth or consequences?"

* * *

Jake determined to turn it around.

A day at Sandia Casino was far from common place and closer to heaven. "Your stress melts away on these Vegas-style games," he said to a new friend. She smiled sweetly in her pink lamb's wool V-neck sweater matching hot pink nails. Her fingers flicked the cards in a sassy way, tapping with an intensity that distracted from his usual clarity playing poker.

A few more rounds and he would regain his momentum.

Her button pulled through the loop, straining from supporting two ample sisters, crying to be touched. Black lacy underwear peeked from beneath. He tapped his chest in frustration.

"Oh God, help me," he said.

"Are you some religious fanatic?" she asked.

"Just a normal guy with the usual concerns."

"Glad you don't have issues," she said deeply relieved.

They met on Fridays for a few weeks as Jake attempted to make it lucky, having fun while earning an income. Sade was his good luck charm. She also seemed to enjoy his company. His wedding ring napped in a pocket. The delicious buffet was a sidekick fueling him for more action.

Driving home through the rugged landscape was more stressful.

Jake handed Lisa a ticket for speeding. "Twenty over," he said, "But I couldn't have been going more than ten. The bumps and curves slow everybody down. The officer was a jerk! I'm so annoyed."

A flat tire delayed his return home the next week.

"Wasn't my fault this time … Things happen, Lisa. Do you want me to stop driving the blasted car?" Less is more and her failure to respond packed a wallop. "I even skipped the buffet—give me credit!" he said defensively.

Her eyes penetrated his soul.

"Guess I said too much! Why can't I keep my mouth shut? What kind of wimpy god would allow such a life?"

"Brooke encouraged me to let others see the shattered places in my heart … that's where the light of Jesus shines through!"

It wasn't that simple.

Little food in the refrigerator; his marriage going up in smoke—he couldn't divulge his despair to family, friends, or church.

"Perhaps the noise of this world distracted your focus on priorities," Lisa said slipping into bed next to him.

Chapter 7
Solace

ONE LAST TRIP UP the mountain to retry his luck brought more problems and less cash than Jake could afford. Convincing Sade she needed to move on with someone more her style proved to be costly. "I'm headed to the ocean anyway. It's best we part company."

"Call me when you get there and I'll meet you anywhere," she offered.

"I have financial responsibilities to my children and their mother," Jake said, hoping to finally break free. "If things don't turn around soon, I'll be homeless."

"I'm in love with you and intend to keep you in my scope for a good long while," Sade said. "Worst case scenario, you can move in with me."

Jake arched back breathing deeper.

"It's over, darling."

"No, it isn't," she whispered in his ear. "I think I'm pregnant,"

She cried on his shoulder as dishes were cleared from the table. He was a loser. Many others said the same thing. He needed to get away to think.

She clung. He gave in.

Her glittery gold dress dazzled his yearning eyes, revealing a powerful reward beneath the surface. Holding her brought back emotions he tried to suppress. Insisting on a moment to confide where no one could eavesdrop, they moved to private quarters. The sensations of her body pressed against his were more than he could resist.

It was all a big mess.

She assured him she would make it easier; eliminating the extra burden, if he promised to reconnect after his divorce was finalized. Jake pledged his assurance for their bright future. In reality, feelings for her were long gone. Attempts to contact Sade would eventually stop.

A chance encounter with Pastor Davis on the way home spun a different light on his evening. "Just getting a snack to eat after job hunting," Jake said in the Kwik Trip. He reached for chips and a Coke—pushing guilt down and manufacturing a story that would convince cynical listeners.

"Those buffalo wings are tasty," Phil said.

"Short on cash tonight and left my cards at home. You know how it goes when you're looking for work."

"Hey Jake, we need an extra set of hands for our white water rafting trip with the youth, next Saturday up at Lookout Canyon. No cost to chaperones. We could sure use your experience. Some of our assistants have little knowledge about outdoor sports. Any chance that could work for you?"

"Don't think I have anything. Sounds like fun."

"I would appreciate your help."

Pastor Phil said nothing if he noticed the missing wedding band.

Lisa wasn't so kind. Jake did his best to weave a convincing tale about taking it off to check oil.

After a fun filled day rushing rapids, Phil Davis talked with the teenagers around a campfire. "God has seasons and reasons for everything He does. Can't figure out what He's doing? What He's waiting for? Maybe He's getting ready to use you as a positive example in this world and knows it's going to take lots of work."

"Will we see you tomorrow?" he asked Jake.

"Sure will."

Perhaps by coincidence the sermon was from James 1:2-4. *Count it all joy when you fall into various trials, knowing the testing of your faith produces patience. But let patience have its perfect work, that you may be complete, lacking nothing.* (NKJV)

His parents came over in the afternoon.

"Good thing we finished our home exterior ourselves or it would have cost a fortune," Jake said to his father. "Just bought caulking, flashing for around the chimney, new weather stripping for around the garage door, and a fence post today. I'm trying to caulk defects in the wood siding grooves so water doesn't get in there. Still need to finish painting the lower edge of the dark brown horizontal trim and some soffit in the front. And we have trim boards for around the patio door since we took the old ones down"

"Need any help?" Adam asked.

"No thanks, Dad. Just trying to pass time doing something constructive."

Looking for solace Jake drifted through painfully tedious days. He avoided contact with family, friends, and neighbors—hoping they would forget his shame in overspending, then losing a great income. New gadgets to play with were the last things on his mind. Latest car models, hottest fashions, chic restaurants, no longer obsessed him. Funny … now that he had plenty of time to enjoy those diversions. How could he know his empire would come crashing down so easily?

Where was God in all this?

Trekking up mountains, surfing in the ocean, hunting for an elusive job that would satisfy consumed his time instead. Spending time with his wife and children held little significance. "That's what started this downward spiral," he reasoned. *If only* became his way to escape.

Nagging him was the one person who was supposed to comfort his soul.

"You can't afford going on vacation if you don't have money to pay for it," Lisa said. She offered no alternatives.

"Don't forget our financial situation, my love? I'm looking for a job."

He arranged to visit numerous localities that offered a fresh start. His bigger picture was completely out of focus.

Lisa's excitement skyrocketed, scheduling eight new piano students from coupon slips on the bulletin board inside the grocery store. "Hooray! At this rate, we can pay our utilities."

She painstakingly took every opportunity to spend their dollars as frugally as possible. Cleaning houses was her next potential money-making venture. With little food in the refrigerator, a few weeks from signing up for welfare, someone knocked at the door.

"Hello?" Lisa said, looking around.

On the ground lay a basket with numerous groceries inside.

"You're never going to believe this but someone mysteriously showed up at our front door with food; and after knocking just disappeared," she told Jake.

"Maybe it was a delivery. Did you see a truck?"

"Nope. Nothing."

"You should have gone outside and walked around. Maybe if you had been more observant …"

"But no one was there."

* * *

The 4th of July community shindig presented a fun opportunity to celebrate Alex's first birthday. Wagons covered with balloons and streamers paraded down streets while festive booths and tables offered assorted treats. Lisa made angel crunch cookies with Rice Krispies sprinkled in candy confetti. Red, white, and blue ribbons filled the air with occasional pops from stray balloons.

Photographers snapped multiple photos—one unknown woman in particular kept clicking pictures of Jake.

"Any idea who she is?" he asked Lisa.

"Apparently an admirer."

Lizzie practiced riding her new red bicycle from Pampa and Mimi. Lisa chased the birthday boy, just learning to walk, around the neighborhood. Jake sampled treats and avoided paparazzi intent on recapturing him on film.

"Where have you been hiding?" Sara Thomas, a neighbor three doors down, asked Jake. She brushed crumbs from her shirt. "Sorry. I've been busy in my kitchen but finally have time to talk."

"Is your husband here today?"

"We divorced last year. He was never around anyway."

"Sorry to hear that."

"Miss seeing you on the news every night. You added so much to that show—with your charm and all."

"Thanks for the compliment." He hugged the dinky redhead who looked fresh from the bakery. She even smelled like cinnamon rolls. Her body melted into his for a moment like a glove on a cold hand in the winter.

"Ummm," Sara said.

He hugged her tighter.

"Uh … if you ever need my help."

She glanced up with intrigue. "What a great neighbor! I have a few light bulbs that need changing and other work only a tall guy could do."

"Lisa has this cake for Alex but after that …"

A drum cake with cherries was center of attention for the whole group as little Alex tried to grab the glowing candle. Lisa caught a cherry covered in frosting before it landed on the ground.

"Blow it out!" Jake coaxed his son, unsuccessfully.

Lizzie held her brother's hand as they sang.

Lisa cut the confection into pieces before attempting to carry her sticky birthday boy home for a bath. "Can you stay with Lizzie for the lights?" she asked Jake. "I'm going to call it a night after Alex falls asleep."

"Like a good father."

Sparklers and kid-safe sizzlers were planned for the pre-show. Father and daughter enjoyed a brownie and lemonade in between rounds of pinwheels, dazzlers, and rockets. The atmosphere was charged with electricity. Smiles abounded as oohhs and aahhs began.

"After the fireworks?" Jake whispered to Sara.

Worked out to be a fine time for both families.

Several remaining tasks needed to be finished—requiring assorted trips to help his neighbor in the coming weeks. "Don't forget to change our porch light," Lisa said one day, before a piano lesson.

With neighbor Sara bringing over bakery treats as a special thanks for Jake's help, they bonded closer. He had no idea when she might stop over—and certainly no control when Lisa was gone. Finding them home together peering over old photos was harmless. Lizzie even laughed with them. Turning it into a monumental crime came easy for his protector, however. She glared after Sara left.

"How often has this happened?"

"Nothing's happened before!" Jake insisted.

"This is my home, Jake She isn't welcome here when I'm gone," Lisa said. "And if I ever find her here again, God help us all ..."

"Think you're forgetting the scripture that says we're to love our neighbors."

Overwhelming tears in the middle of the night awoke Jake. Lisa's sobs from the bathroom continued intermittently, despite his efforts to calm. What more could he do?

"I need a man who can ..."

"Wake up, Lise. It's just a dream."

"The problem is my husband."

"Have you no compassion? I didn't do anything wrong. I'm just trying to be neighborly."

"Try being a husband and father, first."

That stung. Jake wanted to fight back ... but why? What was the use? He'd botched many things but his intentions had been good. Life was tough for the couple who meant to impact their world in dramatic ways. "Maybe we'll catch a sunrise and find great joy in the morning," Jake said trying to lighten Lisa's spirit before falling back to sleep.

She appeared to cuddle closer.

*   *   *

"Aunt Abby's home from the Dominican Republic to see family, visit supporters, and reorganize her finances," Jake said at breakfast.

"I forget what she looks like," Lizzie said.

"She's in that picture on the refrigerator."

"Why does she take care of those children?"

"Cause she likes kids ... silly."

Within hours Abby was hugging and kissing Lizzie and Alex—her two favorite kids in the whole world.

"Who wants to play find-the-butterfly?" she asked. They energetically joined in; carefully watching a colorful woven *butterfly* discover hiding places, then search for new ones. Alex chased Abby around the room until he fell asleep on her shoes.

Acting stories in mime was something the newest actress had never experienced. Talking with her hands, forming objects and making signals, required thought and skill. Lizzie refused stopping even for a bedtime snack. "We're not finished, Mom."

Even Jake was having fun.

"Why do you need to leave? You can sleep in my bed," Lizzie said.

"I know, Princess—wish I could but my mom is waiting for me. I haven't seen her for a long, long time."

"Can my friends come over when you come back?" Lizzie loved the pantomime part best and wanted to include them in scenes. "It's so fun when you're here Aunt Abby."

Instantly a hit, she came to Lisa's rescue with babysitting, making dinner, etc. over the three months she was in the area. Having attention from a dearly loved aunt was something Lizzie and Alex would remember. Her gentle ways and wise insight with discipline gave a fresh dimension to parenting for a struggling mother who was beginning to wonder why she had children in the first place.

"We're not alone in this world Lisa," Abby said, "You have someone who can support and encourage you no matter how difficult it seems. Don't forget who loves you the most!"

Chapter 8

Donuts & Kites

"MY BRAIN WORKS BEST when it's fresh—just like food," Holly said at breakfast to Adam. "I always have better insight first thing in the morning than late at night when grogginess sets in."

"So what's your advice today?"

"How about inviting Lizzie and Alex for sleepovers every Friday?"

"Every Friday? What happens to our date night?"

She pushed his arm in a playful jab. He responded by pulling her forward in a full kiss before lifting her off the floor. Holly tried to eat his ear before reaching to tickle him. Giggling, she landed on her toes. "I'm gonna be big trouble if you refuse my request."

"Promise you'll keep our romance alive?"

"We spend quality time every day! But two very precious grandchildren need more of us in their lives."

"You win! Race you to the car."

"It's only Thursday."

"Well we better double our time together if we're busy on Fridays—and there's no better time to begin than now."

Lizzie and Alex waited eagerly for Friday to come. Pampa picked them up and unloaded suitcases at the porch. Mimi was waiting with cookies and milk.

"Where's Baby?" Alex asked.

"Abby already went back home, honey."

"She takes care of hungry children," Lizzie said. "Maybe we could send them cookies." She looked up with bright eyes.

"Not mine!" Alex said.

Adam laughed picking him up and reached for Lizzie's hand. "If we hurry, we can see some baby sheep before it gets dark."

Sitting on the porch with flashlights after the moon came out, Pampa sang songs. Lots of them! Some were funny; others were sad. The best were ones about animals—especially after helping care for farm pets.

"I like sheep," Alex said, remembering the little ram that ran alongside him bleating.

"He wanted your cookie," Pampa said.

Reading from the Bible became a special tradition that took on new meaning as bedtime stories. Lizzie wanted to begin in the front of the Children's Bible and go to the end of the treasured book. "I think we need to read this more often," she said when they finished.

Learning about Biblical characters soon took priority over favorite stories Mimi told. "We can listen to those later," Lizzie explained to her brother.

Learning to pray was poignant with tender hearts touching the face of God. "Please help Daddy get a job. We don't have any money," Lizzie said, beginning to cry. "And my Mommy gets angry."

"They shout very loud!" her brother said, his face animated.

"Alex and I want to be happy."

Taking turns saying what was on their minds was not only revealing but challenging for grandparents who had encountered their own struggles in marriage. "Please forgive us Jesus, for not being more available," Adam said later.

"And we'll try to make it up to them," Holly added.

Saturday morning Mimi made donuts from refrigerator biscuits— poking a hole in the middle with her grandchildren before cooking them in oil in the frying pan. After cooling, powdered sugar was sprinkled on top. Lizzie wore an apron matching grandma. Alex had a chef hat like his grandpa.

Gobbling them up together brought smiles.

Pampa talked about God's rules, calling them "*do nots*". Mimi shared stories about when she made mistakes and didn't listen to God. Using creativity, they tried to teach important spiritual concepts. Curious to know more, Pampa and Mimi taught Lizzie how to dig in scripture.

"Whether or not we make a difference is in His hands," Pampa said.

"I long for them to love the Lord with all their heart, soul, mind, and strength," Mimi said. "Father, please show us how."

Holly painted a beautiful picture with three precious children holding donuts sitting at a table. The wall art above them said, "How sweet are your words to my taste, sweeter than honey to my mouth!" Psalm 119:103

She hung it in her kitchen.

"Can I keep that when I grow up?" Lizzie asked her grandma.

"I think that is a great idea!" Holly said.

They enjoyed their weekends with grandparents so much; Jake began feeling guilty not spending quality time with his children. Inspired by his parents, he attempted to spend more time together. The first afternoon flying kites with Lizzie and Alex brought more frustration than joy.

"Run faster. It will never get up," he shouted to Alex.

"It's going too high. Pull back, Lizzie!" Jake yelled. The tail broke. String twisted into a ball of horror. A tree grasped the colorful creation tight in its leaves, promising never to let go.

Tears and shouting brought Lisa to intervene. "She's only eight years old, Jake. It should be fun."

"I'm trying."

"How's a two year old supposed to run fast enough to get a kite off the ground?"

Jake stormed off.

She picked up debris he left lying on the ground and took the kids inside.

* * *

"How was the worship service this morning?" Adam asked Jake on Sunday afternoon.

"Didn't make it."

"Why?"

"Sick kids—I guess."

"But you could have gone alone, right?"

"Don't worry. I will next week."

"Half-hearted commitment is no commitment, Jake. Insincere worship equals no worship. Where do you stand with God?"

"I'm struggling not to fall asleep over spiritual issues."

"Sorry to hear that … So you have no desire for direction from a sovereign deity?"

"God has more important things to do than concern himself with my mistakes. He's busy elsewhere," Jake said.

"Like stubborn stains on a favorite shirt, there'll always be something you wish you could change. Some bad habits are like addictions that can't be overcome without help. Some character flaws are scars that never go away without surgery. When all else fails and you're ready to give up, that's when God does His best work. Maybe you should try to get back in touch. In spite of your disappointments, I doubt He's ready to give up on you."

His words reverberated in his son's head all week.

On Sunday, Jake slipped into Grace Fellowship after the opening prayer. An usher nodded at him with a smile. The pastor's wife glanced over and beamed. Phil Davis asked the congregation where they turned in time of need.

Jake reached in his pocket for gum.

"Beware. The devil may trick you. He knows when you're lonely, discouraged, and ready to give up—and he wants to help you get there faster. When's the last time you refused to listen to his taunts and kneeled before your Savior instead? Jesus knew about pain and loneliness. His closest friends and disciples fell asleep during his darkest moments."

He looked at Jake.

"Do you feel trapped by circumstances? If you could change anything in your life right now, what situation or relationship do you want relief from? How are you going about it? Pride and sin keep us off our knees and cause us to rationalize. No matter what—don't allow confusion and frustration to build into self-pity, resentfulness, anger, or bitterness. Our struggle should never consume us."

Jake shrugged his shoulders.

Fortunately the pastor's eyes had turned elsewhere.

"Spilling your guts to a Psychologist can make you feel better but doesn't mean the Almighty has heard. Sin separates us from our Father. When's the last time you considered giving up wrong attitudes and motives? Did it bring you to your knees? Don't let sin take you on a disastrous plunge down a slippery slope."

Jake left during the closing prayer.

He had other things on his mind.

Selling pizza wasn't his idea of a great career but Jake kept his game face on. "Beats fixing broken tail pipes and checking cars underneath their bellies. Those dudes start with oil-soaked-clothes before they navigate upside down in the dust. I end up pretty clean, with the exception of greasy hands, and at least eat Pepperoni once in a while," he said to Lisa.

Charming as ever, Jake also raked in tips.

Spending extra-time chatting with customers increased future business—and they ended up asking for him specifically to deliver. Sometimes his route ended at a party.

"Don't wait up!"

"Do I ever?" Lisa asked.

"Tonight won't be a good time to start. I'm catering a big bash for my boss. It'll end late and there's always cleanup. I'm going to handle most of these holiday gigs for him. We need the dough, my love."

Mounds of bills and coins ended on the kitchen counter by morning so Lisa didn't mind. It was her job to transfer those into food. Making tasty morsels with cheaper products took planning—but then, she was great at that. She was a professional. Did a fine job cleaning the house, as well. Some husbands were expected to help with mundane woman chores but not this liberated male.

He had it under control.

*   *   *

Sensing her loneliness over the holidays, Holly invited Lisa to a Christmas Bazaar for girlfriend festive shopping. "It's free with over 80 crafters and handmade items including a bake sale, raffle, and children's exhibits. Please come with me?"

Lisa had no extra money to spend but enjoyed a fun afternoon gathering creative ideas and laughing. A special surprise was wining 2nd place in the raffle—with two tickets to the *Christmas Home Tour* and a gourmet chocolate Christmas Tree.

"A double win," Lisa said, handing the tickets to Holly. "You'll enjoy this tour more than we would." The chocolate she would keep.

Holly introduced her to a close friend, artist Sandi Welch, as they were leaving.

"Glad to meet you, Lisa. Come over to my studio to craft a toy turkey with your kids," Sandi said, pushing glasses up on her forehead before patting her head looking for them to write Lisa's phone number down. "I think we'll make great friends!"

Lisa tucked her business card in a glittery green shopping bag.

"We need to meet Adam at the River of Lights where he's taking Lizzie and Alex to see animated displays of zoo animals," Holly said. "The holiday light show features thousands of Southwestern plants and holiday scenes for more than 90,000 visitors each year."

Lisa knew.

The large cobalt shrine, juxtaposed in the background, framed delicate angel and snowflake luminaries before casting a myriad of colors on the water. Lisa stared into the streaks of gold reflections pointing from her to someplace past the horizon. She reached for a rail, following Jake's father up the steps. Lizzie was far ahead racing with Mimi for cocoa on a nippy winter evening. Alex was asleep in Pampa's arms.

Overwhelmed with sadness, tears blinked from her eyes but no one noticed.

She remembered celebrating her engagement on a luxury helicopter tour of the River of Lights, watching thousands of twinkling lights transform the Bio Park Botanic Gardens into New Mexico's largest walk-through holiday light show. Jake had been romantic, kissing her hand tenderly between numerous kind-hearted comments. It was fun getting re-acquainted and planning for a wonderful future together. Marriage and death changed many holiday traditions but the wonder of Christmas remained the same.

This was just a new angle.

Time would tell what the future might hold.

Knocks on the door brought Jake to his feet. "I have something for you," the uniformed guy said, handing him a package.

He pushed the door shut with his knee before presenting it to Lisa.

"Is this from you?" she asked.

"No."

"Then where did it come from?"

"Check the label." There was no return information and the origination stamp was illegible.

"Huh? That's interesting."

Jake cut the tape. Together they peered in and pulled packing material out—as a card fell on the floor. "Yeah, knew we'd find who this is from," he said. The envelope held a $100 gift card to the local grocery store. No signature. No name. No message.

He pulled tissue from the package eager to see the contents as Lisa watched bewildered.

"Yeow ... Oh, man ... What in the world?" They both gasped as $100 bills fluttered out. Jake tried to catch as many as he could.

"How many are there?" she asked.

"Too many to count."

Three minutes and twenty seven seconds later they knew.

Jake paced back and forth. He scratched his head and went back to the pile, afraid to touch any for fear they might turn into coal. There were too many possibilities to consider. "Why couldn't the sender have left a clue?"

"$5,000—I can't believe it!!!" he said.

"Let's have a New Year's Party with one of them," Lisa said quietly. "People are starting to wonder about us. This would be a fun way to rekindle friendships and get back to how we used to be. We can still be an influence for good."

"Maybe you're jumping to conclusions, Lise. We're still not out of the woods. I have no income. I lost my job. Remember?"

"You can drive faster delivering pizza," she said.

"Uhh ... small problem. Probably going to give up that venture soon. The Escape needs some repairs."

"How about being a lumberjack in the Rockies?"

"Or a sailor to the South Seas?" he suggested.

"No, I don't think so."

Lisa discovered a wooden name plate resting on the bottom of the box—engraved with *Jake and Lisa Clark*. "Oh, Jake. It's beautiful!" she said, showing her husband the treasure.

She traced their names tenderly before placing it on the table.

Jake didn't know what to think.

They snuggled on the couch in a lighthearted moment as he rubbed her back. She stroked her fingers up and down his arm.

Cookie needed to go outside to do his business.

"We're going to make this work. I just know it," Lisa said.

"Until then, I have some errands to run. I'll be back in a couple hours."

They had different roads to travel.

Mixed signals coupled with conflicting emotions placed the two fragile ships dangerously close at times—at opposite poles on other occasions. Part of you is shoved away in a closet until you deal with grief. The will-to-survive part of tragedy requires a shout out to anyone in sight.

Two sweet children kept bringing them back together to the middle.

"Respect other people's space," Lisa's mother always said. So even though it was the hardest thing in the world, her focus remained on that goal.

* * *

"Congratulations!" Joe Garcia said on the phone. Jake tipped his chair back on its legs. Silence.

"I won a Pulitzer for my work in Djibouti?" Jake asked.

(Laughter)

"The Scripps Foundation recognizes excellent work through National Journalism Awards and you're a finalist for small-market television stations and online community news sites. Your expository journalism series with investigative reporting has uncovered irregularities in our Indian Nations and brought scrutiny to these issues."

"Ya don't say!"

"You'll split that $10,000 with Brianna Smyth. Don't get all excited."

"But I did most of the work?" Jake said exasperated, his cynical tone quickly turning angry.

"Irritated by the rules? Don't go after the little guy. I'm just a messenger," Joe said, trying to regain Jake's respect.

"People are individuals and I appreciate our differences. Thanks for the call, Joe."

"See you around, good buddy."

Relishing the highly regarded award for journalism, Jake contemplated the uncommon circumstances it was based on. His hard work resulted in betrayal by Mike Hintz—whose own admin screwed up the promo and created the mess. Because she had a private rendezvous with Mike was none of Jake's business, she said on three occasions. How could Jake have known what was going on that morning and how did Mrs. Hintz find out?

His ideals had also been jerked away when he discovered Brianna moved in with Paul Esse the year before—while pretending to have a special dalliance with Jake.

In the end, Paul received kudos for Jake's masterpiece series. A flash in the pan; right place at the right time. He also stole the prized co-worker's affections. Jake wanted to punch him.

Two adversaries at the station tried to falsely destroy his reputation and get rid of him. Jake had no intention of going to the stupid awards ceremony, if there was another way to get his prize. I don't want to see any of them ever again. Maybe a job in Alaska rushing Huskies in the Iditarod would be a challenging escape.

The Yukon sounded better and better.

Searching ads for a new vehicle motivated Jake to find something purposeful to do with his life again. Prices were high but so was the cost of living. He asked his father for advice.

"Sons look at their father in a certain light. Want them to provide wise insight when they need it. Any pointers you care to give me?" Jake said on the phone to his dad.

"In high school, I earned my position as quarterback of the football team because I knew how to play the game. There's no reason to back away from your goals Jake—pursue them even harder but don't lose sight of your first priorities. I'll contact Josh and David to see if they know of any possibilities out in California."

"Just so you know, I'm gonna be off on my own for a while," Jake said.

"I assumed you'd job hunt alone?"

"Lisa has issues with everything I do."

"Where are you going with this?"

"We don't click anymore."

"Come over for dinner tomorrow and we'll finish this conversation."

"Sure ... Dad."

"Ever wonder why the problem keeps resurfacing?" Adam said to Holly. "His self-centered affections offer no love to others."

At dinner the next day they had more to say.

"How would you like to change course—adjust your sails? Are you ready to enter new territory?" Adam asked his son.

"Buy a boat?" Jake grinned. "Sure."

"How would you like to live off luscious fruit from a land full of milk and honey? No longer eat manna from heaven for breakfast, lunch, dinner?" Holly asked.

"Are you guys on something?"

"God's at work restoring relationships and building new ones. Language is a bridge to people. We've asked many questions over the years. His answers have led to unexpected places," his father said in a serious tone.

"How does this involve me?"

"Our lifestyle should be a foretaste of our eventual destiny in heaven. Angie is already there waiting for us," Holly said.

"She's been out of my life for a long time. I don't think it serves any purpose to continue grieving over what might have been." His lips tightened and he clasped his hands. Sometimes he hated his mother.

"But you haven't shed one tear for your adorable daughter, Jake?"

His face hardened. "You start talking about a thrilling adventure embracing life and suddenly jump into a tragic death? I don't get it. And I'm not going to be your whipping boy. I did nothing wrong."

He jumped up and slammed the door on his way out.

"Remember that story you used to tell him?" Adam asked Holly.

"Once upon a time, a mysterious ship docked at the wharf in Harbor City ... with an eerie light glowing below deck ... It was twilight … with dark clouds filling the once orange sky … Jake saw pirates creeping over the side … one spotted him watching from his grandfather's bait shop on the shore … and even though he had nothing to fear, Jake began to run as fast as he could."

"Wonder where he'll end up?"

"Doesn't matter. He's not going to get away from God."

Chapter 9
Fog

EARLY MORNING SUNLIGHT STRUGGLED to break the stranglehold moisture played with high humidity. Unseen clouds remained completely hidden. They tried to shake loose as rising temperatures held them in a security pat down. A welcome breeze would improve visibility but none was in the vicinity.

"Good thing you didn't go hunting today. You'd be shooting innocent squirrels," Lisa said.

Jake cleaned his rifle as he waited.

He'd been attacked by a hive full of angry hornets, enslaved by their captors—forced to make honey which they knew nothing about. Her words stung worse than tentacles of a gigantic jelly fish hanging on the last bite of lunch in the sea. Gone were Lisa's former, kind-hearted comments of a woman in love. Here to stay was a cup of poison too bitter to drink.

And she acted like nothing happened.

Her story had absolutely nothing to do with reality. Jake repeated the words to himself, mimicking Lisa.

His stomach started to growl.

"Want something to eat?" she asked cheerfully.

Her coffee smelled good with a hint of vanilla so he stood to get some.

"I'm sorry, Jake. I should have been more respectful even though I was trying to be honest."

"Ya think?"

"Hooray, he can speak," she said to the wall.

She handed him coffee in his favorite mug and started making an omlete. "Can we just kiss and make up? We need to redeem this day somehow. Looks like we'll be together for the whole morning."

"Okay."

"Before or after breakfast?"

Her questions were beginning to get to him.

A call after lunch caused Jake to go outside. Lisa pretended to dust in the foyer, trying to overhear. Some of the conversation was heated. "I simply can't … No, that's the end of it … I tried sweetheart; it's just not possible." He moved farther from the door. "How many times have I told you about my intentions … I did everything possible to keep my promise … We can finish this conversation in person … Do not call back tonight."

Walking back inside, he leaned over to pick up his shoes. "Need to go help the Pizza guy on a run."

"That was a woman."

"Yeah, his daughter was giving me a message for him."

"It doesn't make sense, Jake."

"Nothing in my life does." He hurried to the new Honda.

"Maybe we need to take another trip together." Jake said when he returned.

"So we can suffer more pain? No thanks."

"Then I'm going to California to catch a few waves while I figure this out."

"We have no money, Jake."

"Well, I can't contemplate life here while you're on my case. I've got some changes to make." Heeding wisdom wasn't always Jake's strong suit. He packed a bag and kissed Lisa on the cheek before heading west the next morning. "I'm supposed to meet my cousin by 5:00 pm. Have a couple job interviews. I'll call in the next day or two."

Reflections on the Pacific Ocean would take minimal time—unless partying with relatives and surfing used his waking hours. Surely he would call immediately if he found a job, though it's doubtful he would start instantly.

She waited five days for an answer.

"This new job changes everything—it's time to move on," he said.

"How soon?"

"I interviewed for a consultant job as a Talent Scout in Seattle. Need to go up next week to finalize everything."

"We're moving to Seattle?"

"I'm moving up alone temporarily … considering life there, before I make a permanent commitment."

"I don't understand. What does this mean?"

"I don't know, Lisa, but I'll tell you the details when I learn what's involved. In the meantime, I need a new wardrobe for the bright lights, camera, and action. We're talking big time here. These people are headed for Hollywood and fame."

"Will it involve travel?"

"Of course. Where the star shines, I'll be just around the corner."

"Sounds kind of funky."

"I knew you'd be blown away. The guys I work with wear snazzy designer suits. You haven't seen anything like this before! I'm talking glamour and glitz. And don't worry—you'll be wearing great gowns like this cobalt velvet Jovani with bare back and slit up the thigh that will require Jimmy Choos for the Oscars."

"Sounds like you just won the lottery."

"All that and more."

"So when are you coming home?"

"Just long enough to swing by for a few hours and grab some things before I head to Seattle day after tomorrow."

His phone dropped off and Lisa sat back in shock.

Flying by the seat of his pants, Jake blew in and then took off in the middle of the night. "I don't want to bother anyone until I get my first paycheck and find stability. We'll buy a second car as soon as I can make arrangements. I'll fly back to see you in a few weeks."

He reached down to tuck her in before kissing her on the check. She tried to stand up but he gently pushed her back. "Don't wake the kids," he whispered.

Then he was gone.

She lay in bed thinking until the sun came up. This was different from anything she expected. Things would surely calm down in a couple days. Lisa had kids to think about and a house to take care of.

Explaining where Daddy had gone was actually easier than she expected.

"Just got tickets to the sensational Four Bachelors Concert," Jake announced on his first day of work. "Wish you could go with me on Saturday, Lise."

"Me too," she said wishing they were together again. Part of this scenario didn't make sense. "I'd like to fly up and help find a place for us. You probably need my insight about what will work best for the kids."

"I'm staying in a comfy efficiency apartment with monthly rates. This will do temporarily. Money's pretty tight until I get into a routine."

"When do you get your first paycheck?"

"Not until I get my portfolio lined up. I'm working on commission."

"So how long does that take? Don't you get a normal paycheck in addition to the bonus?"

"It's not a bonus. It's my pay."

"I thought this was a lucrative position."

"It will be. Hang in there with me."

"Jake … On which day will we get more money?"

"Gotta take this call, babe. I'll call you back."

His voice mail picked up for the next three days and Lisa left multiple messages to call back. "Why can't I reach you?" she said when he called.

"I'm out of the office talking to clients most of the time or in the conference room where we can't take personal calls. You're gonna have to bear with me while I learn the ropes in this new job. I don't want to upset the boss."

"It seems like you have a big secret life and I'm not part of it."

Lisa tried to understand but Jake wasn't able to communicate clearly. His thoughts jumbled. It seemed he had marbles in his mouth—or maybe in his brain. It appeared his income would take a while longer. She threaded food on skewers to make it look like there was more.

Stretching bread and potatoes only goes so far.

Five days passed before Lisa heard from her husband again. She was busy with Little League anyway. "Alex looks so cute in his little uniform! He's just adorable! When he hit the ball yesterday, he broke out in laughter and forgot to run. After the game, he always looks around for you. I don't know what to tell him, Jake."

"Stop! He doesn't know whether I'm there or not, Lise. You're twisting this to make me look bad. It's more important I find a solution to our financial problems right now. We'll have no future unless I do."

With more time alone to think, Lisa started attending Grace Fellowship again. Most days she slipped into the children's area with a flurry of parents, kids, and teachers interacting; and kept dialog about Jake to a minimum.

One sermon was about reasons why God sometimes delays answers.

"We can't live in sin, disobedient to God," Phil Davis said. It would be good for Jake to hear this message, Lisa thought. His refusal to talk about spiritual things indicated something sinister was going on deep down.

She opened her Bible to Psalm 84:11.

"It has to do with an intimate relationship; walking uprightly; a heart bent to please; willing to be obedient," Pastor Phil continued.

She was trying so hard.

*　　*　　*

Arriving home after grocery shopping, Lisa pulled into the driveway—part way. She noticed a white heap at the side of the road.

"It's Cookie!" Alex shouted.

"No it's not," Lizzie countered. "It can't be. He's inside."

Lisa knew better.

She opened the car door and went to check as Alex joined her. Bending over his body they paused. His paw was limp but he was still warm. She picked him up and cradled him. His fur smelled of peppermint soap from his bath the evening before. The red collar with engraved nameplate would become an epitaph for his grave. Alex pulled at his leg. "Wake him up, Mommy."

"He's gone to heaven, AJ."

Nothing to do but carry him to the house. It took an eternity. Alex followed while Lizzie sat in the car.

Lisa found a box and draped a piece of yellow satin in the bottom before laying Cookie in the middle. She tucked the corners over his hardening body. A few tears dropped down as Alex found a special doggy-toy and put it next to the family pet. Lizzie entered the house and walked past towards her room. "Do you want to say goodbye?" Lisa asked.

"What's the point? He can't hear me anymore," she said slamming her door.

Alex helped carry groceries in before they found a place in the yard to bury him. Ice cream had melted so she dumped it in the sink. Frozen vegetables could be refrozen. The bread was soggy but could be used along with most of the other food. The doggie treats caused her to break down in the middle of the floor.

Alex sat beside his mother patting her back.

Then he climbed on her lap. His kisses and hugs caused her to cry harder. "I love you, dumpling," she finally said.

"Let's call Daddy. He'll know what to do."

The phone rang three times before a young gal answered. "Hullo?"

"Oh, I'm sorry," Lisa said. "I have the wrong number."

She tried again. The same voice picked up. "Hullo?"

"Uh ... is Jake there?"

"Nope. He went to get some night crawlers but will be back before we go fishing. Are you his mother?"

"No. Will you tell him Lisa called?"

"Sure. No problem."

He never returned the call.

They buried Cookie under the oak tree near a fence where he loved to hide bones. Lizzie sang a song she made up and Alex said a prayer. Mr. Brown, an elderly neighbor, came over to apologize for accidently hitting him while swerving to miss another car. "Looked like he was trying to chase the car when you left," he said.

The door might have been ajar when Lisa carried Cookie into the house. Her keys were still in the ignition when she went back to get groceries.

Lizzie had been the last one out.

The next time Lisa reached Jake, he seemed out of breath and in no mood to talk. "Cookie died last week." She told him about the accident and how painful it had been for Lizzie.

"What do you want me to do about it, Lise? I'm not God."

Talks with Jake took Lisa from climbing out of a pit and plunged her deep into depression. She was seldom able to reach him directly and he hardly ever called back. "It's been almost two months and we've had little contact. Where's the money from your paycheck?"

"Needed the first check for living expenses in Seattle. That's my priority. I'll send the next one to you on Friday. Thought my dad paid for the utilities. You should still have a little left in the savings account." Female voices laughed in the background.

"Thought you were home alone."

"I was but the neighbor just stopped over."

"The one you went fishing with?"

"Didn't remember telling you about Francie? We're getting to be pretty good friends. She knows how to keep a lonely guy from going crazy."

"Sounds like more than one female?"

"Yeah, three of them tonight. We're going out to dinner and then down to watch boats. Her friends are awesome."

"Is that why you don't have time for me?"

"Do you want me to sit on the sofa like a recluse every night and cry in my soup?"

He had no intention explaining about the thump on the floor or the incessant giggling close by with an occasional clearing of her throat. Lisa couldn't see him motion to Francie to stop nibbling on his hear.

"Things like this never happen to others, Jake."

"Happens all the time. Look around at all the divorces."

"Are you suggesting ..."

"It is what it is, Lisa We're so different. Diversity isn't working for us."

"Have you considered what could possibly be wrong in our home? Do you have any concern for my welfare? What about your children?"

"Are you blaming me again? Look in the mirror is all I can say. You were the one not watching her, Lisa. If you had just stayed in the hotel room or been …" He paused to tell the girls he would meet them at the corner. A door shut and the background went silent.

"I wonder where we went wrong." she said to Jake. "Do you think God is capable of getting us out of this mess?"

"I'm in love with someone else, Lise. I don't have room in my heart for both of you. We'll see what the future holds. Really can't tell how this will unfold right now but it feels so right. Francie makes me feel like a million bucks."

"Ever walk on rose petals? They're easily crushed," she said before hanging up.

Crying seemed out of the question. Her sockets were dry.

Spending time at Grace Fellowship provided the only anchor she could find in her tempestuous sea. Slipping in beside Brooke, Lisa felt safe and welcome. Rev. Davis spoke about how ignoring termites causes great palaces to collapse and how the tiny critters cause unbelievable damage.

She tried to take notes but the words flew by too quickly.

"Everyone has a relationship with God but some don't relate to Him. They feel He's distant; out there somewhere! They have no sense of connection and spend little time together. May attend church occasionally but become satisfied with the superficial—what you see, touch, feel on the surface—never go deeper. Truth becomes clearer as we apply it to our life. The Bible isn't a mystery novel. It provides stability, an anchor in a storm no matter the strength of wind or waves. Serenity, peace and contentment follow. There's something awesome about a creator beyond beautiful snow-capped mountains, bubbling brooks, a majestic sea of stars."

"Can you explain it to me?" she asked Brooke after the service.

"Sure. How about on Tuesday morning?"

"It sounds wonderful; I really want to understand."

They dug deeper into scripture than Lisa knew possible.

Brooke explained how the Holy Spirit can do nothing when we're proud and try to handle our life alone. "We can't control our own destiny, regardless of how hard we try. We need to realistically look at ourselves. Do I thirst or hunger to know my Creator better? Will I spend time in His presence and allow Him to change my thoughts and actions?"

Agreeing to study together each week, Brooke decided to mentor Lisa until she could fly alone. The butterfly with a broken wing would find healing in the only one capable of working miracles.

The following Tuesday they met again.

"What does Psalm 42 say to you? How does this apply to your life? Look beyond what you can see. The more you listen; the more you'll hear. The more He excites you; the more time you'll spend together. You're going to learn more that you can imagine, Lisa. God can restore what seems lost or forgotten. Sometimes our lives seem stretched out like a wilderness filled with barren patches of failures and regret. Lost opportunities litter the landscape of our past and we have no hope. We think our lives are broken beyond repair but that's not true. We can't change the past, but God can restore our present and our future. You'll find yourself being used in ways you never expected," Brooke said.

"How can one person do everything?" Lisa asked her mother-in-law.

"You don't need to, sweetie. Someone wants to help you. And don't forget Adam and I will always be here for you."

"How long has this been going on? Why didn't you ask for help?" Adam asked.

"We were so caught in our pain, we failed to properly grieve," Lisa said.

"Then you plan to make changes?"

"I can only speak for myself. Our pastor's wife is mentoring me and walking me through the grieving process."

"Reflecting later, people always say—we wouldn't have missed this for anything," Holly said. "I can't promise how He's going to bring you through this but I know He works miracles. We're supposed to thank Him in advance."

Chapter 10
Marathon

"CONGRATULATIONS!" JOE GARCIA SAID to Jake on the phone. "You're the winner of the Worchester Prize for Excellence in Reporting on the Environment—with your six part series on, *Restoring the Oceans to Pristine Condition.* The $40,000 prize money is the largest cash prize for journalism in the world."

"What a lucky coincidence!"

"The purpose of the prize is to recognize outstanding reporting with the potential to bring constructive change and increase public awareness. Your originality and excellence were noted as newsworthy for an elite group of journalists. Winners are required to attend an awards ceremony and assist with marketing—including at least fifteen radio and television interviews, so expect requests for videotapes and b-roll footage. This is your chance to go big-time in the national media, Jake. Welcome back!"

"Appreciate the news," Jake said beaming from ear to ear. "Hate to cut you off, Joe, but a client just walked in. Let me know more details if you hear anything."

His dreams had just come true!

Taking the afternoon off, he headed for Bachman's Beauties to finalize a deal on a houseboat he'd recently considered—with expense no longer an issue.

If he hurried, he could catch Francie and tell her the good news.

"Hallelujah!"

Luck was with him and she joined arm-in-arm as he became proud owner of the *Forbidden Odyssey*. It would take work getting her back to seaworthy condition but with his adoring friend's help, the new abode could exude warmth in no time. The engine would be tweaked. Deck and rails scrubbed and polished—would gleam in the sun. Inside living quarters were ideal for providing the comforts of home; with the potential to take him places he only imagined. Taking her out on open water was a fantasy he could feel in his bones.

The little dinghy was a bonus.

"Thank you God," he said standing on deck with his arm wrapped around a cherished companion.

Francie's cute brown eyes peeked from thick lashes as he kissed the top of her dark curls. She giggled. "You're the best thing in the world for me right now," he said in her ear. She leaned closer and purred on his chest. Her fun-loving-ways were a magnet for joyful living, frolicking wherever he wanted to go with complete abandon. His apprehension being alone in an unfamiliar environment had been eliminated the moment he met the attractive female. She enjoyed his companionship as much as he craved being around her. Appreciation from a bubbly young woman who catered to his manliness frosted the cake.

She had no flaws.

Not even a hint of jealousy surfaced when her friends playfully interacted with Jake or appreciated his charms, just as stable relationships should offer.

They lingered while the sun went down past a glowing crescendo, until the moon came out in full glory. Stars twinkled overhead as they christened the Forbidden Odyssey with a cheap bottle of chardonnay.

Jake's spirits had never soared higher!

Waves rushed against the side of his new home while he slumbered—on the old mattress, musty but firm—keeping him awake longer than he intended. He'd forgotten an alarm and overslept. With his phone dead, and the day unplanned, he stopped at Starbucks for breakfast.

How good could life get?

It had been eons since Jake had a wad of cash in his pocket and felt like a real man.

*   *   *

She slammed the door to her room and uttered words forbidden at school. No one cared about her anyway, so it didn't matter what anyone thought. Lizzie put in earphones and turned her music louder. She had no intention finishing homework. She was just a kid and needed space. If her stupid mother had been more accommodating for Dad, he would never have left either. Maybe she should go visit him and they could live together.

True, they had never really developed a close relationship, so far— he hardly knew about her life—but that would change if Lizzie visited. He was her father after all.

Surely he cared.

"I don't care what you say," she said when Lisa entered her room. "I'm going to live with Dad."

"Really?"

"He's been planning this for a long time."

"When did you last talk about it?" Lisa asked.

"It's none of your business."

Lisa left the basket of clean clothes on the floor and walked out of the room. Then she came back in and kissed Lizzie on the cheek.

"I'll miss you dreadfully," she said to her daughter.

Rev. Davis must have known what she was thinking when Lisa slipped next to Brooke—a few minutes late, with Lizzie. "What's going on inside of you?" he asked, beginning his sermon. He looked around the congregation. "What's causing stress or discouraging you? Caught in the middle of a fog? Perplexed by situations beyond your control?"

Lizzie nudged her mother.

"Psalm 42:11 says, *Why are you downcast, O my soul?* In times of great sorrow, in the middle of battle, where do you turn? Apparently God understands and wants to talk about our concerns. David's question was repeated in Psalm 43:5."

"Disappointments come easily and are unavoidable. They may be caused by the inability to satisfy people closest to you; by lack of respect and appreciation for what you've done; blaming God for bad things that happen; or strongholds—sin—that trap you in the cellar when God wants you on the roof to see a sunrise."

"If your house should burn to the ground and you lose precious treasures, you'll have reasons to be discouraged but don't have to be incapacitated. Disappointments are inevitable but discouragement is a choice."

"He wasn't just talking to me," Lisa said driving home. "I'm glad you were with me this morning Lizzie."

Lizzie smiled.

"I want to sit with you next week Mommy," Alex said.

"Kids go to children's classes," Lizzie said. "Don't they, Mom?"

"When you get bigger, I'd like to have you sit by me, A.J."

Fighting between brother and sister followed.

Lisa tired of the meaningless chatter and blocked it out. She couldn't wait until Tuesday when Brooke came over. Music on the radio helped ease her frustration. "You did me wrong and I'm gonna move on ... you can't hurt me no more ... I've got my eyes on a star ..."

* * *

Empty drawers in the dresser didn't help ease her loneliness. Lisa pretended they were full. Wonder if he ever thinks about me? Does he think about the kids? She could call Jake to chat—but her pain would surely increase. It always did! *Did you mean anything you ever said? Is there anything about me that you like?*

"How could I get it so wrong?" Lisa asked Brooke on Tuesday.

"Maybe you're seeing an elegant tapestry from the wrong side?"

"Notice my garden this morning—It resembles my life."

"Don't give up, Lisa. He's in control no matter what it looks like."

"Why does he allow my pain to continue? Why did he promise not to give me more than I could bear ... and then abandon me?"

"Are we talking about Jake or God?"

Lisa laughed and blew her nose. She re-poured hot tea and reached for a Mint Rhapsody. Brooke chose Spiced Chai.

"God understands tears when our heart is broken," Brooke said. "If you make good choices, your feelings will ultimately support those decisions."

"When we dated, a canoe capsized dumping both of us into the water. Jake playfully acted like he was drowning, thrusting his arms in the air and gurgling. He had no idea how serious it appeared. Sitting on the bank later—drenched—I asked, 'Can a person really make sure he goes to heaven when he dies?' That's when I prayed with Jake."

"Did you just want an insurance policy to stay out of hell? Or did you want Jesus to change your heart? Are you aware what really happened that day?"

"I know I've sinned and don't deserve talking to an Almighty," Lisa said.

"There's a Harvest Festival coming up—a women's retreat—that I believe you would enjoy. Why don't you sign up? I'll talk to Phil about getting you a scholarship, if Jake's parents can watch your kids. Call me when you find out."

All the details worked out for her to attend the conference.

Lisa determined to spend time pulling weeds and thistles while she tried to hold her family together.

Arriving with other giggly females over piles of suitcases and mounds of bedding at the rustic lodge in a mountain valley, high in the Sangre de Cristo Mountains north of Albuquerque, the Conference Center welcomed guests. "No matter the season or the situation of your life, you'll find a sanctuary for your mind, heart and spirit here," the volunteer said. "Relax, recharge and meet God personally. There's something for everyone in an atmosphere and environment that nurtures spiritual journeys."

Checking in and finding rooms took hours but each minute was a delight. By the time Brooke and Lisa connected, she had three new friends—one she had never met and two were casual acquaintances from Grace Fellowship.

In the morning, coffee wafted down hallways waking those who wished for an extra hour of sleep. Sausage and eggs waited with the famous cinnamon rolls that melt-in-your-mouth.

Lisa was an early bird, eager to find strength to continue her difficult journey, and quickly discovered a favorite place to meet God—beside a stone fireplace in the massive lobby. Warmth from the glowing embers penetrated her body and spirit. She sipped steaming coffee while waiting for the day to begin, savoring newfound moments of peace as ladies sauntered by in their crisp outfits.

She pulled her favorite navy sweater tighter around her shoulders. The fresh mountain air was invigorating.

"Hey Lisa, How'd you sleep?" Brooke asked her cherished friend.

"I'm here to learn as much as I can," Lisa answered. "I'll catch up on sleep when I return home."

"Wish all my friends were as wise as you," Brooke said.

They joined a table of hungry friends for the first of several delicious meals.

Within minutes, an attractive woman with silvery hair stood up and adjusted her cranberry jacket over an ivory silk shirt. Her black pants had creases, looking like they'd never been worn. A silver cross was at her neck.

"When was the last time you were dazzled?" she asked. "For me it was this morning as the sunrise reflected over the mountains with glorious ochre and tangerine shooting rays into the darkness of heaven, as a dazzling ball of gold made its way onto the horizon—popping his head to say, "Good morning dear friend.""

"I'm trusting God to work miracles and make us winners!" she said with a smile.

"Nothing can stop us but ourselves," the speaker began. "Whenever God takes his people into a new territory, he goes first to prepare the way. He does things we can't imagine. The things you're just now catching a glimpse of, he's already been actively involved in. He melts hearts of strangers before you arrive at the party. Fighting giants, tearing down walls, preparing great and tasty feasts—nothing is too hard for him. Nothing can stop his plan. No power on earth can oppose him."

"What if we resist?"

"He won't move you into the Promised Land with sinful behavior. A sovereign Almighty can't tolerate sin. Read about the Israelites. Character and integrity take time to develop. Rahab was busy cutting deals, lying, prostituting herself. Lots of work needed to be done but her faith saved strangers. The red cord represented blood over her door. Conditions for belief are the same for everyone. Salvation never changes. Remember the Israelites in Egypt on the night of Passover? Rarely will he keep us where we've already been. Moving forward requires we leave something behind. It's not about where you came from but where you're going."

"Get ready to move with the cloud."

Holly and Adam were surprised to hear about emerging details of life in Seattle from grandchildren. Some of what Lizzie and Alex revealed must be a misunderstanding. Lots of questions were waiting for Lisa when she returned.

Adam was curious about the houseboat his son purchased and was settling into. "Must be why I've been unable to reach Jake," he said. "Maybe there's no cell tower near the bay."

"I can't reach him either," Lisa said.

"Does he contact you regularly?"

"Jake's never had much contact with the kids—never really bonded with Lizzie and hardly knows his son. His life pretty much revolves around himself. He calls on occasion."

"And if you had an emergency?"

Lisa burst into tears.

*   *   *

"Jake … nice to hear your voice. Tried to reach you all weekend," his father said.

"Out watching a perfect sunset." Jake said. "What do you need?"

"I'm not the one who needs you, Son."

"Is there a problem?"

"You're the one who made a commitment to Lisa. Did the elaborate gifts, cards, and never-ending promises over the years mean anything to you?"

"Uh Dad, I have a friend over right now."

"Do you require Jesus stand at your front door and knock before he can spend time with you?"

"Friends can stop by my place anytime."

"Are they more important than your family?"

"I'm still running around trying to find a stable life for my kids. Haven't found what I'm looking for," Jake said. "Until the sun comes up, gonna catch more fish."

"It's obvious you need to do some soul-searching. Change your thinking and your actions will change. I'll call back later."

Adam hung up.

"God hasn't forgotten you during these dark seasons of your soul, regardless of how it feels," Holly said to Lisa. "We come to know Him best when we need him most. I can promise you personally that hope is waiting at the end of the dark tunnel."

Lisa needed to hear words of encouragement.

"You bring out the best in your adorable kids," Holly said. "Good work! Great interactions. Keep it up! You deserve rewards—and don't forget the gifts He already gives—butterflies, rainbows following the rain, colors of fall, and many more."

Adam challenged her to watch the power of God in a variety of situations. "Fixing our problem is not His goal. Transforming us into His image is. He's all about what's inside."

"Can I pray for your family?" Adam asked before leaving.

His words lingered in Lisa's ears long into the night. If only Jake would listen to his father ... either of them.

* * *

A picture of Jake on a sailboat, holding up a huge red snapper, was in the mail—along with a pamphlet requesting donations for an 18 mile run around the bay. "Ends with a fish fry in support of the American Heart Association," he noted on the bottom.

"Sounds like an exciting life," Adam said to his son on the phone.

"Just trying to help out and make a difference in this world. You always ask what I'm doing."

"And what are you doing with your wife and kids this week?"

"Don't have any extra time this week."

"What about next week?"

"What's your point, Dad?"

"We all encounter circumstances in life. It's up to you how to respond. You make it what you want it to be."

"So I signed up for a grueling marathon."

"Where will that get you?"

"Healthier and happier."

"And explain to me how your family fits in?"

"A friend just stopped by. Need to go now. Give everybody my love."

"1 Corinthians 9:24 says, *Don't you know that in a race, only one runner gets the prize? Run in such a way as to get that prize,* Jake."

When Adam got off the phone with his son, he planned a family marathon so everyone could be involved. He drew a map of the yard; inserted posts at varied positions to mark *miles*; set up benches to rest; placed coolers of water and juice in prime places; and Holly baked an assortment of yummy treats for sustenance. With numbered flags on their backs, the entire family minus Jake set out on a fun-filled family marathon.

After a laughter-filled morning, Lisa was deemed the winner.

On Tuesday, Brooke added her own rules for Lisa.

"Non-Runner Marathon Tip #1—Eat jelly beans at every mile marker. They're game changers, if not life-changers."

"Non-Runner Marathon Tip #2—Always run the race with a good friend who talks and prays a lot. Talking because it keeps your mind off the pain; praying because it keeps the pain from messing with your mind."

Sunlight streamed through the gorgeous stained glass when Lisa entered Grace Fellowship on Sunday. A twist of blue and green sparkled from the corner. *Where did that little lamb come from?*

She'd never noticed him before.

"Is your life wrapped up like a big present—yourself!!!?" Rev. Davis asked. "Are me, myself, and I your favorite friends? We're not being dishonest or unethical when we think about ourselves with no need for God's help. It comes naturally. We're central and need to consider what we say, do, how to respond in circumstances. But that's not where it should end. Do you insist on handling things alone; never consider you may need someone else's help? God multiplies what we anchor in his hands. Doubt and confusion will compound our difficulties when we attempt to serve two masters."

"What do you refuse to let go of—have a death grip on? What we hold tightly, we sometimes lose. Insecurity produces fear. I want this so much ... I've gotta have you!!! When anything becomes more important than the Almighty God, it becomes an idol. We may not lose what we cling to but we'll lose something much more valuable—things we treasure most—joy, peace, contentment. There's no room for His blessings when we clutch our own priorities."

"Do you hold on to hurts, refuse to let go of the past? Unforgiveness shows on our faces. The grips of animosity, resentment, bitterness show in our health. He doesn't intend for the past to carry into the future—you'll miss blessings planned for tomorrow.

Glancing in the church bathroom mirror before leaving, Lisa noticed a bit of gray hair popping out of nowhere. Frown lines accentuated her aging eyes and lips. Maybe she needed new makeup ... or a face lift.

Chapter 11

Acne

THE NEIGHBORHOOD BABY SHOWER for Angelica Garcia, filled with adorable nighties, hand knit booties, a beautiful quilt made by a doting grandmother, and other infant paraphernalia, brought back deep emotions for Lisa. As she gingerly touched each of the presents, thoughts of becoming a new mother preoccupied her involvement in reality. "Oh, I'm sorry," she said to Sara, who tried to pass a rosy satin blanket to Lisa.

Tiny pink cupcakes on thin slices of cake decorated like diapers were served with pink M&M's. Lisa busied herself picking them up, one by one, and pretended to hear the neighbor's conversation—laughing from time to time.

She didn't remember saying goodbye. Calling Jake was all she could think of. Luckily, he answered.

"Hi. Are you busy?"

"Just got home. I helped a co-worker paint his boat this morning."

"Are you finished repairing your houseboat?"

"Almost. Just a couple more tweaks and I'm taking the Forbidden Odyssey out for a spin, to watch her purr on the open sea."

"I miss Angela!"

"That was a long time ago. Nothing I can do. Get over it."

"It's hard taking care of the kids alone, Jake."

"Sometimes you need to buck up, grit your teeth, and move on. You can do it, Lisa." A knock on his door, giggle in the background, whisper in the foreground, and she knew what would come next. "Gotta go now. I'll call next week," he said.

"About the utility bills …"

A dial tone told her the conversation was over.

Lizzie slammed the door, shouting words she couldn't say at school from the bathroom. Her tone was becoming increasingly difficult to tolerate; didn't matter if her antagonizer was a teasing brother or her mother.

"Come out here right now young lady."

"I hate you."

"Doesn't matter. You have responsibilities." No response for a minute brought repeated threats from Lisa. "Lizzie—can you hear me?"

The door opened and a cantankerous adolescent walked out, earphones in place. "I'm Betsy, in case you ever want to talk to me again," she said, brushing past her mother in the hallway.

Lisa reached for her arm and then held back.

She needed to talk with someone first.

Kneeling by her bed, Lisa poured out her heart. "These termites are eating me alive. I'm on the verge of collapse. Jake's not even parenting from a distance. What was that wooden name plate with *Jake and Lisa Clark* engraved on the bottom about? Why would someone send such a stupid gift?"

"Lizzie's struggling in school and at home. She's becoming a young woman and torn—because childhood issues can't be resolved. Her friends tease about wearing non-designer clothes, living without her once-famous father, and being unable to hang out at inappropriate places. The bullying is painful."

"Alex is only five and doesn't know his father. He pretends to be a person he believes would be acceptable—but obviously misses the mark. I need creativity in dealing with this lying child. He's so sweet and means well …"

Holly and Adam knocked at the front door.

"Got it," Lizzie said, warmly greeting them. "Hi, I'm Betsy!"

"You don't say," Adam said hugging her. "You sure look like a Betsy to me."

"She looks like a monkey to me," Alex teased.

"Mimi and I love monkeys," Adam said, suddenly grabbing both grandkids. They giggled, tried to run, and Holly stepped in to make a family hug.

"Come join us Lisa."

She did—reluctant at first, but with coaxing melted into the joy of the moment. Confiding some of what transpired in her heart spilled out to godly, caring in-laws during the evening but her deepest secrets would remain exclusively with God.

Lisa copied Holly's quote in the front of her Bible before they left.

Spiritual transformation requires great pressure but ultimately turns coal into diamonds. Refining gold always involves intense heat.

After they left, she tucked kids in bed and went back to an intimate conversation with the one who loved her most.

Driving home, Adam and Holly remembered when they lived with so much playfulness toward each other; observers were intrigued by their relationship.

Adam reached across and stroked Holly's hair.

After the marriage deteriorated beyond any hope of reconciliation, in their desperation they discovered a sovereign Creator who waited to restore the fairytale romance. If only they had known earlier the difference a miraculous spiritual transformation would bring. Early memories of love were rekindled by revisiting places enjoyed during their courtship. Going through picture albums and souvenirs, ideas popped into their creative minds.

"We're not going to get into situations that include conflict any more—are we?" Holly once asked.

"Maybe we should," Adam said. "There's much to be learned from fighting fair. Every relationship has conflict and couples need to understand the difference between attacking versus addressing issues in a healthy way."

"What about the Amore Resort and the Cozy Cove?" Holly asked.

"Absolutely!" Adam answered. "I'm not afraid of a little puny lifeguard anymore." His thoughts drifted to the summer Karen dumped him for the Argentine swimmer. His heart was broken, crushed that she could lead him on for so long. God was there all along protecting him from a conniving female who knew no love from her fractured past.

"Thank you God for bringing Holly into my life," Adam said, his eyes brimming with tears.

"Wonderful new memories—filled with joy—replaced our pain," she said.

"My brother Josh found true love after his bitter divorce; and my brother David met the love of his life in his late thirties. He and Julie are still like two peas in a pod."

"I think you should take a trip up to Seattle to talk with Jake," Holly said.

"Exactly the same thought in my head these past few weeks."

"Let's pray about the details," they agreed.

*   *   *

"Just haven't met you yet …" kept ringing in Jake's ears.

He reeled in a scrawny fish and scratched his finger unhooking the mackerel. Deciding whether or not to throw it back, his stomach growled.

"You lucky sucker!"

Francie stormed off after a magnificent excursion out to sea, sleeping on the Forbidden Odyssey for only two of the three-day getaway. She seemed the perfect companion. They laughed hilariously at their joyful lives, thrived under intense sun, and regaled the night away—planning a rite of passage with tattoos in appropriate places to seal their increasingly strong commitment when they returned to Seattle.

The houseboat gleamed in the bay but sparkled farther out on the open water. Warmth from the sky met a breeze and the couple cooked bratwurst, fresh fish, and grilled vegetables over a rack of coals on the deck. Delightful desserts Francie baked for the voyage were tantalizing under a full moon. Whatever possessed the ambitious go-getter to climb into his dinghy and paddle to shore had nothing to do with him. He would retrieve it later but had no intention of rekindling flames with this feisty ex-lover.

His mind was made up.

She questioned his promise, demanded proof he could not give, and Jake simply refused. He owed her nothing.

Salty air licked his soul as Jake guided the treasured vessel back into its assigned slot. Her car was gone from the parking lot. Where was the Intrepid? Francie swore she would destroy it as she paddled away. "Go home to daddy," Jake had yelled back. "You need to grow up before you play with real men."

He threw her clothes in a trash bag and scooped up her toiletries—not caring that a couple landed on the floor and in the toilet. "No one does this to me."

"Wish I'd never met you," he said on Francie's voicemail. "Your stuff is at the end of the dock, in case you still need it." A peaceful evening and good sleep helped shake the anger from his head by morning.

There were more fish in the sea.

One client, with a luscious physique and more talent than the others, developed a special chemistry with her promoter at their first meeting. "Maybe we can spend more time together after my tour ends next spring," Adele said in a drawl, batting her thick eyelashes. Her southern accent and soft, demure demeanor were opposite of immature Francie.

Imagine giving up a stable wife for such a selfish tumbleweed.

"Hey sugar plum ... want to spend the holiday together?" he asked another female who caught his eye in the market. Her smile intrigued him and he followed her down the street. "We already know each other," he said at the corner. "You went to the Four Bachelor's Concert with me last year."

"Did you lose my number?"

"You're not gonna believe it but I moved into a new apartment the next day—and really did."

They reconnected licking candy canes on his deck.

* * *

"I have tickets to a Chamber Music Festival with A Glass Duo from Poland. Can you join me?" Holly asked her daughter-in-law.

Lisa was delighted. She hardly ever left home anymore except on Sundays.

The glass harps chimed in harmony with *Dance of the Sugar Plum Fairy* by Tchaikovsky, followed by Ave Maria, Swan Lake, Fur Elise, and Toccata and Fugue in D minor by Bach. Lisa's spirit soared as her ears took in the melodious feast. Her fingers tapped her thighs in rhythm, moving in circles as his hands tenderly caressed the goblets. Tiny lights overhead flickered in unison. Reflections in water-filled-glasses mesmerized listeners watching intently. Canon in D by Johann Pachelbel was her favorite. She closed her eyes and pictured Jake sitting next to her. "Father in Heaven, if you can hear me right now, please take the nightmare of my life and give me joy."

She left the concert in peace.

Running her fingers over the rim of a goblet at dinner—the music played in her soul again. Amazing! Just like that.

Decorating the Christmas tree alone without Jake was sad for her; but thinking about baby Jesus coming to a sinful world to change hearts brought joy. Someday she would be in heaven with Him, together with her precious daughter who had gone on ahead.

Whatever happens, I'm never going to be alone again.

Armed with parenting tips from Jake's parents, Lisa explained to Betsy and A.J. her rules for the house. She would attempt to teach them skills necessary to navigate through their no doubt rocky lives. When temperatures rose, higher than steam coming from the kettle, she'd step back and re-evaluate.

Adam and Holly were carefully watching and would continue to mirror her authority in that home—until God chose to include someone else.

*   *   *

For Betsy's 12th birthday, Holly described Aunt Abby's Royal Tea Party and was charged with repeating similar festivities. Elegant invitations read, "A Royal Princess Party will be held on January 16 at 10 o'clock in the morning."

Sandwiches were cut in diamond shapes; petit fours decorated with little flowers followed. Tea was served in fancy china cups with cream. A silver bowl held tiny pastel mints. The girls learned to curtsy, sit properly, and wave like a princess if they ever rode in a carriage.

"Every princess wants to be loved," Holly said. "Regardless of who loves you, God loves you more. He starts your day with sunshine. He sends robins and flowers to delight you. He loves to hear your voice."

"A princess should be lovely to watch. Look in the mirror to see what others see. A Royal Princess has inner beauty the world can see when they observe her actions and attitudes. Refuse to do what is wrong. Don't allow yourself to think about inappropriate things. Fill your mind with good and worthwhile thoughts. Philippians 4: 8 says, *"Whatever is true, whatever is honest, whatever is just, whatever is pure, whatever is lovely, whatever is admirable—think about such things."*

As an afterthought, Holly organized an all-day *Over-the-top-Oasis* scheduling deluxe manicures and pedicures with Lisa and Betsy for the next day. Hot pink nails thrilled Betsy; Lisa chose red; Holly picked a French nail manicure. Lunch at the Enchanted Tea Room preceded shopping at Charming Charlie's.

"It was so much fun I wish we could do it every week," Betsy said.

"I'll treat you both to a Valentine surprise if you join me next weekend," Holly said.

Three lovely females were escorted by a handsome Adam, accompanied by a young boy who enjoyed being the center of his doting grandfather's attention. Love was obvious in a once desperate family, touched by God himself.

Lisa was excited about a Heart-to-Heart seminar Brooke invited her to attend. The informal all-day conference promoted connecting with an Almighty so we can better build our relationships with humans.

To begin the day, a magnificent magenta, salmon, and lavender sunrise with fluffy cotton candy stripes against the fading gray sky invigorated every inch of her body. "God is an amazing artist," Lisa said.

"Imagine what He's doing with our lives," Brooke replied.

"I'd love for Jake to see what's inside me."

"Maybe he will before long. Who knows?"

"I'll leave that in his hands."

The opening welcome and special greeting stirred more feelings of warmth. "Good morning, friends! We're glad every single one of you is here—and for one reason. Psalm 16:11 says, *You will show me the path of life; In Your presence is fullness of joy.* If that's your desire, you came to the right place."

"God wants us to express our concerns, needs, issues that frustrate—but he requires honesty, openness, transparency—in a two-way relationship. Those who have meaningful relationships know how to talk to the ones they love. They don't worry about how, they just start connecting. They don't fret over fancy words or deep thoughts. They just tell God what's on their hearts and let Him sort it out. Even Jesus spent time each day in prayer, and if He needed it, so do you."

"When you pray, how much time involves you talking? When you're finished voicing your thoughts, how long do you listen? We're going to discover He longs for us to know how he acts, thinks, and talks. Scripture teaches spiritual truths so we can better understand God's thinking patterns, his behavior. We were made in His image and time together is essential. Don't have time to talk to the Almighty Creator of the universe? Is he an enemy or your friend? Either way, you need to get down on your knees."

"While you're at it, you might as well inspire others to climb to new heights."

Running her fingers over the rim of a goblet at lunch, music played in Lisa's soul again. She cupped her hand in a heart over her plate. What was that verse she just heard about finding fullness of joy in His presence?

Chapter 12

A Father's Love

A CAPSIZED SAILBOAT EXCURSION catapulted Jake into the hospital for a few days of complete bed rest. "It's just a concussion—with a broken arm," he explained to his father.

"Stop living life for what's around the corner and start enjoying the walk down the street," Adam said to his son on the phone. "You need to live every day as if it's gonna be your last. One day you'll be right."

"Just doing what God made me for."

"Why not find a career that best suits His purposes?"

"I need a good income."

"Accumulating wealth—what does that have to do with quality of life? Money is like seawater—more you drink, more you thirst. You're willing to take risks to increase your financial portfolio but refuse to think about how you might impact your own children and what's good for them? What if I had done the same for you?"

"You weren't always there for me, Dad."

"I'm sorry about that Jake. I've already asked for your forgiveness. Storms expose our weaknesses."

"I made big mistakes, as well; and I'm trying to figure out what to do next."

"An Olympic champion once said to focus on one task and goal at a time," Adam said.

"That's too simple. I've got wants and needs of my own—in addition to looking out for my clients."

"Children in the desert longed for tasty turnips in Egypt and tried to hoard manna overnight. Turned out to be infested with worms by morning. Tragedy intrudes in our lives—smelling awful—and maggots eat the remains. Beware! The more you look at temptation, the better she looks."

"Lisa believes our relationship is salvageable but I'm no longer in love with her. She's a chore on my to-do-list. Truth is … I can't stand being around her."

"What about your children? Do you care what happens to them?"

"Only so much I can do."

"Alex started school this year. What's his teacher's name?"

Silence.

"Who is his best friend? Silence. What color are his eyes, for Pete's sake?"

"I plan to spend time with them this summer."

"And after that, what are your plans?"

"Dunno. I'm in no shape to be a parent right now. Handling all the bad stuff back home makes surviving difficult."

"I didn't invest years teaching you solid values to watch you continue making foolish decisions. The Bible is more than words on a page of history. It's a serious thing to hear truth and disregard it. Whatever comes between you and God is a disaster waiting to happen."

"Don't worry about me, Dad. I'll figure it out."

"I'm getting a ticket and flying to Seattle. We need to spend some time together. I'll let you know the specifics, soon as I can."

Leaving a busy terminal for whatever peace could be found on the bay, Adam spent time talking with his Creator in the taxi. All men dream of finding passion, depth, meaning in their quest for significance. What is Jake trying to hide? He lies about intentions; lies about his actions. You must be disgusted."

Adam started to hum a favorite song. "It crossed my mind how life might be … turning back this page of time. It all comes into view … I realize I'm nothing without you. Don't let me lose sight of who I am …"

He wasn't alone.

Eating a hot pizza on the deck of the Forbidden Odyssey, together with his son for the first time in a year, they reunited under the stars. "Nice home, Jake—could only be nicer with your family living here beside you."

"Glad you like my pride and joy, Dad."

Fishing poles propped in the corner begged to be handled and Adam had some ideas. "Wonder if you ever have memories of that coming-of-age camping trip we took for your sixteenth birthday?" he asked.

"Yeah, that was pretty awesome."

"Did you decide to include God in your adult life—as a way to ensure success?"

"What do you mean?"

"Are you so focused on what you want that you completely leave Him out of your life?"

"Man seeks God by climbing higher—which offers a great view to inspire—while giving the climber a chance to recharge on the summit," Jake said.

"So you do spend time with Him?"

"Yeah," Jake said reaching for another piece of pizza. "Once in a while."

"Will you join me at Timberwolf Park for a cookout tomorrow night?" Adam asked.

"Sounds like fun."

When they arrived at the wooded area, perfect for picnics, Adam challenged his son to start a fire from scratch. It had been years since that boy-to-man event on his sixteenth birthday. *Funny how you can forget such simple things.* As if by providence, a spark lit. Leaning closer, Jake changed his method—now puffing small bursts of air, as though breathing life into a doll. He focused—intent on winning the challenge, determined to succeed.

Tiny white wisps floated up, gaining momentum as they rose. A burst of yellow soon joined. Finally! Smiling a big grin, Jake added twigs and branches until the kindling erupted into a serious blaze.

"Started to wonder if you lost your skills," Adam joked.

After cooking bratwurst on sticks over the flames, they settled on the ground to chat. Jake stirred the fire, adding more logs in between. "Kind of like our relationship with God," Adam said. "The original spark lasts for a second or two. If you want to eat dinner or keep your hands warm, you need to keep it going."

Over the campfire they discussed how life involves a series of decisions—career, finances, children—some major issues, some not. "What's the bottom line? How do we determine what's wise?" Jake asked.

"We should carefully consider consequences. If Adam and Eve had a foretaste of the future, they would never have eaten that apple. If the Israelites returned to Egypt for turnips, or if David realized what his one night stand might lead to, their lives would have been entirely different. If Jonah anticipated what being in the belly of a whale would be like, can you imagine how fast he would have run to Nineveh? Most of the time we're clueless how our choices will end."

"I know ... but we're human, not all-knowing like God."

"If Noah refused to build a boat, never having seen a drop of rain, imagine the result—God doesn't make all details crystal clear. We have a belief system based on: what mama always said, our worldview, or convictions based on the Word of God."

"Doesn't it have to make sense?"

"If so, the car wouldn't have crashed or a wife wouldn't have gotten sick. God is sovereign whether we understand or not. He's gonna turn it into good, no matter what, when we surrender our lives to Him."

That brought up memories of life before the coming-of-age camping trip. After his Dad's accident, changes began in their home. Looking at a beautiful sky filled with stars back on his sixteenth birthday, Jake determined to include God in his adult life—it was the only way to ensure success.

"It's time to go home, Jake."

"So soon!"

"Not to the boat ... home to your family."

"Can't really relate to what's going on there anymore."

"I bet you miss them more than you're aware."

"Maybe."

Looking at a sky filled with luminous stars, Adam again explained that God cares more about satisfying the deepest longings of our hearts than providing a show for us to enjoy. "When your heart is in agreement with His will, you'll think about all you might have missed!"

It was hard concentrating the next day. Spending time with his father was refreshing in one sense but distressing in another. Maybe he was getting too old for a major change in his thinking.

"What happened to the stinking salt shaker?" Jake said.

He spotted it on the table. Adam left things in awkward places, though he was trying not to be a nuisance. "Glad you came but I'm ready for you to go," Jake said too quiet to be heard.

"Hope I was a blessing this weekend," Adam said before leaving.

"I'll think about what you said."

Jake watched his dad head for the gate after going through security. Adam turned and waved with a pensive look on his face. It looked like he was going to make another comment but stopped. "I love you, son!"

Traffic was heavy returning to the boat.

Flopping on the bed, he picked up Lisa's picture. "We could have had it all. If only …"

Lisa poured her heart out over a peppermint latte while shoppers lingered nearby. Who cares? Life was probably miserable for them, as well. "Day after day my confusion grows. I'm beginning to believe it's a waste of time thinking about my life."

Brooke touched Lisa's arm, "Count your blessings, instead."

"My treasures have turned to ashes. There's nothing left."

"That is only one way to look at circumstances."

"I have a constant reminder of more serious problems with Betsy and Alex asking questions.

"They need simple, positive responses. Never hold your children as captives. They need to hear you talk about the situation positively and watch as you problem-solve issues. They should never be required to shoulder responsibility for a breakthrough or take on guilt for causing more pain. But no matter the trial, we're never called to go through it alone. We always have a great Helper on our side."

Brushing her hair back, Lisa leaned to pick up her tattered purse. "Thanks for listening, Brooke. It means a lot!"

"Same time next Tuesday?"

"I'll call if something comes up." She smiled walking out, knowing something always does.

At least she had Brooke.

Breaking through a long-forgotten grieving heart would take a miracle but she had already seen evidence of greater miracles. She copied 1Cor. 2:9 in the front of her Bible. "Eye has not seen, nor ear heard, nor have entered into the heart of man the things which God has prepared for those who love Him."

Lisa found a note from Brooke tucked in her pocket when she got ready for bed.

> *You are God's letter to the world around you. What they see in you, and hear from you, is a message about Christ to them. Maybe this scares you? You don't think people will see in you what God wants them to see? Well, better shape up then, because He has chosen you to represent Him whether you like it or not. The good news is that He is doing the writing, not you. Ask God to make your life a great story for others to read today.*

* * *

Back on the Forbidden Odyssey, Jake contemplated the promise he made to his father. Maybe it was another mistake.

His biggest struggle was finding courage to contact Lisa; begin communicating about the past in the middle of painful circumstances that had separated them. Where would he start? Doing so would require admitting guilt, taking blame, being willing to surrender regardless. Family relationships are hard. People get feelings hurt so easily.

"God will bless you in ways never imagined!" his father said.

That required trust—Jake didn't know if he had it in him. His feelings were all over the place. He needed to vent; tell someone his story but it was scary having a conversation about death—especially one he had no control over, one he possibly caused with his own selfishness that day on the sand bar.

Lisa had never forgiven him. He could tell by the look on her face.

To make matters worse, he and Lizzie were not close. They had a surface relationship with fun, games, and activities, but no deep understanding or shared emotion. After pouring his heart into precious Angela and having his soul broken in half when she died, attempting to feign closeness with another female just wasn't in his heart.

It is what it is.

Jake's world was spinning out of control when Alexander was born and no one could fault him for trying to find another job after false accusations and lies emerged. His record was impeccable. He'd given KMOL everything he had, including his family.

He would become a more involved father—learning the names of Alex's teacher and best friend. Sons look at fathers in a certain light and Jake wanted to be there for him. Lizzie needed him in her life, too.

But returning to his place of despair?

He needed to give it more thought. Fortunately, his ex-fiancée, Francie, was out of the picture.

Chapter 13
Café

"Sure hope you enjoy your yummy breakfast this morning! Let me know if you want anything else," the perky blonde said before returning to the kitchen. Her pony tail, pulled high with a red bow, captured most of her curls.

Wired to enjoy female companionship, Jake was heartened by this new server's kind-hearted response. He contemplated how life might be with his world brightened by someone who genuinely cared about his interests.

Life had been lonely lately.

"How did a guy like you start eating alone in this place?" she asked, big brown eyes searching his soul, when leaving his ticket on the table.

"I catch a bus down at the corner," Jake said.

"Come every day?" He nodded. "Good! I can't wait 'til tomorrow." She beamed from ear to ear. "Now don't go struggling with problems at least when the sun is shining? Okay?"

She seemed to have none of her own.

"Breakfast should always be this wonderful!" he said before finishing the last few bites. He left a big tip—hoping to empress.

He watched the red uniform pull against her fanny, sashaying up her thighs as she moved away. Her hand in a pocket pulled it higher. She bent down to grab a napkin on the floor, leaving little room for the imagination. He licked his lips, readjusted himself in the chair, and spilled the last few drops of coffee on his shirt.

Nothing much fazed Jake for the next twenty-four hours.

His bus was late. A taxi splashed muddy gunk on his dress shoes. Two clients cancelled meetings. His boss set up a required conference during the only appointment that showed up. After lunch, he discovered he left his attaché at the café with papers needing signatures.

Being preoccupied at the office was nothing unusual, however, for many co-workers. Most Talent Scouts in Seattle lived vicariously through their talented discoveries.

"The air conditioner isn't working again!" was repeated throughout the afternoon by several people, but feeling warm was no problem for Jake on this particular day. His day dragged on with visions of what could be. The night was even longer with shooting stars and a couple entwined on a yacht moving in unison under the moonlight.

Howling wind after midnight caught nearby trash and danced debris around the water. A tin can rustled against the dock. Dogs barked multiple times as vessels jockeyed in and out of slips.

"Thought about you last night," he said to the perky blonde, on arrival at the café early the next morning. She handed him the attaché case.

"You didn't tell me your name."

"Trisha," the chef called from the kitchen. She smiled and ran off.

His breakfast looked delicious and smelled better than ever. Hungry as a wolf, he emptied the plate in minutes. Jake reached for his coffee and gulped it down. "Slow down big guy! There's more in the kitchen." Her touch on his shoulder reached all the way to his heart.

"Would love to get to know you better," he said leaving for work. "Any plans this evening?"

"Maybe tomorrow."

That all-encompassing female mystique was so powerful he rushed through two meetings, grabbed a newspaper, and headed home early. Again he couldn't sleep. Joy comes in the morning, he repeated over and over. But wonderful breakfasts with a cute waitress weren't enough. She always had excuses.

He worked up courage. "Would you like to meet at the Docks Diner tonight? Then, I'll show you one of the most dazzling sunsets you'll ever see from my houseboat. Is 7:00 pm too late?"

"Perfect."

He washed the deck, scrubbed the entry door, and showered. *Just enough time to light a candle after the sun goes down.* Magazines were straightened. Music was ready. Romance was in the air. Trisha looked fresh as a daisy in her yellow sundress with a white lace insert at the bodice. Creamy sandals showed off her tanned legs. She smelled of French vanilla. They dined on shrimp bisque and lobster Alfredo. "Thought about you a long time last night," he said, finishing his last bite of praline cheesecake before smacking his lips.

She smiled a charming smirk. Her eyes went crinkly.

He winked.

Walking along the pier, Jake playfully pulled her into his arms. A fish jumped out of the water nearby. "He thinks you're a catch too." Her lean muscles showed she was in good shape—a lifeguard, he soon discovered.

Arm-in-arm against the rail of his houseboat, they watched sea gulls chase fishing boats into the harbor, headed for the marina. Sailors scuttled around containers ready to offload their catch. Proprietors waited on the dock to cart off fresh seafood. Hungry animals longed for a taste. The Bait House was restocking for evening activities and the cleaning station was ready for disposal of accumulating fish guts. An occasional aroma was overridden by the salty breeze.

Jake grabbed drinks while she used his privy.

They chatted about love of marine life, changing weather conditions, and safe background stuff. She had needs for security and a loving home. He had his own. She laughed at his jokes and seemed to appreciate his depth. Kissing started casually in between comments ... becoming more intense as the sunset deepened. The sky exuded shades of glorious hues never before known to man—sunflower, ochre, melon, peach, tangerine, salmon, persimmon, ginger, crimson, fuchsia, magenta, violet, lavender, cobalt.

With his hands wrapped around her waist, she leaned back against his chest and they watched a tugboat move sluggishly across the horizon, dragging a disabled yacht. Fishing dinghies headed for the rocky eastern shore. Tiny lights flickered around the metropolis, gearing up for another enchanted evening. He crossed his arms around her chest, pulling her tighter. Her body melted into his.

They danced on the deck, mixing fast songs with wild gyrations and romantic tunes involving passionate embraces. He promised to play her favorite music inside.

"You know, Jake, going out with you is kind of like riding a roller coaster. No end to the thrill! It's sort of fun having you in my life but I'm afraid you're into token relationships. What makes you think this could last?"

"Can't we take it one step at a time? See where it leads? I'm too old to chase you around but I can give you what you need."

"Will it be another girl tomorrow?"

"I just want someone to hold tonight." He pulled her closer. The moon shone on the waves reflecting up on the side of the mooring.

Something inside Trish bristled. "Why do you have her picture on your dresser?" She twisted away. "I want a guy who can love me exclusively? You charming fellows always have someone else's picture in your wallet. I really need to go."

"Pretty please? You're perfect for me."

An unlit candle waited for another chance to flicker. Beautiful music longed for a new opportunity to be enjoyed. Ocean views bathed in moonlight went unseen as a tantalizing evening of romance slipped from view. Delicious Ghirardelli chocolate teased with luscious flavor but remained untouched by lovers entranced in her mystique.

Jake went to bed with a heavy heart.

In the middle of the night Trisha's phone rang. "Hello?" she answered groggily.

"Please don't hang up. Listen for a minute, Trish."

Unsure how to continue, he sat up. "I can't sleep; I keep thinking about you." A barking dog pierced the night air and footsteps ran across the footbridge.

"It's just too complicated. I'm no longer interested in somebody who has another female in his life," she said, determined to hang up and move on.

Her gentle voice, the rhythm of her words, their chemistry reached down to his soul—he couldn't let her go. "Wait a minute; I need you."

Jake knew what his heart was feeling but his brain always seemed to get in the way. Seconds on the clock ticked slowly. "Give me a chance. Lisa means nothing to me anymore. I'll end it permanently. I'll do anything you want."

"I'm starting classes at the university next week. My time will be filled with studying. It's better this way."

"That won't keep you warm on a lonely night."

"I know but it's a choice we need to make. Maybe I'll ask for a cozy comforter this Christmas. Goodbye, Jake."

She had been in his arms for such a short time and suddenly it was over.

Hedonistic efforts caused relationships to disintegrate for Jake. Looking for answers, he decided to phone home in the morning. It was sort of a promise to his father. Something was stirring in his soul.

"I've been waiting for you to call, Jake. Flirt with your spouse, not others."

"Don't know what you're talking about, Dad?"

"A female answered your telephone last night and said she was having the time of her life with you. Another Tina Parker? When I identified myself, she said I had an awesome son; she could see a great future with you. I didn't know how to respond."

"It's over!"

"Why do you do that?" Adam asked. "You repeat foolish actions over and over."

"Attempting challenging feats; trying new adventures; risking what I already have—anything out of the ordinary just to have another thrill. Maybe that's why I chose a career in the world of *breaking news* and enjoy exciting travel," Jake said.

"At the end of your life, what will you be remembered for? Whose life will you have impacted for good?"

Adam's words reverberated in Jake's head long after they hung up. Will I ever be as wise as my father? Yeah, his stories of desperation were true; but my circumstances are drastically different. I want you to be proud of me, Dad.

Then he remembered Alexander.

Hanging precariously from over thirty floors up, a window washer abruptly encountered problems. Jake watched intently from his office. Filthy windows blocked some of the view but his eyes remained glued on the helpless man. Desperation knows no bounds when your life is hanging by a thread. Wonder what kind of family he came from? Where could he possibly be headed in life with that kind of career?

Emergency technicians feverishly attempted to rescue him.

Experts scrutinized the situation and hoisted an inspector up on a scaffold to oversee the plan. No mistakes could be made. Jake gauged the predicament with apprehension. Without warning, a cable snapped, delicate framework buckled, and the stranger bounced from platform to wires before plunging to the pavement below with a splat. "Whoaaa!!!"

The inspector followed—tragically—to his death on concrete the city engineers intended would provide a better quality of life for citizens.

Jake grabbed his chest. His heart felt sick. Two lives were shattered in an instant. Sobs rose from his throat and he bent down for support. He lost his balance and ended on the floor. Everything was in motion. He got on his knees. Pain gripped him in a vice. Blackness from that one rogue wave washed over him. He couldn't see his hands as they covered his face, soaked in a deluge of tears.

"I need your help, God!" he begged.

Struggling like he'd never done before, Jake pulsated between anger and despair. His emotions were reeling like a Ferris wheel vaulted into the heavens. Somehow, no one heard his anguish except for a sovereign Creator.

He couldn't bear to look out the window as sirens rushed in.

As soon as he got to the houseboat, Jake called Lisa. He checked his watch for the time as her phone was ringing. Oh please, dear God, let her answer.

"Hello."

"Hey there, I'm glad you're home," he said.

Silence followed. Lisa struggled to find words.

"Dad gave me a picture of you last week. You look really cute in that red sweater. How are you doing?"

She gasped. "It's been three months since I last heard from you, Jake. What do you want from me?"

"I've made some bad decisions. Guess I'm good at doing that. I want to see you again, Lisa." He sat on the bed, staring at her picture. She looked pretty in a new way. Her smile was genuine. Her heart had always been faithful to him. Her loyalty was more than a guy could ever hope for. His memory flooded with happy moments, enough to make a movie. If only he could get rid of the bad ones.

"Do you think you're immune from accountability? God doesn't see it that way. Do you really think our marriage is salvageable?"

"I'm working on this. Give me a chance to figure it out. I'm ready to try again?" His words tumbled faster than his brain could control. His heart was racing. His hands were sweaty holding the phone but he had no intention of hanging up. Not for a while anyway. He continued. "I picture you in my arms and think, *Man, I'm never gonna dance with anyone like you ever again.*"

"Slow down. Tell me your plan. I'll have to think about it."

As usual there was none.

"I'll figure something out and call you back," Jake promised.

"If I come to see you again, it better be a great dance—for the rest of my life. Anything else is unacceptable. We have children, Jake. Parenting is our responsibility. Even if you shrug off your role as a husband, you'll always be their father."

"I won't let you down this time!"

"I hope not!"

Lisa could hardly believe what had just happened. She got on her knees before calling Brooke Davis. Last time they talked, her pastor's wife said, "We all encounter difficult circumstances in life. It's up to you to envision a good future. How we respond to situations is the key. And remember, you don't have to do it alone. He will walk beside you every step, perhaps carrying you if necessary."

"… I don't know what to do next?" Lisa said in disbelief.

"Let's ask Him for wisdom," Brooke said. All those afternoons of in-depth counseling and encouraging one very lonely, discouraged woman were paying off with a tremendous difference in her continuing to reach for the stars on her sad journey. Only God knew what the future would hold.

What ensued the next day was nothing short of a miracle.

Radiant sunshine streaming through beautiful stained glass windows at Grace Fellowship—was only half as bright as the laser lights flooding Lisa's soul. A big smile was engraved on her face. Friends greeted her warmly but she hurried to sit down, preferring to talk to God and quiet her heart before the service began.

Brooke slipped in beside her.

"What's going on in the secret places of your soul?" Rev. Davis asked.

"Often we try to get away with wrong thoughts, motives and attitudes. We don't care if God knows. Hiding sin in dark corners never pleases God. You need to ask—what is this really costing me? Make sure you listen to Him carefully. Let Him honestly examine your heart. The question isn't if God is on my side but whose team am I on? From now on, do things his way—not yours. Without Him you can go nowhere. With Him, nothing can stop you. You'll still have battles to fight, struggles to endure, but it will be worth it someday."

"Memorial markers signify events that have impacted our lives. A wedding ring is one plainly seen by others. Other events speak of God's intervention. Trust Him in ways you've never trusted before. Situate yourself in places where your only explanation can be that He is sovereign. God has amazing things he longs to do. If we knew, it would blow our hats off. He wants to take us to deeper depths and higher heights ... in order to touch other people's lives. Some don't know He exists."

"Is this too good to be true?" Lisa wondered driving home.

Running her fingers over the rim of a goblet at dinner—music played in her soul. She held her breath.

Reading a *Fresh Start* devotional, her spirit soared.

"When you don't know what to do, climb higher. When the bigger view is blocked by trees, climb higher. When fog settles around you and obscures the view, climb higher. The truth of God's word gives a higher perspective on your circumstances and by reading it, you climb higher. Before God gave Moses the Ten Commandments, He told him, *Climb up higher.*" (Exodus 24:12)

Looking for the wooden name plate with *Jake and Lisa Clark* engraved on the bottom; she found it in Jake's lower drawer. Cradling it to her chest, she longingly whispered a prayer. How she missed his arms around her.

Fearful of becoming overjoyed prematurely, she placed it back in its hiding place, stuffing an old sweater on top.

"Don't let the allure of happiness disappoint you, Lisa."

Rising tide surges in confidently but will move back out to sea within hours.

Chapter 14
Symphony

HEARING JAKE'S VOICE TWO days in a row was reason to celebrate. Every atom in her body wanted to shout "Hallelujah"—but with emotions so powerfully charged, she feared breaking into tears may possibly send a wrong signal. Lisa's heart palpitated trying to calm herself and talk sensibly.

"I reserved tickets to the Seattle Symphony and want you to fly up for a concert in twelve days," Jake said. "They'll play Canon in D by Johann Pachelbel; I know how much you enjoy that music. Can you make arrangements for the kids at my parents' house? I've already talked about this idea with my father."

"And after the concert?"

"A weekend blitz will follow, to show you all the things I've been doing this past year."

"Where will I sleep?"

"On the houseboat—I guess."

"Should I bring anything special to wear?"

"Bring something dressy for the Symphony, a casual outfit to hang out around the Marina, and something in between for anything else."

"Will we have a chance to talk seriously?"

"I'm sure you're angry about the past and some of my actions but I don't want to end up fighting the whole weekend. We'll save that for later. My plan is having fun together."

"I'll be devastated to hear more ugly secrets, Jake."

"I'm not the same guy who left you, Lise."

"It's still kind of scary for me. I don't know what to expect."

"Trust me—I know I'm asking a lot—but it's time for reconciliation to begin. We'll leave the future in God's hands. I just want to enjoy your company again."

They said goodbye and Lisa held the phone to her chest.

She wanted to hear his voice longer. It would be interesting watching the colored threads of her tapestry, in so much disarray on the back, turned around as a thing of beauty. It was more than she could imagine.

Time would tell.

*   *   *

"Destiny takes us on difficult journeys to places where dreams disappear; goals go unfulfilled; our enemy tricks us with lies," Brooke said. "Many of us feel empty with little to offer, failing to realize the strength we have inside. God wants us to know how strong and beautiful we really are." She sipped Chai tea, thinking about her maternal grandparents who had been missionaries to India.

"How can I become stronger? I hardly know what to say to him," Lisa said.

"We want recipes, instant solutions to problems, but you get to know God better while studying His word one step at a time—just like we get to know people. You can't rush true friendship. Start praying about something specific every day this week. Watch God at work."

"I don't know how this can work after years of intense pain," Lisa said. "Jake's caught in a pattern and lacks motivation to change. He's incapable of understanding his actions cause permanent harm."

"Don't give up on difficult family members. The best is yet to come!"

Brooke wanted to describe more about her mother's personal struggle with God after finding her parents massacred in a raid on believers ... in their home on the mission field. The visual was too much for an eight year old suddenly left alone in a hostile world. Foster parents pretended to take her into their loving family but what went on behind closed doors was more traumatic. How a sovereign Father rescued her and turned her life around was a miracle.

Someday Lisa would hear this story—but right now her personal struggle overwhelmed anything else.

* * *

The flight into SeaTac was bumpy with high humidity interacting with the sea breeze but Lisa concentrated on how she would be received by a once adoring husband. True to his nature, he met her at the entry with a bouquet of colorful mixed-flowers and a box of peppermint patties. Lisa reached for the gifts.

"Thanks, Jake. You remembered!" she said, smiling.

"Glad you made it."

He started to pick her up in his arms, to twirl her around in the air—but hordes of passengers and congestion around them prevented that show of affection. "I made reservations for you to stay at the Hilton this weekend. Their deluxe accommodations are nicer than my houseboat; you'll feel more like a princess staying there." He reached for her suitcase.

The ride to the hotel took minutes.

Jake checked her in, and then left.

She unpacked and organized her belongings for the awaiting adventure. Giddiness rose within her as she dressed for the evening and waited for her husband to return. His knock on the door sent shivers up her spine. Would he try to seduce her? She was glad for the private place to retreat, if necessary. Staying on the houseboat would have been a painful reminder of who else had spent time there. No one likes the other woman, anyway.

Jake was dressed in a tux and held out a wrist corsage.

"Do I look okay?" Lisa asked—not envisioning quite as fancy an event. "You didn't say formal attire." The aqua dress draped her slim figure in a stunning display of personal assets but certainly wasn't fit for a ball.

"You're delightful," he said, kissing her check.

Dinner with gleaming candles surrounded by a seafood buffet provided an ideal place to reconnect. Lisa felt comfortable—just like old times—and Jake was a true gentleman. He looked in her eyes when he talked and watched her every move. Maybe she was reading more into the moment than was wise but sometimes you need to take risks.

"We have life's basic essentials: food, clothing, and shelter—but what about our emotional needs?" she asked over dessert.

"Can we keep it simple tonight? I want to enjoy this moment with you."

She smiled.

Burgundy velvet seats in the antique auditorium were worth the money he paid for tickets—even without the performance. They talked until the prelude began. She had many questions still to be answered but paused periodically, waiting for a better time. Jake perched his right arm around her shoulders and touched her left forearm with his other fingers in harmony with the orchestra. The evening was better than any she could remember but the beautiful melodic music raced the challenging hands on a clock to see which would finish first.

"Music is food for the soul," Jake said while strolling back to her hotel. He kissed her on the cheek before leaving. "See you bright and early."

"Don't forget to set your alarm," Lisa reminded him.

At exactly 8:00 AM, dressed for a fun day in the sun, they set off for a tour of Jakes' life—with a quick stop in his office where two people were busy on phone calls. Breakfast was at a quaint café; and then a hop on the bus headed them to the marina. Lisa was most interested seeing the home on the dock where Jake spent his private time.

The azure sky and sapphire water were separated by grays and tan, accompanied by occasional bits of color on the wharf. Billowing white sails dotted the horizon along with gray fishing dinghies and charcoal tankers headed somewhere. Closer to the pier was a greenish row boat needing an oar; and a rusted bait house smelled fishy with a nearby cleaning station.

"Nothing like I imagined," she said walking over the footbridge and along the gangplank. He helped her up the broken steps.

"Welcome to my home," Jake said proudly.

The deck creaked as they moved across to a sagging door—perhaps lopsided because it was one hinge short. Dirty windows were spotted with beads of salt and streaks of moisture. A Pepsi can rolled past in the breeze.

"Phew! What's that smell?" she asked without thinking when he opened the door and motioned her inside. Three old green chairs were scattered near an upside down barrel holding an antique lantern. The trunk in the middle held assorted marine magazines and wrappers of candy bars. A sink of dirty dishes was surrounded by the tiniest kitchen she had ever seen. "Nice to see you do eat healthy once in a while," she said.

Jake pulled two bottles of water from the pint sized refrigerator and handed one to Lisa. "Let's take a hike around the marina."

"Can I use the bathroom first?"

"Sure. It's right here," he said opening the door to a closet.

She inched her way into a cubby even her washer wouldn't fit inside and pulled the door closed. The tiny sink sat on top of one single pipe. Jake's bag of toiletries hung on the hook—with a towel sharing the same spot.

"You have no shower?" Lisa asked when she finished.

"It's outside on the back deck."

"Huh …"

He pointed to the round disk with a hose connected to a water supply when they went outside. "Can't people see you?" she asked bewildered.

"Not if it's dark."

She spotted an old shower curtain tied to the corner with a bungee cord.

"Now I see why you booked me at the Hilton."

"Ready to enjoy my reality life?"

Stepping warily over planks of rotted wood, Lisa fixated on the pier and walkway around the wharf until Jake reached for her arm. They retraced numerous steps around the marina he'd taken over the past year. He explained bits of history she might find fascinating.

A crab sandwich at the Docks Diner and they were off for more scenic recollections. Lisa stopped to pet a stray gray kitten searching for food, or maybe her mother.

"There's just so much we're leaving unsaid," she said at one point.

Jake tried to reach for her hand.

Lisa retied ribbons at the edge of her capris. She swatted at a mosquito, intent on feasting on her arm. A boat dispensed a warning horn to alert a neighbor passing too close.

"We're good together without negative issues making the water murky," Jake said leaning back on the dock after dinner.

"That's the difference between heaven and earth," Lisa said.

After a dramatic sunset on the wharf with apricot and crimson waves dancing between azure and sapphire, they tried to sort it out on the pier. Each had their own preconceived notion about why the relationship faltered, without going into specifics. Not one word was spoken about their firstborn. The darkness of the water was a stark contrast to the shining lunar illumination overhead.

"Kind of like us," she said.

"Are you referring to me being responsible for the negative part of family dynamics and causing our marital relationship to disintegrate?"

She repeated her take on what happened again and again, trying to get to the bottom of personality issues they evaded far too long.

"That's not what happened."

"Amazing! How can you understand when you won't listen?"

The temperature suddenly turned chillier. Lisa shivered in the wind and wished she brought her favorite sweater.

"I don't want to go there right now, Lisa."

Neither did she.

Fog crept in quickly. By the time they realized what was happening, it was too thick to safely make it back to her hotel. They could barely find the Forbidden Odyssey. Lisa clung to Jake's hand as they inched their way up steps and across the deck. The creaky door opened and he knew exactly where the light switch was—bringing them back into a world where they could see.

"You can sleep back here," he said, showing her the door to his bedroom area. "I'll catch a few winks in my hammock on the deck."

She looked around the cramped space holding a built-in-dresser, hook for clothes, and plastic chair beside a pathetic cushion on a platform. The faded olive quilt covered a swath of semi-sheer ivory percale. Pillows resembled folded towels. Her picture was in the farthest corner on an end cap. A porthole looked out to a blanket of nothingness.

She undressed and pulled on an old t-shirt Jake had in the drawer before climbing into his bed. Wind whipped at the wall.

Lisa struggled with her thoughts.

A faint foghorn sounded in the distance.

Hearing her scream during the night brought Jake rushing in to comfort her from a nightmare. He caressed her head as she wept in his arms. "I'm sorry, baby. It's just a dream." Her hair was damp as Jake brushed it to the side. Nothing more could be said. By morning everything would be forgotten. He slipped in beside Lisa as her tears subsided—cradling her body on the lumpy mattress. "Heavenly Father ... we need your help so desperately," he said to himself.

True, his enthusiasm for spiritual things wasn't the same. "Needs to be rekindled," his father said, over the campfire at their recent father-son talk.

"Is the quiet voice of God working on your conscience?" Adam asked his son. "We do the greatest learning in our deepest valley."

How did he know?

Rubbing sleep from her eyes, Lisa woke to the smell of fish frying in a pan. She stood up on a wobbly floor and tried to remember where the bathroom door was. Jake was deep in thought drinking coffee on the deck when she emerged.

"Morning sailor," she said.

"You look pretty cute with your mascara smeared and no lipstick."

They laughed and Jake stood to turn the fish. "Help yourself to some of my gourmet coffee, made in Seattle."

Eating on paper plates with stainless Boy Scout utensils, the couple talked about Jake's plans for a variety segment he was promoting at the local TV station with a talented reporter he met recently. "You're gonna love Tiffany. Everybody does," he said.

"Oh, no. Not again."

"No, Lise. I promise you're gonna like her."

"Why?"

"She cares more about listeners than anyone I know. Her focus is on doing an excellent job at whatever she's doing while the limelight is on others—never her own abilities, though she's highly talented."

"Everyone knows you can't succeed without discipline yet few possess skills necessary to achieve the desired results."

Lisa looked at Jake intently—wondering if he truly was listening—before continuing. "In a sense, the key to discipline is goal-setting."

He nodded.

"When's this variety show going to debut?" she asked.

"Week from Monday, if we get the go-ahead from her boss."

"Will you keep your job when you get this venture going?"

"Temporarily. I'm backing off from new clients and transferring commitments of established stars ... but intend to start several other ventures in a few weeks."

Lisa paused abruptly and looked down. "Does that include being a father?"

"I can make room for that."

"They need you, Jake."

Her mind was preoccupied with children she birthed and didn't notice Jake had gone outside. She looked through the dirty window to see what he was doing. A neighbor apparently needed help navigating his pontoon out of a berth, around the mooring.

Lisa decided to freshen up before cleaning the galley. When he returned, she was finishing the last dish.

"Hey, I like having you here."

Lisa smiled. "If you show me where the Windex is, I'll wash your windows."

"Great idea. I'll help from the other side."

Working together as a team was a long forgotten memory. Lisa struggled to keep her emotions under control. Jake knocked on the glass and motioned for a drink. She happily obliged.

Sitting on the waterfront together brought her nightmare back into view.

With sobs, she recounted her dream in detail while Jake tried to close his mind to why it was his fault Angie died that day. "Angela was being sucked out to sea with that horrendous wave. I tried to grab her legs but couldn't hold on; the surf was so strong. I was clinging to Lizzie with my other arm—trying not to drop her. You were busy at the end of the sand bar trying to catch the biggest fish I've ever seen. While I shouted for you to help, a tanker blared his horn. You couldn't hear a thing."

He went into the bathroom for a long look in the mirror. Taking time to wash his hands, he finally returned.

Lisa had wiped her eyes and was rearranging furniture.

"We better get you back to the Hilton to pack. Sometimes the traffic gets heavy going to the airport."

The former news anchor reported it correctly. They made it just in time.

Jake held his hands on her waist, fully planning to kiss her goodbye—when an agent picked up her carry-on and abruptly motioned for Lisa to start a new line going through security. Another man moved in close behind. She turned to speak, but hesitated and just waved. "Don't forget me," she mouthed, as a line formed behind her.

Jake blew her a kiss and turned to leave.

He glanced behind him but she was gone.

Thinking back, Jake remembered how his obligation to present broadcasts in a professional manner, void of personal emotion—while remaining a charming anchor—seemed effortless at first. His personality was perfectly suited for such a role. Unable to let heartbreak over sad stories impact his focus to communicate grim reports clearly required sensitive balance.

Bearing unimaginable pain after his daughter's death was more difficult than his soul could handle and talking about it with anyone, including Lisa, was awkward. Many factors were too highly charged to discuss. Maybe refusing to think about the tragic loss of his firstborn was a way to escape dealing with her absence?

Angela … how he missed her!!!

Frigidity in spousal communications no doubt began destroying his marital relationship. Few words with Lisa, beyond superficial day-to-day living, left Jake craving intimacy from someone who cared.

Lisa camped on his aloofness in spoken words and failure in non-verbal behavior. Instead of supporting him, her intent seemed to look for flaws. You can't build loving thoughts and initiate caring actions toward someone you're seething with anger toward—especially if they're to blame for a horrific accident.

Perhaps glancing around at other females was an attempt to make her pay.

Being maligned by jealous co-worker Paul Esse, who eventually stole his position and livelihood, and his despotic boss Mike Hintz who was intent on stripping Jake of everything he worked hard to achieve, added fuel to the fire. Not to forget—little food in the refrigerator with a new baby; his marriage going up in smoke; and pride rendering him unable to describe his growing desperation with family, friends, or church.

Secrets are sometimes simpler than truth.

Jake grabbed a thirst-quencher and noticed a tug dragging another disabled frigate through the channel. Weary journeymen watched helplessly from the rail, stymied in their efforts to succeed in a business venture now abandoned. A nearby fisherman hurled scrawny perch back into the abyss. Deep below the surface, foraging sea life no doubt scavenged for tasty lunches.

For one refreshing moment sky and sea appeared at peace to the naked eye.

Searching for food Jake discovered a clean galley, sparkling head, and piece of paper lying on a straightened quilt.

"Someday we'll talk …"

"We talk about superficial things, sleep in separate houses, and only God can do anything about it at this point," Lisa confided to Brooke. "Three years ago, Jake said his heart wasn't right toward me. I wanted to take action and change the situation but I'm convinced God wants him to take the initiative. It's hard to believe he ever will."

"Waiting is one of the hardest things in life," Brooke said sipping her Chai tea.

"A counselor told me this was his way of punishing me—harboring resentment and unforgiveness in his heart."

"No matter what you're facing, a lonely carpenter understands the complexities of every situation and hasn't forgotten you. You'll make it to the other side on your weary journey through valleys, up rugged mountain trails, across steep ledges. He has solutions for your circumstances and may spare you from stormy waves, or protect you in storms like His disciples experienced."

Lisa listened intently while enjoying Hint of Mint tea.

Brooke shared her mother's personal story about how an orphaned missionary kid who knew little about life outside India, came to live in an abusive home where God was proclaimed loudly on Sundays but hidden in a closet during the week. What transpired in a short time caused the ten year old to hate people and the Almighty she once knew. Her private trauma led to secret choices that contributed to harsher consequences—until a touch from the long forgotten Savior, rekindled a fire that once burned bright and turned her mourning into great joy. "If God can't do the impossible, then He isn't God!"

Lisa brushed away tears, intending to talk about her own parents' untimely demise the following Tuesday. She was certain they knew nothing of the transforming power of a lonely carpenter. If only she had been stronger and able to offer insight about her convictions earlier.

"He has a journey for us to walk and a destiny for us to fulfill," Brooke said. "The best part—we don't take the path alone."

*　*　*

The Jacob Clark & Tiffany Reed "CAR Show" debut involved few hitches and rave reviews. Ratings surged the following week. Jake called Lisa within minutes of going off-air after each episode.

"I'm proud of you," Lisa said, ecstatic about the news.

The second call was answered by a different voice. "Hi."

"Lisa?"

"No. I'm her daughter. Who is this?"

"Uhh … your father."

"Do you remember me?" Betsy asked.

"Of course, Lizzie."

"I'm Betsy, Dad … I'm not a child anymore."

"I know. I always forget. How are you doing?"

"We need a father in our lives—somebody to care when we have needs; a person to listen when our heart breaks; someone to cheer when we succeed. Not just for myself but also my brother."

"I'm sorry for being gone so much but I want to spend time with you in the future."

"What about today?"

"That's why I called."

"But you didn't sound like you even knew I existed."

"I was surprised to hear you answer the phone. Your voice sounds different than when you were a child."

"A long time has passed since she died, Dad."

"Uh, I er we need to …"

"Excuse me?"

"It's hard to share my thoughts about the past but my kids have always been important to me."

"Did you only love her—my sister?"

"Angela is gone."

"Just to heaven, a little early."

Betsy uncovered tears she never knew existed. Hearing her father cry unleashed a torrent of her own emotions and made her very uneasy. Maybe he would hang up and never call back. She had no idea what to say next. Lucky for her Lisa entered the house and Betsy handed her the phone.

"Hello???"

"Will my children be better off with me back in their lives?" Jake questioned

"Of course."

"It was hard talking to Lizzie—maybe I'm not capable of being the father she dreams about having in her life."

"There will always be regrets and cynicism but parenting isn't something we do by ourselves. We have a helper and I'm learning to lean on him."

"Hey, I have a great idea. When you see I'm walking down a dangerous alley, give me a warning sign. That might be helpful."

"Like what?"

"You can tap your head like you're thinking."

"And that will cause your brain to kick into high gear?"

"Yep!"

"If it doesn't?"

"Thumping me on the head, will mean … now, sucker."

Lisa laughed. "Might be worth a try. You seem predisposed to go down the wrong path at times."

"That's why I chose you, darling."

Whether it was a chance encounter or a glimpse of destiny—Jake's ratings at home also surged.

Chapter 15

ABC ...

Jake groggily reached for another cup of coffee only to find the pot empty. "Enough of that," he said, turning the hissing machine off. "Probably should eat something instead," he muttered—but lingering memories of the moon's reflection over the ocean three weeks before crowded any chance for real productivity. Rubbing his eyes, he stared at the bottom of his cup.

Lisa's words rang in his ears.

Why couldn't she understand? It was all so simple. Well, maybe it wasn't. Her way of responding to difficult situations was certainly opposite his. He tried umpteenth times to explain thoughts and feelings but was rejected at every turn. Now the blame was all his? Not from his perspective. Trying to communicate with Lisa was difficult after Angela died but every day since brought up more issues. They tried to figure it out on the pier.

The darkness of the water was a stark contrast to the shining lunar illumination. "Kind of like us," she had said.

Lisa was referring to him being responsible for the negative part of their family dynamics and causing the marital relationship to disintegrate—while taking credit for being a supportive wife and providing positive feedback. She repeated it over and over. *That's not what happened.* Frustration made him want to give up ... but he had already yielded to that many times.

A yearning in his heart kept bringing him back to reconciliation.

True, his enthusiasm for spiritual things wasn't the same. "Needs to be rekindled," his father said, over the campfire at their recent father-son talk. "We do the greatest learning in our deepest valley. Is the quiet voice of God working on your conscience?"

How did he know?

Thinking back, Jake remembered how the crutches he built his life on were knocked out, one at a time. Bearing unimaginable pain after his daughter's death was more difficult than his soul could handle. Being maligned by a jealous co-worker, who eventually stole his job and livelihood; a despotic boss who stripped him of everything he worked to achieve. *The noise of the world distracted my focus from what should have been my priorities.*

Now what?

Jake noticed a little blue church being built down the street ... like bees at work. Every day held intrigue. He couldn't resist chatting with workers and occasional staffers interested in the latest development. "Deviations will be minimal but necessary for each phase," the foreman explained. "Keep watching!"

He was right.

Immediate changes were almost negligible—from a distance—but the overall transformation was phenomenal.

Eager to open the doors, Pastor Turner sat on newly poured steps observing the bay community. Jake passed, whistling on his way home from work. Their eyes met. "Howdy, friend ... My name's Bill." He tipped his cowboy hat. A thick Texas accent made it hard to discern what he said.

"I'm Jake."

"Saw y'all passing through here. Are you neighbors?" Savoring his words for just a minute made him easier to understand.

"Not for long."

"How's that?"

"I'm headed to Albuquerque to reunite with my wife," Jake said, opening up to the stranger. "Rebuilding my family might take time but I have a glimpse of hope right now." He had lots more to say but cut it short.

"Good for y'all!"

"Setting aside personal ambition will be difficult—but my life's in God's hands from now on—and I'm excited to spend more time with my kids."

"If you're fixin to be around longer, you'll fit right in with our group meetin' around the corner in the converted movie house. Stop over before you take off. Y'all might glean some wise advice to take with you on your travels back home."

"Might take you up on that offer. I'm here a few more weeks and have no idea what the future holds."

"If you could do anything, what do you have a hankering to do, Jake? We're most satisfied when we're fulfilling a purpose."

"How do I go from head knowledge to heart knowledge?"

"Get out of the boat!"

Jake laughed, thinking about his love for water vehicles and current home situated on the sound. The prospect of leaving them behind was worrisome enough. Now there was more? His knees started shaking.

"Not sure how to start?" Bill asked. "Get feedback from godly people closest to you who can give insight from their perspective. Prayer confirms and regulates. He'll show you what to do next."

Early Sunday morning Jake shaved, pulled on his best pants and shirt, and entered the lobby of Twin Cinemas as a custodian unlocked the front door.

"Howdy. Coffee's almost ready and the crowd's right behind you."

Jake turned to see three couples opening the door. Seven other parishioners were behind them. All were friendly and the greetings turned into longer conversations. Pastor Bill Turner was busy shaking hands when he spotted Jake.

"We'll, I'll be …"

"Thanks for the invite," Jake said.

He found a seat near the back.

Heartfelt singing about a cross and a Savior followed. "Hear the sound of hearts returning to you … Hosanna … 'cause when we see you, we find strength to face the day … In your presence all our fears are washed away."

"It's one thing to say you love your wife but another to honor and care for her," Pastor Turner said in his sermon. "Are you treating her with love and respect? Guys usually treat their wives like they treated their mothers—even if she lives far away or is no longer alive. Your lifestyle and how you talk about your mother clearly reveal your attitude toward her."

For the first time in his life Jake considered the place his mother, Holly Clark, consumed deep in his sub-conscious. Had he shown her love and respect? Did she feel as inferior as Lisa did by his words and actions?

The sermon continued.

"Family provides a place for support, encouragement, love, guidelines, essential needs and stability in a hostile world. This group of people interacts with us personally, in contrast to aloof and disinterested bystanders. Experience offers deeper levels of knowing another—at our best and sometimes worst! Someone bigger than you and I determined what group we would be born into and thrive in best. Thank Him and give your relatives an opportunity to prove His plan is flawless. Families who know forgiveness from a risen Savior go the farthest."

"Maybe that's why we're still together," Jake said to the pastor afterward.

"Hang on to that guidebook and talk to Him in-between. He can even restore years the locusts have eaten. I'll be praying for you, Jake."

"Thanks, cowboy Bill ... God bless your ministry."

"Y'all take care."

"Guess I needed to hear a different dialect to understand what's important," Jake said on the phone later that afternoon. He tried to use Cowboy Bill's Texan drawl.

"Just be you," Lisa said.

"Seriously, there is a new man in my mirror. Are you ready to meet this guy?"

"It's kind of scary when I'm around you. Remember when you told me you wanted nothing to do with me and had no interest in ever seeing me again? Even up in Seattle, you cut me off and said ..."

"What does different mean to you, Lisa?"

"I don't know where you're going with this but I'll listen."

"We do the greatest learning in our deepest valley. I'm finally taking credit for the negative part of our family dynamics and causing our marital relationship to disintegrate. I'm sorry, Lisa. Will you forgive me?"

"There really is a God, if that's true."

"I was bull headed, on a path to self-destruction. No one can fix or cure it when you determine to forge ahead blindly; but you get stronger in the tough times."

"I released you to God and allowed Him to intervene."

"That's why I need to ask you a question, in private—face to face. Can we meet up at Lake Tappahannock next weekend?" He had the script ready for a beautiful love story taken from the Bible about a Jewish bridegroom getting ready for the most wonderful relationship ever known to man. Since Jake was known for keeping secrets, this would be the last one he would ever keep from Lisa.

"Okay, I'll make arrangements," she said.

"See you soon."

Clearing out the long-abandoned-garden distracted Lisa from thinking about possibilities. Part of her was euphoric able to enjoy a happy home; the other half couldn't stop worrying. Anxiety over the past usually blurred her dreams for the future. It was a struggle. Yanking unwanted growth took extra strength—but would be worth it someday. This reunion would surely take all she had to give emotionally and she was already exhausted from the painful past.

Wait! This would be a piece of cake!

Jake abandoned her but the story wasn't over. What could his question be? They were still married ... legally. He couldn't get down on one knee.

Waist-high weeds covered rocks in the back corner.

All the perennials had been choked—but more were on sale in the newspaper. She wiped her brow. A glimmer of yellow caught her eye. "Yes!!!" Her favorite was still alive. Leaping with joy, she startled a tiny brown bunny. He didn't know which way to run. Where was his mother? Lisa crouched slowly, trying to not frighten him further.

His fur shivered as he panicked, heart thumping through his skin. Tiny eyes darted back and forth frantic for an escape from certain death. Time stood still.

"Oh I wish I could help you, little one," she whispered. Her tears started slowly. She bent lower.

She covered her eyes with her hands and sobbed. On her knees down in the garden, Lisa found relief from a heart long broken.

"Wonder what Jake will think?"

Chapter 16

Sunrise On The Lake

THE COZY SECLUDED CABIN on Lake Tappahannock was an ideal location for their long-awaited reunion. Jake was overjoyed to see Lisa drive up, running to meet her before she could get out of the Honda. The patina of a cherished work-of-art longing to be admired caught his breath. "Sweetheart, I haven't slept for days!"

She melted in his arms.

"Do you have any idea how much this means to me?" he said.

Lisa struggled to find words. She had been the one to listen in the past. Nothing like staying in character. Jake understood. "It's alright, Lise. Take your time. We have the whole weekend."

She looked more beautiful than ever with sunlight on her chestnut curls; Amarige exuding from her being. Her demeanor and essence spoke volumes. How could he have longed for other creatures, far inferior? Why had he missed out on God's finest for so long? Jake shook his head in an attempt to clear his mind.

He took her hand and they headed to the cabin.

Stepping stones wiggled under their shoes as they walked down a winding path. Somehow Jake felt strong. Climbing steps to the porch, Lisa stumbled—but regained her footing, leaning on his arm. "Lucky for me, you're beside me right now," she said.

"I intend to be a husband you can depend on."

"That's nice to know."

"It can only get better for us, sweetheart."

Lisa smiled. "I really like these rocking chairs. Hopefully we'll spend some time out here on the porch."

"We sure can."

He opened the door. Inside the cabin radiated a warm, welcoming touch from a man in love. A bouquet of wildflowers rested on a table *made-from-logs*; a hand-woven basket filled with wrapped surprises nestled on the bed. The red bow was a last-resort but looked enchanting. Jake painstakingly prepared everything he could think of to delight this female. She really mattered—finally.

"This looks wonderful!"

"I hoped you would like it. Before you get settled, can we sit down together a few minutes?"

"Okay ..." she said with a quizzical look but sat beside him.

He put his arm around her shoulders and turned slightly, excited to speak while looking in her sparkling eyes. Just like Jake promised, he had a question—and a proposal. "I fell through the cracks but want to get back to what He planned for us," he began. "At the end of the story, I'll ask my request."

Lisa listened attentively.

"Life is often complicated and it isn't hard for hearts to get confused. That's why the Bible says, *To guard over your heart with all diligence, for from it flow the issues of life.* (Proverbs 4:23). "Our hearts are where living takes place, attachments are made, and where love happens. You don't want just anybody getting inside your heart, unless you're sure they want God's best for you."

He smiled, and her eyes misted. Jake reached for her hand.

"Our heart is a mixing bowl of issues in life; whatever's cooking inside will affect everyone around. That's why we need good ingredients: kindness, compassion, love, joy, forgiveness, and hope. In the end, the condition of our heart determines how life will turn out ... Hey there, don't cry."

"It's what you do to me. I get excited and then you let me down." She wiped her tears and started to stand.

"This can't wait. Betsy and Alex's fate is in our hands. I've spent way too long trying to figure it out. I promise you, we won't be the same."

Lisa walked toward the door in frustration.

"Let's go down by the lake right now. I'll finish later."

Paddling a cranberry canoe around Lake Tappahannock reminded Lisa of old times. Laughing at ducks with babies following behind their mama; then watching an eagle soaring overhead—was quite a contrast.

Jake splashed water on Lisa. "Come on. You can smile."

"Are your arms getting tired?" she asked.

"No chance … not as long as I'm with you!" He proceeded to do twenty pushups on the dock after they finished, proving his point.

The sunset was spectacular for the observers entwined on a wooden bench by the long dock. Luminous gold rays rose into brilliant ginger, while rose mixed with crimson before merging into mauve, violet, and rich purple—huge clouds of it—layering into the deepest cobalt possible in one single sky. Nestled in each other's arms, they watched stars emerge from a moonlit ceiling. Constellations frolicked in unison moving slowly around the North Star with meteorite showers filling in the empty spaces.

A comet leapt from Mars to Jupiter.

Lisa didn't remember climbing into bed.

"The sky's gorgeous this morning. Coffee is ready. Come watch with me as the latest masterpiece unfolds," Jake whispered to his sleeping wife.

She stumbled out of bed and dressed quietly.

Another stunning work of creation unfolded as the day presented itself. Nothing like the evening before but a beauty all its own. "No two sunrises or sunsets are ever the same," Jake said. "My mom's an expert at appreciating nature. She taught me lots."

"Is that where you got your gusto for living?"

"I suppose." A growling stomach made them both laugh. "Hey, let's run into town for a yummy breakfast. Saw a cute place I want to take you," he said, reaching for her arm. "Shall we … my beautiful princess?"

"Fairy tales don't always have happy endings."

"This one will. It's a sure thing."

Hospitality flourished in the quaint nearby town of five stars—only two streets wide. A gas station, restaurant, and three stores filled the business district. "Do they even have a hotel?" Lisa asked the friendly waitress.

"We have two Bed and Breakfasts."

"And a post office?" Jake asked.

"Over in the grocery store."

The scrumptious garden omlete filled with tasty home-grown veggies was mouthwatering. To-die-for strudel muffins bursting with juicy blueberries joined the gastric gala. They lingered over mocha supreme on the outdoor patio under an ivy-covered trellis with miniature roses. Pots of geraniums, sweet peas, and honeysuckle provided a sensational aphrodisiac.

"Life's a journey from Main Street to Gooseberry Lane—we'll come again," Jake said driving back to the lake. They passed a woman hanging laundry on a line, children racing on stilts, a gardener picking weeds from his vegetable plot, and a mailman delivering three boxes to a gift boutique in a small house—advertising a Grand Opening the following Monday.

An afternoon filled with Beach Olympics offered nail-biting fun for the couple. They threw Frisbees over colorful distance markers; harpooned pointed sticks into circles of rocks; skipped stones over the lake; and looped string braids over specific branches. The never-ending-because-of-too-much-laughter wheelbarrow race was a brilliant idea of Jake's.

He stopped now and then to hug Lisa between events. They were in their own world as squirrels stopped to watch.

"Are you aware what happened twelve years ago?" he asked suddenly.

"Uh huh. How could I forget?"

Jake tackled her in an exuberant embrace meant to comfort. Falling to the ground in a heap, the wildlife scattered. Lisa got a speck of sand in her eye.

It kept watering.

He pulled a clean hankie from his pocket.

"My intentions were good. I was trying to rekindle our relationship on that wretched trip to the east coast. I had bigger plans for our anniversary up in the Big Apple."

She began to sob so he pulled her closer.

Neither said a word—like had happened so often over the preceding years. They sat on the ground and built another wall of silence. A deer jumped through a clearing, unaware anyone else was on the property.

"You had my heart and soul," Lisa said. "I trusted you."

"I'm sorry."

Lisa blinked back more tears.

"It's gonna work out; I promise."

After gazing into the water a while longer, Jake got an idea. "Are you hungry?"

Lisa's stomach answered.

"Let's start a fire. We're gonna have a cookout." Jake pretended to do sword swallowing with a stick and tried to do a hula dance as kindling took off. Logs finally settled down, ready to properly cook food. They grilled hotdogs, pineapple chunks, and marshmallows for their own private luau.

Jake sang love ballads as they dined.

Watching flames turn into ashes, Lisa described about cleaning her neglected garden—anxious over a painful past blurring her dreams for the future. "When the glimmer of yellow caught my eye, I knew our traumatic history would soon be finished. Then I saw the tiny brown bunny. He didn't know which way to run. Where was his mother? I tried not to frighten him further—but flashing back to you abandoning me brought sobs, and I scared him away."

"I'm sorry for causing you so much pain, Lise."

"The best part, Jake … I found relief for my broken heart down on my knees, out there in the garden." She broke into tears again. Hugging her was all he needed to do—for that moment.

"How 'bout making some cocoa?" he said.

Jake stirred the fire to re-ignite dying embers.

"I'm still waiting to hear your secret question. How long do I have to wait? We're still married … well, legally. You can't get down on one knee," she said.

"Au contraire, mon petite."

It was time.

Jake got down on his knee before Lisa in the presence of God and a thousand stars. "There's something I've been waiting to ask." He looked up in the sky with moist eyes and smiled.

"Need your help, Jesus ..."

He began again. The words seemed like out of a novel. "Once upon a time, a long time ago, a foolish young man chased breaking news stories. Thrilling jaunts and action galore in front of cameras was right up his alley. The only thing better was seeing a certain lovely female walk past the set when he started working at KMOL."

"Hi there! Remember my first greeting after not seeing you for years?"

Lisa smiled demurely, just as she had many years before, listening intently for the rest of the story.

"Fortunately, I knew where you lived."

"It seemed perfect back then," Lisa said.

"Our family just pretended to have fun. Think about the hostility my childhood home held? My parents never figured it out until I moved away. Emotional conflict, constant bickering, and intense resentment were inhabitants that wouldn't leave. To keep myself from exploding, I disappeared as often as I could."

"I'm beginning to understand where you might be going with this," she said.

"Paddling down that river when the canoe capsized—dumping both of us into the water—it wasn't an act pretending to drown. You have no idea how serious it really was! I was scared to death committing to a lifelong relationship. Didn't know if I had what it would take to make a permanent commitment. I lacked self-discipline."

Lisa laughed.

Jake grimaced and then tapped her knee.

"Sitting on the bank, when you asked if a person could know he would go to heaven when he dies, I forgot my fears. It felt important sharing the truth with a valued friend there on the grassy slope. I never told anyone my beliefs before; I'm not sure my faith was more than an insurance policy. Somehow I felt providence brought our destinies together for a reason. I figured being on the same team as you guaranteed a personal win. I knew we would take the plunge together some day."

Lisa twisted her ring—not daring to expose the dark feelings it evoked, but grateful she hadn't discarded it on many occasions.

"Do you remember when your Mom gave me a Bible—with the note tucked inside? It said, *Did you know this is a love letter written to you by God Himself? It's fresh and new every morning. I hope you enjoy reading it.'* That precious book kept me from jumping ever since that day on the beach when ..."

Emotion took over. Jake joined her grief.

Tears flooded Jake and Lisa's eyes as sobs filled their throats; their lungs pulsated for a breath, gasping for air just like their firstborn must have desperately needed when that one rogue wave knocked Angela down on the sand bar. Focused on their own needs that morning, neither watched the struggling toddler sink into sand and breathe no longer.

They now clung to each other—and to God—a huge difference from how they originally dealt with Angie's death.

"I have a gift for you," Jake said, breaking the intensity of their sadness. He reached into a cardboard box sitting beside the extra firewood.

Lisa pushed glittery purple and blue tissue aside and pulled a journal from the silver bag. "You prankster! Not again." She shrugged and then opened it. On the first page was a carefully designed formal contract between both of them ... and God.

Jake held his hands together like he was begging.

"Please, Lisa. Will you make this commitment with me?" His eyes looked deep into hers waiting for a reply. "Tina Parker asked me before our wedding, 'Are you positive Lisa's the right girl for you?' My answer? Absolutely!"

Lisa was deep in thought a minute before answering. "You stole my heart years ago. If you promise to take care of it forever ... yes, I'll spend the rest of my life on earth obeying God with you," she said.

"HOORAY!!! Dad's challenge is coming true. Remember when he said, *If a miracle will convince people, why not be one?*"

They kissed like they meant it for quite a while.

Angie rang melodious bells high above the earth in joyful celebration on that glorious twenty-first day in August, twelve years after she arrived in heaven. Fellow angels most likely crowded around preparing for another party.

"Does anything make God happy?" Lisa asked walking back to the cabin.

"Absolutely. He wants us to have His best—if we're willing—and that makes Him happy."

Scattered around the hardwood floor were tiny red rose petals. "Ever walk on rose petals as they're crushed?" Jake asked.

"Cute idea!"

"Grab my hand Lisa. Through us a wonderful fragrance will be diffused to people we meet, onlookers in our life. Mockers may try to discourage but we're the sweet aroma of Christ like II Corinthians 2:14-16 talks about. He watched from above while we bogged down below."

"Not anymore."

"Hallelujah!" Jake shouted.

"Don't get too comfortable if you want to really make a difference in this world. Most of our lives are filled with routine and normalcy and that's okay. What matters, though, is whether that's all there is. Most of the moments when God shows up in a big way are those times when we step into faith territory attempting to do things that are beyond us," Lisa said.

"We won't see what God intends to do until we give him a chance."

They snuggled in a cozy and secluded cabin, tucked away from cares of a world in turmoil until the moon reached its fullness. The sun would peak its head in a few short hours. Lisa stood up to readjust her wrinkled clothes. Jake watched, with a huge smile on his face.

"Have you ever seen a woman undress?" she whispered.

Chapter 17

Double Rainbow

STEADY RAIN BEAT IN rhythmic sync on the gabled roof but the entwined couple slept soundly—until drops seeped through the cabin ceiling and landed on Jake's face. He woke with a jolt and sat up. Lisa purred like a kitten beside him. Watching his beautiful wife brought feelings of joy and satisfaction he missed.

"Morning sunshine," he eventually said. "It's late and we have journeys to begin."

She brushed her hair back and stretched. "I don't want to go home alone," she said wistfully.

"Then come with me."

"I can't, Jake! We have kids to take care of. I wish you were coming with me."

"It won't be long before we're together again for good."

"Betsy and Alex will wonder what happened up here. What should I tell them?"

"I'll call them at my parents before you even get home."

She stared at Jake with her mouth wide open. "And you'll say what? Now I'm really curious."

"Tell them the truth; I'm in love with their mother and can't live without her. We'll need to move you all to Seattle or find me another job back in Albuquerque. In the meantime, everyone can fly up for a vacation."

"And stay on the houseboat?"

"Why not? The kids will have a blast on the high seas—just like pirates."

Lisa laughed so hard her sides ached.

"Call me the minute you get home. Promise?" Jake said, kissing his wife goodbye before fastening her seatbelt and shutting the car door. "Not sure how I'm going to survive without you but I can always wait on the dock."

As Lisa drove south, a rainbow filled the sky from east to west causing her to pass under a natural bridge toward their waiting children. It hung in space for several minutes. Her heart fluctuated between giddiness and sadness leaving Jake at the most perfect moment she had ever experienced. She could still feel his body.

"You're never alone," he said before she left.

Jake briskly cleaned the cabin and loaded belongings in his trunk. "Just whistle while you work …" he sang. A second rainbow filled the sky above him briefly taking his focus away. "Please God, give us direction and make the details work so we can be a family together soon."

He contemplated various factors returning home.

Spiffing up the houseboat for a quick sale took priority but days passed fast with much to do. Lisa would have better ideas when she arrived with the kids on Saturday. A stop at the local Good Will provided bedding for Betsy and Alex in the crowded living area. Jake rearranged furniture and bought a piece of plywood to make a semi-private cubby for each. Red satin sheets would hopefully delight his lover in the bedroom.

Laughter could be heard around the marina when Betsy and Alex took their first tour. Jake tried to pay attention to Lisa, unsuccessfully, as he answered questions and bounced from son to daughter.

"Is this really a house?" Betsy asked.

Sunglasses kept her skepticism a guarded secret but the tone of her voice hinted of the truth. She pulled honey blonde hair back in a purple scrunchy. "I don't think this is a very good place to live, Dad," she said with emotion. Her flip flops pattered on the wood walkway.

Alex was intrigued with the boats. His big green eyes opened wider when a catamaran came into view.

Jake explained about each as best he could. "A few have places to sleep. Others are for transportation on the water. Just don't go away from us without permission, okay? Some things are dangerous around here."

"Where are the other kids?" Alex asked, looking around.

"There aren't many—a couple live down at the end of that pier. Most of the people who live here are adults."

"That's boring," Alex said.

"Why don't you live in a nice house?" Betsy asked.

"This is the best place to live," her brother argued.

Neither could understand what the houseboat's name meant.

Sitting on the deck of the Forbidden Odyssey that evening Jake learned a lot of new information including facts that Alex could run faster than most boys, hit lots of homeruns in baseball, and hated mushrooms. His son's best friend was Mark E. whose favorite activity was soccer, they walked on stilts made by his grandfather, and A.J. liked to kiss the girls especially Courtney. Lisa listened with great interest.

"Do you only kiss your mother?" Jake asked Alex. He shook his head.

Lisa laughed. "Not anymore. Now that he's in school, there are more important females to pursue. Think he takes after his father." Jake gave her a quick look of disapproval.

A.J. climbed on his mother's lap. "I still love you, Mommy."

"I love you, too, my little strawberry shortcake." She tried to eat his ear but he squirmed off her lap and sat by the rail watching a trawler out in the sound.

Jake discovered his daughter's best friend was fifteen year old Mark O. who had wavy brown hair, was good at math, lived four streets away, and liked to kiss Betsy. "You're way too young for that," Jake insisted. "And you're not going out alone with any guy until you're sixteen."

"He invited me to the Spring Fling at school and we had lots of fun."

"I hope Mom was with you the whole time."

"No, his father dropped us off and picked us up."

"The only male you're gonna hang out with from now on is me, or your brother Alex."

"Tell him to stop Mom," Betsy pleaded.

Jake regretted not having spent more time with both his offspring. They seemed quite interesting and well-adjusted in spite of his lack of parental involvement. "We're going to do things different from now on. Some will be good but a few procedures will make us uncomfortable for a while. Each family is unique so I'll figure out how we can be the best one possible. People can't get any closer than that. I'll try to listen—and learn what's important—so talk to me if you have questions."

"What if Mom says we can do something different that you do?" Betsy asked.

"She won't."

Jake looked at Lisa and winked. "We're in this together!"

Before she went to sleep, Betsy talked to her brother about changes. Some ideas hit a bulls-eye; others were confused. Their parents eavesdropped through the cracked door.

"Let things sink in slowly as they watch the new routines," Lisa said quietly. "It'll take time to change their thinking but they'll adjust if we stay positive and balanced. You can talk to Betsy alone over the next few days if you have concerns."

"Where did I find this brilliant wife?"

"Right next door."

He reached for her shoulders but she turned and his hand slipped to her chest. Playfully she bent to the floor to take off her shoes.

"You're teasing me."

She smiled, pulling the peach shirt over her head. "Close your eyes."

"Never."

Jake took his shirt off.

Lisa tried to jump under the covers but slid to the other side of the bed on the satin sheets—right into Jake's arms. He held her tight as she giggled.

"Shhhh!!! You're going to wake the kids!"

Betsy and Alex listened silently, interested in the frivolity going on in the next room.

"I think they like each other," Alex said.

"Maybe we'll get another baby."

The two started laughing so much, a creak of the door was necessary to tell them to go to sleep. They laughed even harder under their covers.

"This tooth wiggles," Alex said at breakfast the next morning. Jake reached over to touch it and it fell into his hand.

"Wow."

"Bethy ... Bethy ... I lotht my firth tooth." With big eyes, he held his lip out so his sister could check the empty space.

"You'll get rich now. The tooth fairy pays lots of money for teeth," Betsy advised him. "Make sure to put your tooth in a special place tonight."

The joys of children were more poignant than ever for a couple beginning the renewed task of parental teamwork. For Lisa, each interaction was sweeter than before. For Jake, exchanges offered meaning and significance the absent father had missed. Their offspring thrived from the extra attention.

"I don't want you to leave," Jake said every evening before they fell asleep.

Each morning Lisa said, "Why can't we stay here?"

"I want to live in this house," A.J. said. "Don't sell it, Daddy."

"Why don't you keep the Forgotten Odyssey? We can have a vacation house like other people," Betsy suggested. "We even have our little rooms."

A bad storm blew in their last day together and cancelled planned fun activities. Huddled in the cramped quarters, with excess rocking, made Lisa queasy and Jake agitated. Betsy and Alex fought over trivial issues—bored with games, conversation, and togetherness.

But life goes on despite storms and routine is essential for maintaining a happy home—so suitcases were repacked and goodbyes were said at the airport.

"School starts on Tuesday," Jake said. "You'll have lots of interesting things to do soon."

The protector guided her children to their flight.

The phone was ringing as Lisa walked in their home.

"I'm flying down in a week to talk to Kate Jones at KMOL about ideas for a variety show in Albuquerque. If that concept doesn't work,

I may interview for Project Manager of a Media Company in Phoenix. Either way, we'll be living together as a family soon."

"Would you feel comfortable working back at KMOL?"

"Absolutely. I'm different than when I left, Lise. Haven't you noticed?"

"Just wondered about the people."

"That stokes me more than anything. It would be a great opportunity to interact with them on a professional level and also present my beliefs about life. I've been praying about this for months."

"What would your show include?"

"A contemporary news segment about positive issues and people— maybe they would have nothing in common but unique viewpoints add authenticity in reporting—anyone can present the evening news. It could include extraordinary pictures and unusual sights from old news reports, clips of individuals pursuing dreams, companions with a unified goal, candid and meaningful interactions, events from history that inspire or challenge, with some trivial acts of kindness and caring. I would serve as host in master of ceremonies role with numerous other personalities including former co-workers. My dream would be to influence and impact strangers."

"Sounds like an awesome venture, Jake. I'll pray about this. I'm excited to hear the results of your meeting."

In her heart she already knew.

*　　*　　*

Enjoying Family Reunions at Holly and Adam's ranch was a treat. Spending time with relatives turned out to be more cherished each chance meeting. Relaxed on the sprawling porch celebrating for this event was a highlight Lisa would never forget.

Sitting by Jake, who appeared delighted to be near her and their children, made it even better.

"Only a sovereign Almighty could orchestrate having all of you back in my life." Jake said. He looked around at Jason and Brenda, Abby who was home on furlough with her beau of two years, godly and loving parents, and his precious wife and kids. "Lisa and I are emerging from a nightmare and need time to regroup—but there are needy people around us who need to hear … about hope. Sudden life changes overwhelm people every day. Adversity is continually knocking at doors. I have cousins in worse condition than I found myself. Who cares about them? I do—finally."

"We're proud of you Jake," Holly said. "Let us know how we can help."

"I'm the luckiest one of all," Lisa said, before bursting into tears.

Jake pulled her closer and A.J. scooted next to his mother, gently patting her hand.

"I made many of the same mistakes as a father," Adam said. "Thankfully, God rescued me before it was too late. When your ship started to go under, Son, I knew you would eventually climb to the top of Kilimanjaro successfully and plant a memorial marker on that summit."

Abby was sobbing in a Kleenex and Betsy was close to tears.

"Maybe you can tell us what changed your heart," Jason said, with curiosity brimming from his eyes. "You've always charmed people with your demeanor but now it seems you genuinely care about them."

"It all started around a campfire with my father," Jake began.

"The week-long campout was a coming of age affair. Talking by the fire, we discussed responsibilities people acquire as adults and the specifics of being a man. As we sat under the stars talking, I felt God's presence greater than ever. A true sailor can chart his course by the stars, my dad said. I wondered if that was true."

"A father is responsible for what happens to his children spiritually," he said. "We watched an eclipse of the moon with the sky turning red before getting into our sleeping bags. It was eerie."

"The next morning, Dad made lumpy black pancakes and coffee. I remember being hungry. Don't laugh—you're cooking alone on the last day, he told me solemnly. I thought he was joking. Well, he wasn't."

"Hiking in the woods, we came across a little cabin. Although it appeared deserted, Dad knocked on the half-opened door. It was dusty and the floor squeaked. Some books were in the back corner of a table—with an old Bible. Dad opened it and started crying. This treasure chest will change your life, Jake, he said. He shared his story of despair and redemption."

"I remember the sun shining through a broken window and asked Dad if he would help me talk to Jesus. Getting on my knees, I talked to the Almighty God of the universe for the very first time."

"Has he made a difference in my heart? From that first day. Did I fall under a heavy load of despair after Angela died? Unfortunately, yes … and I failed to cling to him when my boat capsized. I even tried to swim to shore as the storm raged but I'm living proof sailors aren't made on calm seas."

"Whoa, that was intense," Jason said.

"I want to read a Bible," Brenda said. "Wish we had one."

"We have an extra right here," Adam said getting up.

"The most noteworthy thing about reality on earth is a baby came at Christmas to give us the best gift ever," Holly said. "We spend money and buy everything in sight to satisfy longings in our soul—but that doesn't erase sin and emptiness inside. Who would think a dirty stable could offer hope? Surely the Savior of the world would have been found in a beautiful palace, surrounded by royalty."

"It wasn't that long ago I realized the truth about human nature and a sovereign creator," Adam said, sitting back down.

Abby chimed in. "Jake, do you remember when we flew home from California and thought Mom and Dad joined a cult? After hearing shouting and seeing animosity for years, we were shocked—stood frozen in the kitchen doorway—when we found them kneeling side-by-side on the floor praying."

"I know," Jake said. "Hearing Dad's deep voice talking to God late that evening, I thought paint fumes affected their thinking but my sister was convinced even the smartest people can be brainwashed."

"How long did this last?" Jason asked.

"It was more like wisdom took over their previous irrational thoughts," Jake said. "Everything actually turned out better."

"I'm happy you included neighbors in your home on occasion," Lisa said. "Watching you was our entertainment. Jason and I were immersed in pretty negative family issues during childhood. We were secluded from most meaningful events in society—held hostage by fear or maybe bitterness—with apprehension about connecting with people including a sovereign being. My parents were recluses and had contempt for anything religious."

"Didn't realize that until just now," Jason said. "They forbade talking about God in our home, except to complain about idiot crusaders, but they dragged us to church for holidays. Wonder why?"

"It was the right thing to do," Lisa said, "A charade so people wouldn't start talking. They feared being found out for their sinfulness."

"Do you think Mom and Dad went to hell?"

At the thought of Pete and Mary Stewart languishing in hell, Brenda broke into sobs. Holly kneeled in front of her, whispering for a minute—before both stood and went into the kitchen. Their voices continued unintelligibly in the distance.

Jason squirmed as he continued questioning Jake and Lisa. "We'll never have the answers," he finally said.

"What if you're wrong?" Jake asked.

"I'll never know."

"Yes, you will," Lisa said.

Jason stood and thanked Adam for dinner before finding his wife. Betsy leaned on Aunt Abby's shoulder, struggling to stay awake; Alex was sound asleep on Lisa's lap.

A sky full of stars twinkled as everyone went inside to guest rooms prepared for the *Clark Family Treasures*.

Holly's 62nd birthday began with a sunrise that delighted her soul. Adam surprised his wife with breakfast on the porch as family gathered to begin the day. "Finished my chores early so I could spend the entire time together," he said.

"Happy birthday, Mom!" Abby called cheerfully, peeking out the door.

"Yum. The coffee smells good," Lisa said walking toward her mother–in–law.

"Your food smells even better," Jake added, kissing her on top of her head.

"Help yourself. I made enough to feed an army," Adam said, pointing to the kitchen.

When everyone was situated, Jake broke into a prayer of thanksgiving for his mother's life and joy about being with relatives. "Oh yeah, and thanks for the delicious food my Dad made all by himself."

"What are the plans today?" Abby asked. "Everyone's curious to know."

DOUBLE RAINBOW

Adam described his intentions, and others offered a variety of ideas that perked attentive ears. Eventually they looked at Holly for the final choice. She left the specific details for each person to decide—except dinner watching the sunset, and a campfire.

"Words can't describe my enjoyment just being in your presence and talking about life together. Each of you has a special place in my heart," she said with a twinkle in her eyes. "It wouldn't be a birthday without mentioning the guy who created me; and my parents who lovingly raised me. Granny was also a treasured part of my childhood who showed me the path to real joy in His presence."

"Hooray for Jesus and Granny!" Jake said.

"My 50th was not a good birthday," Holly said remembering back. "The special celebration extravaganza was cancelled abruptly when we buried precious Angela three weeks before. No one was talking and the silence was deafening. Adam and I clung to God in our agony but the only thing we could sense was helplessness … and each other's arms."

Tissues were passed around as eyes welled with tears.

"Even Jesus cried when His friend Lazarus died," Adam said, trying to provide some comfort.

"I know where she is," Alex volunteered. "And someday I'm gonna see my sister. I bet she looks like Betsy."

"Not quite as cute!" Jake said winking at his daughter.

"I used to love a solid blue sky with only the sun shining," Holly said. "When clouds moved in, I was disturbed. Did you know that clouds and wind are necessary for beautiful sunrises and sunsets? It's interesting how the things we like least—sometimes are the most beneficial."

"Maybe that's why we go together so well," Jake said to Lisa. She giggled.

"I think you made a good choice," Adam said. "Lisa is delightful and dependable. She's been a great wife and mother."

"Remember the *fireworks* cake with sparklers that singed Jake's hand when he sliced a piece—popping a balloon hidden inside?" Abby asked.

Laughter from the family muffled his response.

"Life certainly started off with a bang for you two lovebirds," Holly said. "Jake provided gusto with his fun loving ways; while Lisa could be counted on to provide insight and stability."

| 171 |

"Together you were like a huge stadium with enough electricity to light it," Adam said.

"Remember what you said to everyone?" Abby asked Jake.

"We want to make a difference in this world."

"And you will!!!" Adam said.

"You've already made a difference in my world," Brenda said "Watching your unbearable pain keep me from noticing my own problems over the years. It gave me something to focus on like a lighthouse. Last night a spark within me was ignited when I asked Jesus to forgive me …"

"Oh Brenda …" Lisa said reaching over to hug her.

"That's wonderful news!!!" Jake agreed.

"I need to talk to you today if you have time," Jason said to his brother-in-law. "I have questions that need answers."

"No better time than right now," Jake said standing.

A flurry of activity took place on the Clark ranch while a precious angel looked down at her family with a big smile.

In the afternoon, Holly shared a flashback from the past to Lisa and Betsy.

"Moving to the country 23 years ago was a momentous change for our family. Sitting on the porch most evenings, we told each other stories. Some were based on real life—others were made up. Abby came up with a rotation plan."

"Dad was always the storyteller on Mondays. His sagas were the most gripping. My turn was on Tuesdays. I used my imagination and provided a mystery to figure out. Jake entertained us with tales from the Wild West on Wednesdays. And Abby told exciting stories like Gigi used to make up on Thursdays."

"How long will it last? I asked Adam one day."

"We'll enjoy the stories as long as we can," he said.

"Little did we know—Jake and Abby would *still* want to sit on this porch telling stories years later?"

"I have a special story to tell Betsy and Alex," Abby said walking up to the porch.

Everyone listened before they fixed dinner.

"The first day of snow, that first winter here, Dad burst in the house to announce, 'Snowball is having a baby!' We all ran to watch as the little lamb was born. The mother was protective as she licked the baby off and nuzzled her. After eating some hay, Snowball called to her lamb with a soft *baa*. Snowflake ran to her mother and took a gulp of milk. Her tiny tail swished in the air."

"After observing the lamb's birth—Dad sat between me and Jake and said, 'I've made a lot of mistakes in the past but I love you and want to be a better father in the future.' He tried really hard to make up for his mistakes."

"Dad was also a very good shepherd. Sometimes he needed to look for a lamb that was caught in a fence and return it to the flock. The sad bleating once caused him to cry. He tenderly balanced the baby with one hand while stretching the fence wire to release it. That mother was sure happy!"

"Now who wants to feed sheep with me?" Abby said.

The happy little lambs were friskier than usual, jumping in playfulness with each other; eager for corn.

Chapter 18

Campfire

SAVORING A DELICIOUS BARBEQUE with family, while watching a spectacular sunset, was Holly's dream birthday. She was still in love with her husband, her children were at peace with God, and the future looked exciting. Her heart was full of thankfulness. Delicate shades of lavender and rose filtered into an azure sea before flaming tangerine and crimson jumped into the mixture, inciting varied hues to disco like they had never danced before. "Watch this carefully," she said to her chatting relatives.

Everyone looked up at the show.

Waves of mauve, cranberry, and peach tried to move in with pizazz. A single glow of buttery gold started shouting from the dance floor—with a message too potent for words. Spellbound, they gazed! When final flickers of radiance streaked from the embers of a slumbering sunshine, they all clapped.

"She'll rise again in another beautiful gown in the morning," Holly said.

"And so life goes on," Adam said, hugging his wife.

The merriment continued.

"Remember when Jake came home from school with his new friend Peter and announced they were going to swim across Lake Hiawatha?" Holly asked.

"Pete was a great swimmer and they wanted a challenge." Abby said.

"A few people had attempted swimming across already so I assured them they wouldn't be the first!" Adam said.

"I had my own struggle with a fragile ego; and without God's mercy and grace, could have sunk to the bottom of a lake much bigger than Lake Hiawatha." Holly said.

"Jake needed to make decisions as a teenager under our watchful guidance," Adam said. "Whether or not he might fail was no reason to abandon worthy endeavors. He needed to consider options and learn to make wise choices. Truthfully, there were times I wondered if we failed as he grew older."

Lisa laughed and Jake tightened his lips and scowled … before leaning over to kiss her.

They discussed teaching kids how to set beneficial long-term goals.

"We made mistakes not being realistic in what we attempted," Holly said. "Let's practice learning how to do that together as a family."

"Brenda and I have a big task reclaiming lost years of wise parenting with our daughters up in Idaho. We need your prayers. They'll no doubt have little to do with us when they discover religion is a significant part of our belief system," Jason said.

"Abby and I also have a big challenge ahead," Ben said standing. He kneeled in front of her and reached for her hand. "I talked to your father this morning and he approves. Will you become my wife?"

"Aaahh … this is a huge surprise."

"I love you and don't think we can serve God effectively unless we're married. Will you marry me, Abby?"

She blinked back tears and consented in front of her family. "I thought you would never ask," she said.

"We were so committed to our first love; I wondered how we could make time for us as a couple. But after listening to Jake and Lisa, I became convinced this was the right decision. We'll continue to be teammates in every area. He has to stay at the center, however."

"By the way, I forgot this," Ben said, reaching into his pocket. He pulled out Granny's antique engagement ring and placed it on Abby's finger.

Cheers were heard by sheep grazing in the pasture.

"A wise woman builds her house—but with her own hands, the foolish one tears hers down." Holly quoted from Proverbs 14:1. "Make us proud, sweetie."

"Thanks, Mom," Abby said, coming over to hug her mother.

Congratulations continued until Adam had a bright idea. "Tonight would be a great night for sharing stories, a cup of hot cider, and songs around a bonfire," he said. Everyone pitched in to gather twigs for kindling, pull logs over, and rearrange chairs around a mass of orange streaks quickly turned into a blazing heap of warmth.

Alex worked the hardest.

Sitting around the fire, Adam started singing, "How great is your God? ... Sing with me ... How great is your God?" They all joined in.

"Just like Old Faithful ... He never changes," Adam said. "But we do, as we get to know Him better. Let's be honest tonight. What do you fear? What has caused deep pain for you? After we divulge personal information, we'll throw our notes in the fire."

He passed around paper and pencils. Adam sang songs as they wrote. "Anyone willing to tell us your personal thoughts?"

Jake and Ben were courageous. Abby, Lisa, and Brenda followed.

"Let's move on to a new adventure. Are you ready to take the BOB challenge?"

"What does that mean, Dad?" Jake asked.

"Share something with every person you meet. Some might benefit from your smile. Others may need to hear a cheery encouragement. A few will have concerns or questions. Watch and listen for what He wants you to do next. It might involve asking someone to join you for coffee."

"So our goal is to bend-over-backwards for people we come into contact with, right?" Jake said.

"Never underestimate what God wants to do in your life. His plans are far more meaningful than the ones we cook up for ourselves. Sometimes feelings of unworthiness drag us down, and other times our imagination is limited. But God has bigger plans!"

A bag of marshmallows appeared with sticks to roast them. Adam rearranged the fire before they sang Happy Birthday to the family matriarch again, in harmonizing rhapsody.

While they turned white puffs into golden creations, Jake talked to Betsy.

"Someday a charming guy will try to steal you away from me and make you his own property. He'll only care about himself though he'll try to convince you that you're his one and only true love. Don't believe him. Run for your life, especially when it feels too good to pass up. If he truly loves you, he'll wait patiently until you're convinced of his intentions. Whatever you do Betsy, don't fall for his lies about how you're worthless without him. I've been a lousy father to you, up to now, and you deserve the best husband out there. To prove your worth, we're beginning weekly dates until someone who cares more about your heart and soul than me comes along. And he better be pretty awesome!!!"

"When will we start, Dad?"

"Tomorrow night."

"But Mark already wants to watch a movie with me."

"He'll have to wait his turn. I'm the new guy in your heart."

She smiled as her father kissed her nose.

"This is kind of better than Aunt Abby," Betsy said.

"Yeah ... for a long, long time." Jake hugged his daughter tight. Lisa watched from the other side of the fire.

As the embers died down, he waited for a perfect moment to tell his family one final secret. Seizing an opportunity, he cleared his throat. "Excuse me. Since I've been known for keeping secrets, this will be the last one I'll hopefully ever need to expose."

Lisa's eyes opened wider.

Jake stared across the fire into his beloved wife's face. He winked, causing her to laugh nervously. "The Bible tells about a Jewish love story where the bridegroom sets out after midnight to consummate his relationship with his betrothed. She patiently waits for his arrival ... wondering when he might show up to begin a mutual life together. Weeks, months, and years pass with no sign that he intends to keep his promise. Then, when all appears futile, he appears and takes leadership over her life permanently. Lisa, it's with great joy I can reveal that I've returned home for the last time."

"My position is secure as a husband and father—and I'll begin an eight-week promo for the best career I could ever hope, with God's help, next week."

"I'm here to stay!!!"

Around the campfire Jake's family held hands and prayed for what might come. Lisa scooted around to hug him. Nippy air was sneaking in but snuggling would keep her warm.

"Have you ever seen the Northern Lights?" Holly asked when they finished.

"I've seen pictures and they're awesome!" Lisa said.

"Watching the aurora borealis is a spellbinding experience. Great arches of shimmering rays—from violet through yellow–green to the orange-reds—dance as curtains of colored lights across the sky. The aura of mystery surrounding these most spectacular natural phenomena eludes even the wisest men. What impresses me most is the Bible describes it perfectly," Holly said.

Adam nodded and interjected, "Psalm 19:1 says, *The heavens are telling the glory of God; they are a marvelous display of his craftsmanship.* Another verse in Romans says, *Since earliest times men have seen the earth and sky ... and have known of his existence and great power.*"

"Discovering that Jesus was more than a cute baby on a Christmas card has been my best present ever," Holly said. "And watching him change my life has been the most spectacular thing I've ever seen—even better than the Northern Lights!"

"What more could happen in one weekend?" Adam asked.

With plans for a Christmas wedding taking shape in the Dominican Republic, Abby and Ben headed south. Hopefully the whole family would be able to join them on the beach for an informal ceremony.

Jason and Brenda flew north to support their oldest daughter Christie who was barely twenty-two and pregnant with her first child, unaware who the father might be—and her nineteen year old sister, Chelsea who recently moved in with her third boyfriend, an atheist who hated the concept of a deity. He would surely make their newfound faith difficult.

"Do you really believe Mom and Dad are in hell?" Jason asked Lisa, before saying goodbye.

"They made their own choice to reject a risen Savior," Lisa said. "There are consequences for sin. No one knows what happened during their final minutes. We could discover a miracle took place on that highway. I do know where Angela is, though, and she's not dead."

*　　*　　*

Jake and Lisa determined to become more active participants at Grace Fellowship Church beginning with the Sunday morning worship service. They were greeted by Phil and Brooke Davis, and hundreds of parishioners who opened their arms and hearts to a dearly loved family.

"Some circumstances in our lives won't change. Are you living above or trapped under them?" Pastor Davis asked in his sermon. "The secret to peace and joy regardless of the situation is contentment. Our struggles shouldn't consume us. Don't fall for self-pity and complaining, or become angry, resentful, confused, without hope. God knows everything that's happening and allows it for a reason. Just because we can't see Him working, doesn't mean He isn't. The more difficult life becomes, the more seriously we need to listen to the spirit within us. Instead of asking why, ask what can be learned from this?"

"Things that used to trouble me don't anymore because I've learned that a loving heavenly father will allow us to go through painful trials so we can grow up. Even being in jail gave Paul a surprising audience and allowed time to write a book. It wasn't a mistake—though you may think sitting in prison for sharing your faith might be. What looks like a hindrance may actually be a resource, leading to an incredible season of fruitfulness."

When he finished praying, Phil Davis headed straight for Jake. "I think you're the one to head our teenage Breakaway in April. The Janssen's were heavily involved but just moved to the east coast with an unexpected promotion. We need someone with your physical stamina, along with your passion for impacting hearts. I know God has been changing your heart and these teens are my deepest concern as they come of age in a dark world."

"Can I pray about that with Lisa and call you later?" Jake asked.

He already noticed several teenagers chatting in the foyer. With the privilege of influencing his own children, and Betsy and Alex becoming older, this would be a dream come true.

Maybe God had ways of restoring the years locusts had eaten.

His first step was to establish a godly home his wife and children seriously needed. The second priority was to put his heart and soul into a variety show that miraculously popped up in his hometown. Several former co-workers needed to be contacted over the next few days to impact that venture most effectively. With God's help, he would finally succeed.

He intended to spend time on his knees before falling asleep.

"Did you really love her more than me?" Lisa asked while undressing.

"Who are you talking about?"

"Was there more than one?"

"Oh no, where are we headed tonight?" Jake asked.

"It's hard to find a place where we truly belong since we're often our own worst enemy. Someday our struggle with brokenness will be over, and we'll be made whole and happy for the first time in our existence."

"Are you second guessing what happened in the past?"

"Do you really love me?"

"I've given you every reason to believe I'm finally telling the truth. You know that I love you. A thousand times more than I did when we got married."

"But did you love her more?"

"No, Lise. They meant nothing!"

"They?"

"Please, sweetheart! Just let me hug you tonight. We'll talk in the morning. You're getting worked up about nothing." He pulled her closer and embraced her body warmly. Touching her lips, he whispered how beautiful she was. His fingers stroked back and forth across her shoulder, slowly sliding down her torso.

Lisa struggled to shake off pictures of Jake touching another female but it was too much to bear.

Her cry of despair touched a nerve in his soul that he didn't know how to handle. Just when things were starting to turn around, now this?

"God help us! Haven't I already paid enough for my sins?"

Thoughts of Tina longing for more of his touch; Kiki begging for him to stop; Sade massaging his body and causing him to tremble; Sara desperate to find intimacy; Francie offering hope of a glorious future in paradise while making him feel like a man; others providing for his physical needs instead of a wife who should have been there for him—left him frustrated and confused.

Maybe the future wouldn't be so bright after all.

Chapter 19

Reflection

SUNLIGHT STREAMING IN THE bedroom window woke Jake, who realized he was alone in his bed. The house was eerily quiet. He took care of personal needs and pulled on his clothes.

Hurrying to the kitchen, he found a note on the counter.

Helping in Alex's class this morning but will be home for lunch.
I love you,
Lisa

He made a pot of coffee and scrambled some eggs. Leftover blueberry muffins looked tasty so he gobbled two, wishing he'd eaten slower as he brushed crumbs on the floor. Yeah, he was a lucky man. He looked forward to lunch with Lisa.

Her Bible was on the table so he opened it to Mark 6—where she had scribbled a note on paper.

I'm sick and tired of being discouraged. How did I get here? By degrees.

1. Look inside yourself.
2. Look up. (You're in trouble if you don't.)
3. Look back.
4. Look ahead. What are your desires? How does God fit into those dreams?

5. Reorganize. What are you doing that you shouldn't be?
   What aren't you doing that you should?
   P.S. Don't forget. It's unwise and costly to act when
   you're tired, angry, or hungry—and will usually result
   in destructive choices.

Jake pondered his wife's thoughts. They made sense. He picked up her Bible and began reading Mark 6, stopping at verse 48 because he was baffled. He read it again.

Jesus saw the disciples straining at the oars, because the wind was against them. Shortly before dawn he went out to them, walking on the lake. He was about to pass by them. Why would Jesus do that? His disciples were struggling in a bad storm? Why walk out close to them if he had no intention stopping to help?

Written in the margin of her Bible Lisa wrote, "I would like to be included in your day but the choice is yours to make. I'll wait patiently until you call. Love, Jesus"

By the time Lisa walked through the front door at noon, the meaning of the verse was clear. "I learned a bunch this morning reading your Bible," he said getting up from the chair. "That gunk that clogs minds needs fresh air from scripture to clear out the cobwebs."

He hugged her. Then he hugged her again. "I'm sorry about last night."

"So am I. My mind goes dumpster diving often in a search for peace. I ask myself, 'Why wade through garbage? What do I hope to find digging in negative stuff—some new painful tidbit of truth? We've been through enough pain already. Why do I insist on inflicting more? Why not pull weeds in a garden, instead?' I'm my own worst enemy, I guess."

"Besides the fact it was mean to say I loved someone more, I was unfaithful, Lisa, and deserve your scrutiny and resentment. You could have flushed my ring down the toilet and refused to talk. Thank God for a second chance to prove my love."

"In my quiet time this morning, I read a devotional by *Fresh Start* about setting aside past failures and moving on. Somewhere deep down inside, we need to dig a grave and bury wrongs we've suffered. Let it become a forgotten spot to which no footsteps mark a path; and then never go there again! It might take more than one try for me, but with His help I'm going to succeed. The only thing we knew for sure is that God is in control and He'll take care of everything. I'm determined to learn to trust both of you."

"Let's keep talking about these issues until we work the kinks out completely. God can't really use us 'til we do."

"When I have questions about the others, just kiss me like you mean it. I'll forget about them quickly."

"Let's practice right now."

They did and lunch was an hour late.

Sitting alone on the patio, Jake and Lisa continued to reflect on the past. "Remember when our minister asked, 'What's the most precious item of value you have to give as a Christmas gift to Jesus?' What did you promise?" Lisa asked.

"I don't remember. Probably nothing," Jake said.

"What I promised and what I gave were two different things."

"Do I have to guess?" Jake asked.

"No, but it's still hard to talk about her."

"Our firstborn?"

"Yes. I used to wait for the day you would talk about Angela without shouting. That happened on rare instances. Most of the time, you were silent as a rock seething with hostility at me. I tried to restrain my emotions to keep you from running farther away. That built an even bigger wall between us."

"It was just too painful. I was supposed to be her protector."

"Same for me, Jake. I was her mother—supposed to be watching her closely that morning. She was so excited to go out on the sand bar with you! I was tired and had a lot on my mind, resentful at you for ignoring us and then going off to have your own fun. It felt like we were a nuisance in your busy life."

"Couldn't be farther from the truth," he said.

"How could I know what you felt when you concealed it?"

"Guilty again. I don't think you understood my need to project a perfect image to thousands of listeners every evening. Being in front of a camera, people think you're a celebrity or some kind of deity."

"Maybe that's what you wanted them to think."

"I did have a huge ego—before my fall from grace."

"How will it be different this time with the contemporary news/variety segment? Will you lapse into your old ways?" she asked.

"Do you mean with females?"

"No. With your pride."

"I think you know the answer," he said.

"Will this really cost something more from you?"

"The key for both of us is to take our eyes off me and put it on Him. That's the difference."

"Wow, Jake! That's powerful."

"So will you be one of the special guests on my show?"

Lisa laughed, prematurely. What she didn't know yet was that her name was on the celebrity list for the first show and not because she had a pretty face.

Previously working unseen in the station's ivory tower—while ambitious anchors, reporters, and distinguished guests made headlines on air in front of viewers—Lisa was nervous. Her debut on the first episode for Jake's new show was only because she believed in what her husband was attempting. Primping in the make-up department on Monday, September 27, she listened attentively as Kate Jones went over plans for their interview. This was paramount for success as an expert on the "happiness in the home" segment to follow.

Minutes from going live, Jake winked at his wife. He made a heart on his chest with his fingers and looked up with a confident smile.

Set crew hustled to get lights, cameras, and props in place as the production crew, cameramen, assistants, and talented personalities prepared for take-off. A malfunctioning IFB threatened to halt the pilot momentarily until a hand signal was given.

5, 4, 3, 2, 1 …"Welcome to the *Ed Jakate Show* where you'll find us from 10-11 a.m. every morning this week … and hopefully for many weeks after that … I'm Jake Clark with bubbly Kate Jones who will enhance our daily exposés with her dynamic personality. Call the station; follow us online; write to our producers—if you like any of the magnificent tidbits we offer and want to see more."

"We need you!!!" Kate chimed in.

He began by talking about students across the country being back at school and engrossed in education and relationships—with interesting shots of adorable faces including Betsy and Alex trudging off to a workday of learning. He promised to offer nutritious afterschool treats later in the show with a renowned chef.

Kate Jones moved into a segment on international competition in education.

A video from Sentani, Papua, Indonesia showed students at Hillcrest International School. "One of the school's trademark activities is a program known as Outdoor Education," Jake reported. "During second semester, the entire student body and a number of faculty members travel to a remote location in Papua, the Indonesian half of the island of New Guinea. For two weeks students and faculty serve local people with community service projects, hosting kid's clubs, and leading worship services in local churches."

"Students sometimes live with locals in their homes," Kate said. "In addition, students are encouraged to interact and learn about culture and history. Each student keeps a journal; and then writes an anthropology paper based on their experiences during the two weeks."

"I understand the students also complete a photo journalism project," Jake added. "Wouldn't that be fun?"

"Pepper, our production assistant, sure had fun putting the photos together for this power point. I would give you an A+ … if I was your teacher," Kate said to Pepper, joking.

"Great idea!" Jake said. "Everybody call and give us an A+ right now. We'll pause for a mini-phone marathon and award some kind of prize for the 10th caller. What do you have in your purse that we can give away?" he asked Kate.

"I'll bake some brownies," Lisa said from the corner, just out of view.

"Come on in, sweetheart! You're our next guest. This fabulous woman has wonderful ideas about making a house kids will love coming home to after school. You'd be crazy to miss the next few minutes!"

He stood to make room for his wife to chat across from Kate, while the station broke for a commercial. Lisa wore a rainbow t-shirt with two big hearts decorated with her children's names. During the hiatus, 27 people called in with excellent remarks.

Excited co-workers watched eagerly.

"We're back with *Happy Family Tips* from our expert Lisa Clark."

"Scientists confirm babies need to be touched, as well as fed, to survive," Kate said. "Growing children need the same. Where do we start, Lisa? What should I do when Johnny walks in the door after a bad day at school?"

Lisa glanced over at Jake who was beaming. "Expressing affection to a younger child is usually pretty easy. They naturally gravitate to your lap and arms. Kisses and hugs work best. Tickles, wrestling, and back scratches are also good. When kids become self-conscious, it becomes more difficult. You can touch a shoulder as they pass and squeeze their hand or arm gently with goodbyes."

She took a breath.

"Always look in your child's eyes when either of you is talking. Your facial expression and tone are more significant than what you're trying to convey. Be available when they want to share. Wise mothers figure out best times for each and watch for signals. Put down your magazine and bend to their level. Our daughter Betsy bubbles over right after coming home. Alex likes to sit on a stool next to me whenever I cook."

"And bedtime might be a more appropriate opportunity to express thoughts at the end of the day?" Kate asked.

"Absolutely."

"Most parents figure the child is just there, basically existing as they grow up," Lisa said. "Adults question negative behavior and actions but ignore feelings lurking beneath issues. Develop an interest in your kids' emotional health with appropriate questions and responses. Inquire what they're thinking or which friends make them feel the happiest … and why. Find out where they like to go and what brings the most satisfaction. Discover secrets no one else is privy—because you're there at the pivotal moment when no one seems to care."

"Great advice! Anything else we need to know?"

"Each home is as unique as the family that resides inside. Keep building your relationships with positive words. Say I love you, often. Whisper it in their ears. Write it on notes. Pin it to their pillow. Say they're special and you love them very much. Tell them you're glad they were born!"

"That would work in all my relationships, not just with children," Kate said.

Jake motioned from the side with his hands formed in a heart on his chest.

Lisa smiled.

Another commercial break left additional advice unsaid. *Happy Family Tips* would return the following Monday for its second episode, an obvious favorite segment of the *Ed Jakate Show*.

New comments from 117 delighted listeners kept phones ringing during that twelve minute segment. More followed.

After the show ended, Mike Hintz stood near the back waiting to congratulate his newest stars. "Tomorrow we'll talk about current trends in wind generators and visit a solar house that will blow you away," Kate said joking.

"Can't wait to see where this is going to take us!" Mike said.

Jake and Lisa whispered prayers each morning for direction, wisdom in choices, and rebuilding relationships. The first week was a huge success.

The happy couple was physically and emotionally exhausted while listening to Phil Davis on Sunday. "What are you hungriest for today? What do you want to do more than anything? Who do you want to spend time with?" He paused.

"Did your answer have anything to do with Jesus?"

"Deuteronomy 6:5 says, *Love the LORD your God with all your heart, soul, and strength*. It's not a casual thing to say you love someone with all your heart. What does that really mean?"

"Does sleeping in a barn make you a cow? Does seeing a picture of the president make him your close friend? If you take a trip to the county fair, does that make you a world traveler? What scripture can you quote without looking in a Bible? Does God fit in your vocabulary outside of profanity?"

"Describe your relationship with Him."

"Engaging in a couple of casual conversations doesn't count as a friendship. If you want a real relationship, you'll desire to know what He thinks and spend time in His presence. When was the last time you told someone He's significant in your life? Does anyone know He lives inside you? When people meet you—they're actually meeting God in person. At some point He'll begin working in your life, making you like His son."

"Where you are is not where God wants you to stay. There is a next stage to your journey. New seasons of growth are coming. It may seem God is silent right now but that's just a test. Teachers usually don't talk when students are taking a test. He's checking to see if we're ready to move on to the next level."

"A guy named Bill was burned over seventy percent in a house fire that cost him dearly a few years ago. He writhed in pain and couldn't imagine going on. After multiple skin grafts and surgeries, his wife Dottie left him for a more handsome fellow. He decided to focus on the Savior who gave him life—changing his heart of stone into a humble servant's quest to obey."

"In months, his face visibly softened from the rough scars and his countenance brought rays of sunshine to those he encountered. Friends were amazed watching the transformation."

"Meeting his ex-wife at a wedding the following year, relatives exclaimed how HER face aged ten years while his was more beautiful than ever. A bigger story unfolded when guests crowded around him at the reception to watch his joy in action and listen as he powerfully influenced people. Dottie sat alone at a back table—rejected by her former handsome beau who recently chose a much younger lover."

"Love rekindled the flame Bill held toward this bitter woman and he set out to make her feel like a cherished treasure. Because Jesus still works miracles in hearts of stone, they renewed their marriage vows two years later on a beach in Jamaica and have been dramatically impacting lives wherever they go."

"Sometimes transformation requires personal sacrifice and is painful.

As He changes hearts and minds, our actions and attitudes become different. One thing is certain—God working in your heart will always stir something in others."

"What is true forgiveness?" Jake asked Lisa after their kids fell asleep.

"Is that when you completely forget the original problem that caused pain in the first place?"

"So how would a person know—if all was truly forgotten?" Jake said.

"They must have forgiven the offense or it would still eat them alive."

"Well, sitting on the patio talking with Betsy last night, I became engrossed in our conversation. I forgot to take my sunglasses off after the sun went down. It got darker and darker … and I could barely see her face. She asked multiple questions and at one point I thought she was you."

"She does look like my more youthful charming self—only with honey blonde hair."

"I had sunglasses on at night. It was pretty dark."

"Go on … what were you saying?"

"Betsy wanted to know why I loved other females, instead of you and her."

"I was unaware she knew anything about them."

"Apparently she heard you crying. It was probably the night I told you about Francie. You must have been muttering oaths about me. Betsy also said she tried to call me on my mobile phone before I moved to Seattle. Someone answered and told her never to call again, to find her own lover."

"Ouch! That must have really hurt."

"Guess she decided never to forgive me, no matter how hard I try. She insisted that when I find another female who likes to be tickled; I'll run off with her and you'll be alone again. She said both of you hate me."

"I told her you forgave me and she said that was a lie."

"In our attempts to build protective boundaries, we become insulated from genuinely caring about others. Walls are built one brick at a time."

"So it's true?"

"You know the truth, Jake. If I can believe you—then you can surely believe me. Look in my eyes."

She gripped both of his hands.

"I forgive you and love you with all my heart!"

Chapter 20
Moonlight Dance

REFLECTIONS OF MOONLIGHT THROUGH the window as Jake brushed his teeth—caused his heart to flutter. "Lise, Let's go outside on the patio to dance. Come with me. Hurry."

"Seriously?"

He pulled clothes back on so she shadowed his actions. A quick glance in the mirror to check her hair and she followed him out the door.

The shimmering moon cast its light on trees and bushes around the property making their yard appear larger. Not a sound could be heard in the quietness of the night. A sense of warmth and tranquility emanated from the kitchen light that glowed through multiple windows.

He pulled her close and started moving slowly.

"There's a kind of hush all over the world tonight ... just the two of us, and nobody else ... and I'm feeling good just holding you tight," he sang. "So listen very carefully, closer now and you will see ... this isn't a dream. The only sound that you will hear is when I whisper in your ear ... I'll love you forever and ever."

She giggled when his lips touched her ear.

"There's more," Jake said seriously.

"When a man loves a woman ... ," he continued singing. They danced in rhythm for what seemed an hour. He stopped to kiss her at the end of each song. "I'll still love you when the moon goes out to sea ..."

Maybe she would never forget the pain from losing Angela but new memories could fill in dark gaps and give her reason to sing despite heartbreak caused by his unfaithfulness. Jake resolved to persevere until the moon shone for the last time. Somehow—with help from an Almighty—Lisa would remember his sin no longer one day.

He touched her hair attentively.

Coaxing her to relax in his arms, he stroked her shoulder, back, and arms. His hands gracefully danced while sliding down an appealing torso to her waist, pausing for a minute to listen to her breathe. His fingers tingled with excitement moving lower as she melted next to his body wanting desperately to be one flesh.

"I could have lost you ... what a price I would have paid," he said.

"We had a heavenly father watching out for us."

"Oooohh, I love you so much, Lise."

"Do you think dancing lessons would help Betsy?" Jake asked before falling asleep.

"Maybe. Time will tell."

"That's not good enough," he said. "I won't stop until two of the most beautiful females in the world are convinced of my love."

"His love is more important," Lisa said.

"That's not my problem. I'm only responsible for doing my part."

A pair of gorgeous pink ballet slippers hung in Betsy's bedroom the next day as a symbol of her father's intentions.

*   *   *

"Come sit on my lap, you sweet little chickadee," Jake said to his lovely wife who was resting on the sofa. "I have plans for you this afternoon."

"I'm leaving in a couple minutes to run dinner over to a family whose mother is in the hospital. I should be back in about an hour. Can it wait until then?"

"Guess I'll take what I can get."

They kissed before he helped carry food to the car. "Hope you can be a blessing to them but remember who is waiting."

"I know. Why don't you take a nap? The kids will be home by dinner."

Her idea sounded better as the minutes passed.

First he leaned back on the sofa. After a quick assessment of the situation, he moved to his bed.

Memories of the University of Arizona filled his mind. Picturing the Library and Administration Building was harder to envision since his life involved spending time with people in busier settings.

Jake's journalism major in college required perfecting his communication skills—in hands-on ways—so he pursued it with gusto during classes and at night. Friends were intrigued with his innovative ways to have fun when stress about the future preoccupied their own minds.

Talking to Lisa killed two birds with one stone. Her voice calmed his soul and gave him a sense of direction. Her insight into the business world was a valuable resource. In front of college friends, Jake bent on one knee and handed her a little box.

"You can't be serious," she said blushing.

She whispered in his ear, "Why are you doing this—with them here? Is this why you wanted me to come to Arizona?"

Ignoring his girlfriend's uncomfortable predicament and cry for privacy, he insisted she open it. Her breath quickened and hands shook as she peeked in the gold container. A scream pierced the air—when a fat bug popped out and slid down her blouse. "Jake!"

He fell on the ground, laughing. "Just want to have a little fun with you," he said, pulling her down on top of him. Embarrassed, Lisa smiled at the crowd watching his antics—then laughed when he tickled her.

"If you weren't so much fun I'd have nothing to do with you," she said under her breath.

An unexpected call from Tina Parker surprised Jake later that week. "I think about you night and day. Are you positive Lisa's the right girl for you?" He was at a loss for words. After hanging up, the sick feeling in his gut lingered but he decided to let her go for good. However, stickers on his car window the next morning convinced him it wasn't her final attempt to win him back.

If only Jake had been stronger fighting off continual urges to get bigger thrills and risk losing what was most treasured in his life.

He'd been foolish, a proud man. Had he been more sensitive to Lisa's emotional needs, many things could have been different—starting with her discomfort on several occasions when Jake caroused regardless of her embarrassment. He saw her concern but games of cat and mouse excited him more. She begged, even pleaded with him to respect her opinion—to no avail.

It somehow gave him an upper hand.

Becoming a father created feelings of euphoria, perhaps extending his pride with double impact to the world. She was so adorable! Everything revolved around this precious creature and it was his job to protect her.

When Angela was knocked over by the wave and ceased breathing on that wicked sand bar, his helplessness was too much to bear. Strangers gathered to gawk at his ultimate humiliation, no doubt aware of the truth—selfish pursuits distracted him from watching the little pixie who was overjoyed to join her daddy on the beach that day; not realizing his mistake soon enough prevented him from helping as she struggled for one last breath; and his job was to tell the breaking news, not make it.

No one seemed to care that she was dying.

Lisa found her husband sobbing on the bed. "Dinner's ready and the kids are waiting to eat."

"I don't deserve you."

"What happened to the guy I was dancing with last night?"

Jake revealed what he had been thinking and she embraced him.

"You're the guy I wanted to marry and you're still the one I want to spend my life with. Nothing else matters, Jake. We're going to make it now!!! Let's trust our Creator. He alone knows how and why we were made with these personalities. Some of the bleakest moments we encounter actually turn into the most cherished and brilliantly colored tapestries hanging on our walls. Looking back, we could never part with any of them!"

The family dinner of ribs and sweet corn was extra special. Cornbread muffins and Adam's deluxe baked beans left little room for brownie sundaes—though nothing was left on dishes when they finished.

Alex had received a baby turtle on the shopping trip with Pampa and Mimi. His plastic home came complete with a spiral staircase and hot tub near the bottom. So far he remained nameless though Lisa called him slowpoke.

Betsy's honey blonde hair was pulled up with a pink ribbon and all she could talk about were beautiful dancing shoes. "We're painting our nails while you guys clean up," she announced to her father.

"If you promise to sit beside me when we finish—while we watch Black Beauty," Jake said.

"I want popcorn," Alex said, stuffing plates in the dishwasher.

As they shuffled for space on the sofa, Jake wrapped his arms around Lisa on one side and Betsy on the other. Alex sat on his father's lap in the middle, with his arms stretched up around his father's neck—until he tired and fell asleep on the floor.

Jake tenderly carried him to bed when the movie finished, giving Alex extra kisses in spite of his being sound asleep.

*　　*　　*

Sunday afternoons with Holly and Adam became a new tradition for family relaxation after worshipping at Grace Fellowship. Grandparents relished extra time with Betsy and Alex, while their parents lollygagged about the ranch in carefree togetherness. Deep conversations usually occurred under an oak tree near the barn—where playful lambs jumped in circles, in hopes of receiving a special corn treat.

"Don't pay attention to them," Lisa said.

"I have other plans today," he said, reaching to pull her down on the grass beside him.

"Not while we have observers."

Jake didn't mind. He slowly unbuttoned her blouse while intriguing her in an interesting discussion. Kisses helped when it slipped from her shoulders. A squirrel scurried past on its way to tell the breaking news.

"Tell me about your parent's conversion," Lisa asked.

"Desperation brought them to their knees after Dad's terrible accident. Everybody thought he would die but my mom seemed happy to hear that news. They sent me and Abby to California for the summer so I'm not exactly sure of all the details."

"When we returned home, a dramatic change was evident in our home. Smiling, with eyes that twinkled, Mom listened when my father talked. Her hostile glare had long been forgotten."

"Listen with your eyes," Granny used to say. "Mom didn't know what she meant but liked seeing the sparkle in her grandmother's eyes."

"Scripture says the eye is the window to the soul," Lisa said. "Peering into the mirror, we don't observe ourselves realistically. We either see nothing or we're overly critical."

"Mom and Dad studied non-verbal communication when they learned to scuba dive—in an effort to better understand each other under water. Did you know most of what we say is conveyed other than by words. They discovered there are certain classic behaviors that give telltale signs about what isn't being said verbally."

"I wish we'd known this during the years we said nothing."

*   *   *

Plans to tell their stories took precedence when Brooke Davis called asking Jake and Lisa to share at an upcoming marriage retreat. "Your testimonies have already impacted several and I'm certain more people will be inspired by your dramatic turn-a-round. We're hoping you can talk together and then each speak personally. If you want, we'll have a bonus time for questions."

Jake and Lisa discussed their options.

"Why is this important for us? What's at stake if we refuse the opportunity?" Jake asked Lisa.

"He never gives what we ask for until He believes we're ready to accept it. Unfortunately, some of us refuse to leave our cares with Him and busy ourselves with what's insignificant."

"I'm guilty of that," Jake said. "Even when we know better, we become isolated in our lives with a hectic pace that consumes time and energy."

"After all those years longing for you to talk about Angie, even just to me—it seems impossible you could do this now," Lisa said, with eyes misting up. "It seems so surreal."

"It's time to talk publicly," Jake said. "I say let's do it with all our heart."

"And will we keep secrets?"

"Whatever He puts on your tongue will be what you should divulge, Lise. What happened in the past will only be significant if someone can be spared from similar mistakes or unnecessary pain in their future. We'll leave the outcome in His hands."

"Just wink, if I should yield to you."

"No, I'll wink because you're cute. The only one we'll yield to is Him."

"Hey, Brooke gave me a note back when I was struggling for hope about the future—about the time your father came to visit you. Those words encouraged me then but seem even more perfect now. It's in the back of my Bible. Just a second … I'll show you."

In a flash, she handed him the note.

You are God's letter to the world around you. What they see in you, and hear from you, is a message about Christ to them. Maybe this scares you? You don't think people will see in you what God wants them to see? Well, better shape up then, because He has chosen you to represent Him whether you like it or not. The good news is that He is doing the writing, not you. Ask God to make your life a great story for others to read today.

The crisp mountain air was refreshing as Jake and Lisa organized a variety of thoughts, ready to reveal their painful legacy of being held captive in a dark cave—where unspoken words remained hidden under the cover of night. The prison smelled of death but shackles lay outside the open door … bolted shut, far too many years.

A large blue conference room, with stage turned homey by a plaid loveseat and coffee table, seated 400 guests eager to hear what promoters described as a life-changing evening. The tapestry above the stage portrayed a county home, with hearts engraved on a tree in the front yard.

Brooke Davis was the emcee.

"Charming Jake and dependable Lisa longed to inspire others from the beginning in their storybook romance but in a shocking twist, they lost precious Angela and experienced unimaginable heartbreak … before sovereign circumstances transformed their willing hearts into a lighthouse of hope. They're here today to share their deeply personal story with you," she said with a big smile. "I'd like to introduce my wonderful friends, Jake and Lisa Clark."

Applause filled the room as they walked to the platform.

Lisa wore a ruffled pink jacket over a white top with a gray flared skirt. Her hair was pulled up slightly at her temples, with chestnut curls spilling down to her shoulders. Jake's shirt was the same baby blue as his eyes and his graying hair added a hint of expertise to his demeanor. They sat on the loveseat. He leaned to kiss his wife, resulting in more applause.

Lisa began her story.

"Everything seemed fine that sunny August morning, following a fitful night for seven month old Lizzie who was teething plus suffering ear complications from our flight to the east coast. I don't remember hearing Jake leave the room but when two year old Angie woke, she ran to the balcony door and spied her daddy fishing on the beach. No doubt God was preparing us for the tragedy with final extra hugs and moments of pure joy. Unfortunately, carefully planned lives screech to a stop. Ours did that morning! People have no idea why God allows terrible things ... but there's usually a reason looking back. When rescue medics tried to find Angie's pulse, my worst dreams came true. Everything stood still. I was filled with unbearable grief—while my husband walked away, attempting to console himself in the hotel. Strangers offered comfort but I was numb. It took a while before I could even talk. God was silent. Perhaps He's angry with us, I thought."

"At times I didn't think I could bear it. I would wake up gasping from pain most nights, remembering awful details that were etched deep in my mind. They say tragic circumstances like these make or break marriages. Ours was almost completely shattered!!!"

"When Angela died, her freshly painted pink bedroom moaned in silence. Her sheets covered in a field of rainbow daisies collected dust. Her favorite books of *Curious George* and *The Three Bears* remained glued to the shelf; and her precious little dolly with curly brown hair sat sullenly on the floor, untouched. We were broken by sadness for months. One day, Lizzie somehow pushed the door open and went inside to play. Sunshine began to pour in the windows again. Birds started singing. Flowers even started blooming in our long neglected garden. Then I found her beach towel."

Lisa held up a rainbow towel with cobalt sailboats, fish, and sea shells—pressing it against her face as she stroked it tenderly.

"After Jake lost the anchor job, none of his new prospects panned out. It was stressful not knowing what might happen. I was pregnant again and struggling to find a place in my heart for another child. I can't describe exactly how I felt but God began to give me peace, just enough to keep me going. A chance encounter with our pastor's wife began a wonderful time of mentoring, as she took me under her wing when my husband moved out. Brooke gave me reason to hang in there. James 1:2 became my life verse. *Consider it pure joy, whenever you face trials of many kinds, because you know that the testing of your faith develops perseverance.*"

"Grieving is difficult but my husband and I were polar opposites—ironically stuck at the exact spot. In my attempt to escape despair and go on with life, I rejected any reflection on my own guilt and blamed him in the process. He refused personal interaction, pretending the event never happened. Thanks to a God who didn't give up on us ... and a husband eventually convicted to pursue what God intended ... we are now back together and committed to finish the work He began in our lives—but this time victoriously."

"I'm still heartbroken about losing our daughter, Angela, but learned much during those trials. Rethinking 'what ifs' wastes valuable time. We can't undo yesterday; it's gone. But we can live for what's ahead. Jeremiah 29:11 says, For *I know my plans for you, declares the Lord; plans to prosper you and not to harm you; plans to give you hope and a future.*

"To be honest, it would be easier keeping this to myself, but I believe He wants me to expose my struggle and let you join me in celebrating. If one person is encouraged hearing my testimony, it will be worth it."

Sobbing could be heard around the room.

Lisa reached for a Kleenex in her pocket as Jake began to tell his story.

"How do you describe heartbreak?" he said. "Have you ever seen a movie where a lion jumps on a man and rips him to shreds?"

"Turning my precious little angel over on the sandbar, I pleaded with God. I felt so helpless—desperately wanting to breathe life into her lungs; see her eyes open; have tiny hands grasp mine. Lisa clung to baby

Lizzie—like a life jacket—watching as her terrified soul mate failed to protect his adorable firstborn."

"My chest tightened; like my lungs were shutting down … collapsing … I thought I was dying. Little did I know that I was! My emotions froze. Seeing anguish in Lisa's eyes drove me deeper into despair. I don't remember leaving the beach when the rescue team pulled up. Guess I pounded on one guy's back, demanding he do the task they came to accomplish."

"My refusal to discuss this catastrophe plunged us deeper into a pit. The dark sea sucked us in like that rogue wave stripped Angie of her life on earth. I shuddered to think someone so precious could be gone in the blink of an eye. For a surfer, the splash of a wave was nothing. Getting caught under the curl was exciting. You always came up for air."

"Lisa looked at me for direction but I was sinking into quick sand faster than anyone could understand. I was a respected evening anchor who informed the public of breaking news—confident, stable, capable of remaining in control when none else could muster strength; secure under a doorway in an earthquake; hunkering down under a sniper attack; reaching the safety of shore after a ship explosion. Jake Clark could handle anything. Crying under an avalanche? Never! You dig out as fast as you can."

"So I tried with all my strength."

"When I came home at night, the darkness sucked me in again."

"Lisa kept her distance from me. I knew her heart was broken, yet she was trying to hold things together for Lizzie's sake. Honestly, I couldn't bear to hear about her pain. I needed for her to be strong. I refused to talk. Guilt added to my grief whenever I took one step in that direction."

"To make matters worse, I reached out to attractive females in a desperate attempt to quench my pain and provide emotional solace. Unfortunately, in my confusion, that led to lack of restraint in matters of the heart and soon included physical interactions that did NOT please God. The more I resisted, the harder my struggle became but sin kept me from going to the only one who could do anything about my immorality. I'm ashamed to tell you that what my parents and wife believed I was capable of being—I blew off because of selfishness and arrogance. It cost me a successful career; and years of sweet fellowship with a wife who continued to love me and innocent children deprived of a father who cared."

"What grieves me most is Lisa's struggle to believe I really love her. I understand my past insensitivity created wounds difficult to heal completely but her insecurities most likely impact accepting unconditional love from someone who loves her much more than I do," Jake said, eyes tearing up.

They nuzzled on the loveseat in front of over 400 spectators.

"I need to pursue forgiveness more fully before this relentless question, deep in my mind, destroys my sacred calling. For some reason, it comes back almost immediately after I release it to God."

"Maybe we need to refuse picking it back up," Lisa said.

Thunderous applause rose as the Almighty Savior smiled down— holding a tiny angel in His arms.

During question time afterward, Jake told about his current Ed Jakate Show and desire to make amends with former co-workers at the TV station. God had already enabled the pilot be extended for a full season.

"Many ugly interactions happened during my reporting and anchor positions—in contrast to what God intended—but that was in the past. He gives second chances so we're back trying to connect from our hearts and inspire the fragile lives I trampled. In particular, I need forgiveness from Mike, Paul, and Brianna so I'm praying for a miracle to take place."

The conference motto, *"He who refreshes others will himself be refreshed,"* from Proverbs 11:25, was immediately accomplished in tangible ways.

"You need to write a book," Brooke said.

"Hahaaaaa!" Lisa laughed—with no intention to add that task.

"David never imagined his slingshot would fell a giant. Esther never thought she would win a beauty contest and save her people from disaster. Moses never thought he would lead his people to the Promised Land. And you have no idea what God wants to do through you either. The important fact is that God made you exactly how He needs you to be, in order for you to do what He wants you to do. Just go for it!" Brooke said. "I can't wait to read more about your story."

* * *

"How can you accomplish new goals, in addition to doing other things required of you?" Lisa asked, when she heard about the new program Jake was offered. "You need a bigger crew to support you."

Holly and Adam volunteered to come alongside their son.

Jake's graduation from high school had been exhilarating but heartrending when his parents realized their years of training were ending. His mother arranged a special open house celebration to commemorate his childhood years and encourage him for what lay ahead. Pictures from infancy through teen years were displayed—with special reminders of memorable experiences that highlighted his brief 18 years. His tattered bunny *Happy* and favorite book "Corduroy" sat in the corner. Holly wiped a tear when she remembered moments with *the apple of her eye*—especially entertaining his little sister. His antics amused everyone who knew him as he joyfully interacted with people. His enthusiasm for life was contagious and his friendly spirit energized numerous people.

"I'm going to spend as much time as possible with my only son until he goes off to college and an independent future," Adam had said.

Twenty years later, they remained active participants in his life.

Keka's Kaleidoscope was scheduled to premiere from 10-11 a.m. on Saturdays. The kids' show would prepare healthy snacks, teach fitness dances, make crafts and art projects, promote animals, study languages, and fly on clouds of cotton candy through stories from around the world. Leaping on a comet and sailing through the stars, above a backdrop of charming houses—each unique in design and home to someone special, the set provided a myriad of sensational delights for children. Whimsical polka-dotted daisies in a garden would have pleased Angela.

A green rocking chair patiently waited for story time.

The first episode highlighted an adorable female Kinkajou Monkey with a honey bear face climbing trees with her long tail. Honey was followed by Candy Crane from South Africa with a ruffled brown skirt over her black and white belly. An intricate cap on top of her head was necessary for mating dances.

Practicing a dazzling moon dance required an appetizing flower cupcake snack for twelve excited children participating—so delightful no one noticed the healthy ingredients. A story about Elsie Piddock skipping in her sleep, by Eleanor Farjeon finished the morning. Jake tapped the rhythm on his knee as he read. "Andy, Spandy, Sugary, Candy, French, Almond, Rock—Bread-and-butter-for your-supper's-all-your-mother's-got!"

Alex was honored to participate with the other contestants for a prized role on his father's show. He continued to jump rope when he got home.

"Think you've got a winner!" Lisa said.

Jake beamed and tried to jump himself.

Chapter 21

Snowflakes

FLAKES OF SNOW FILTERED down as chilly air moved in unexpectedly over the majestic Sandia Mountains. Rarely did substantial amounts accumulate this early. Lisa watched from the kitchen waiting for her family to awake.

Sipping peppermint tea brought her mind back years before.

Holiday activities had usually calmed her parents' negative outbursts—as if a magical fairy took control for a few weeks. Fate, whether influenced by genetics or environment, switched to a new reality while her mother's broodiness and father's passive hostility danced for a brief respite.

Luckily for Lisa, her mother tried to create a soothing oasis from hostility in their backyard … a place for finding comfort from personal demons. Unfortunately, Mary never seemed to find answers and refused to expose details about her past. The young daughter was left reeling in her own struggle with constant criticism and emotional abuse—helpless and hopeless.

She escaped to the garden often for solace.

Contemplating life, Lisa observed neighbors engaged in great joy and frivolity. The nuances between families were astounding. Captivated by a different approach to life and dissimilar responses to adversity, she pondered why and questioned potential good in human beings. Kindness from caring neighbor Holly Clark was powerful. The truth about self-centeredness and pride, part of her mother-in-law's former character traits, wasn't learned until much later—but at the time she seemed like a breath of fresh air for an unloved child.

Holly noticed Lisa watching the sky, reflecting about life one day. "You have a beautiful pink cast. What happened?"

"I broke my leg while skating—it will take eight weeks to heal," Lisa answered. "So I can't visit my grandparents like we planned. They live on a farm and have horses."

"Does that make you sad?" Holly asked.

Lisa couldn't begin to tell anyone how terrible each trip to the farm was. Her parents argued verbally enroute and her grandparents fought with them when they arrived. None of them had one good thing to say about anything ... ever. "Why do we keep going?" Lisa asked her father.

"Someday we'll get our inheritance and stop," Pete Stewart always said driving back home.

"Watching birds and listening to them sing helps me forget," Lisa said to Holly.

"Did you know birds use their voices to communicate just like people? A baby lets the parents know if it is hungry, frightened, or injured."

"How does the mother know which voice is her baby's?" Lisa asked.

"Every bird has a distinct sound. Some birds use a special pattern. Sometimes only the male sings ..."

The pitter-patter of feet and a bubbly greeting brought Lisa back to reality.

"Morning sunshine," Jake said, bending over to kiss her on the lips. A second kiss followed, before interruptions from Alex ended a third. The cozy kitchen provided just the right amount of love and warmth to infuse the entire family.

Plans to make a snowman took shape over a hearty breakfast. Snow angels, a snowball fight between parents and kids, and a scrawny Frosty left the winter wonderland looking like a war zone.

Hot cocoa with candy canes in front of a fire proved those judgments were incorrect.

With children preoccupied, Lisa asked Jake some questions. "Do you realize I'm the first person in my family who professed a spiritual connection with the Almighty? What kind of lives might we have had, if even one of my parents knew the truth years ago?"

"What kind of life would WE have, if you didn't know?"

"Hmmm?" She laughed. "Don't want to even think about those options."

"The point being—that's an exemplary reason to explain what we believe with people who come into our lives. Maybe we're the only godly person they know. We can't leave them to fate or a future chance encounter with another believer, who may or may not value our same passions. I've been a terrible influence for many people over the years."

"Thanks to your renewed heart, my brother Jason was deeply impacted."

"Speaking of Jason and Brenda, I wonder how things are going."

"Recent interactions with both daughters have been difficult. We need to pray for pregnant Christie who's still looking in the wrong places for a boyfriend—guess she moved in with someone else to avoid having to live at home again. Nineteen year old Chelsea's atheist lover forbade contact with her parents. Eli is controlling and appears to have her under his spell."

"Jason knows the depths of depravity his soul and other family members have long been imprisoned. Thank God for salvation, redemption, and forgiveness. We're not in this family group by accident, Lise."

They spent the rest of the morning on their knees interceding for family members, and others who weighed heavily on their minds including Paul Esse, Mike Hintz—and certain females Jake felt guilty of leading down a slippery slope.

Fixing lunch, Lisa envisioned pictures of competitors horning in on the precious treasure she alone should have enjoyed. Resentment filled her mind as the positive morning slipped into a muddy rut. Her facial expressions went unnoticed however as Jake enjoyed a football game between his two favorite teams.

Alex and Betsy joined him.

A phone call from her mother-in-law was a wonderful gift. Both husbands were preoccupied so they could talk undisturbed.

"I thought about you this morning and am grateful for your influence in my life, both as a child and now," Lisa said. "Guess we need to choose neighbors more carefully than a house."

"Someone is attentive to those details even when we're not aware," Holly said. "I wish we could have spent more time together!"

"Same for me. You always have answers for my current struggles."

"What's bothering you today?"

"Discouragement over past events; regrets about what did and didn't happen."

"A myriad of issues clutter our minds while a multitude of emotions accompany our concerns. Sometimes it seems like a merry-go-round. Do you want to share your thoughts about something specific?"

"Not right now."

"God allows things for unknown reasons. *The battle is not yours but God's,* 2 Chronicles 20:15 says. Remember to leave them in His hands!"

"I just can't understand the reason for Angela's death."

"Up in Colorado for Granny's funeral, I tried to find solace but there was none. I'll never forget touching her hand after she died. The warmth was gone—it felt like stone. Then I realized she was never coming back."

Lisa listened in silence.

Holly continued, "You know how I love being in the mountains? This time, the lavender mist at nightfall frightened me. I watched pieces of cliff separate and plunge thousands of feet, shattering on the bottom. One thought gripped me—what will happen to me in the end?"

"At the hospital after Adam's accident, I didn't recognize him. It reminded me of a terrible nightmare that paralyzes you—but you wake up and find it's not real—however mine was. The awful smell reminded me of death and I realized our life *hadn't* turned out the way I expected. For a few days I didn't know if I wanted him to live. Then I recognized the problem was me—I was the one who needed a heart transplant!"

"My focus gets out of sync when I look at me," Lisa said. "I become confused, bewildered, and bitter."

"There are big differences in why people look inward; and variances in attitude regarding what they discover. If you intend to criticize or destroy, stop. If you desire to become more useful, proceed."

"That alters my latest introspection," Lisa revealed. "Sabotaging my own peace, combined with resentment and judgmental demolition toward Jake, serve no purpose but keep me locked in chains. Ironically, my brooding usually follows positive experiences. Maybe I need a warning posted on all self-analysis."

"Sitting in His presence is the best place for that activity—which is essential at times! Don't be afraid of what you find but beware dangers lurking nearby. Distractions take away from our ability to focus so it's vital to set aside time to be still and listen."

"Goes back to spending time with those that matter most," Lisa said.

"Relationships make this world go round and are vital for eternity, as well. That's why Jesus came as a tiny baby, so people would be drawn to him and develop positive connections—even though they didn't know much about him yet. Imagine trying to connect intimately with a stranger who intimidates you? By the time he began his earthly ministry; people had watched him grow and could identify with his humanness."

"I need to get back to my family," Lisa said.

She excused herself from the conversation and joined an exciting football game—minutes before the most exciting play of the afternoon. She plopped on Jake's lap as he pulled her close and rearranged his head to watch. The rush, critical moves, yards, and racing footsteps permeated every ounce of flesh in the stadium and those watching on screens across the country.

Thunderous excitement followed with hugs and kisses turning the event into a family celebration.

"Who's glad Mom joined us?" Jake said.

"I wouldn't have missed this for anything!"

"It's fun to watch guys run without getting tackled," Alex said.

Betsy added, "If the blue guy tripped, the other team would have won."

"Kind of like life," Jake suggested. "Who wants to go outside and play a real game with me?"

* * *

An opportunity to present, *A Christmas Extravaganza ~ Evening of Joy*, at Grace Fellowship became possible because of rave reviews for the Ed Jakate Show. The two night presentation was produced by Jake who remained in control of material inclusion, with Kate appointed as creative director. The event was orchestrated to reveal key changes to his heart and mind that were impossible to address elsewhere.

His entire family would be highlighted.

"Please pray as we offer hope to the hopeless—especially former co-workers," Jake said to Pastor Davis.

Originally, plans included free but mandatory tickets for each performance however Kate believed a minimal donation might make them more desirable. A limited number of complementary passes were available from the church office. Every ticket was spoken for three weeks prior to the December 7th and 8th engagement, so a third presentation was added for the afternoon of December 9th.

Jake mailed tickets to Uncles Josh and David, begging them to bring Grandpa Clark. He gave tickets to the mailman, neighbors, and other professionals he interacted with asking, "Why do you think Jesus came to this world as a little baby?"

As word spread around KMOL, comments were heard about the breaking news. On a whim, Jake asked station crew to volunteer time and talents. To his surprise, several technicians, lighting crew, and cameramen offered their services. Running into Joe Garcia, he questioned his former boss' interest in joining the production.

"Only thing we need is a top-notch director," Jake said.

"For free? You've got to be kidding."

"Trust me—you'll get more that you've ever gotten before," Jake said confidently.

"Hmm … I'll think about that."

Joe turned around a few steps later to say, "Count me in."

A chance encounter with Brianna brought Jake to his knees. "Will you forgive me?" he asked. "I had no right to sabotage what was most important to you."

"You had no idea what was going on," Brianna whispered. "It was Paul's child I aborted."

"Does he know?"

"Yes. I married Paul three years after moving in with him and told him everything. He's forgiven me but still hates you."

Jake gave her two tickets to the show. "Maybe these will help. He's a curious journalist."

"Remember your 25th birthday party at the station?" Jake asked his wife at dinner.

"Who could forget Joe Garcia dressed like a hilarious clown while Paul Esse cut a luscious chocolate cake, with Brianna leaning over his shoulder?" Lisa couldn't stop laughing long enough to hear his response. "Ironically, we all assumed we were bonding closer than ever sharing theories about life, communicating beyond the usual superficial level of conversation."

"Lisa, I long for them to know Him."

"Kind of like a second chance—for all of us."

"In our, *A Christmas Extravaganza ~ Evening of Joy,* they may catch a glimpse of the truth—about Him and discover how He changes lives. I can't imagine a better avenue to tell our story and portray answers to spiritual dilemmas in thought provoking ways. With the personal caring of family relationships, reaching out to friends ..."

"A miracle takes but an instance of God reaching down to people who are in a place to notice His glory."

When patrons entered the foyer of Grace Fellowship, each was handed a sparkling star—representing their own unique self—to hang on a large evergreen tree. As they found seats, Adam began a prelude of Christmas Carols in his deep baritone voice—sitting in a rocking chair on stage, surrounded by family members including Grandpa Clark, Uncle David, Holly, Jake, Lisa, Betsy, and Alex.

"The best way to spread Christmas cheer is to sing loud enough for everyone to hear," Adam said. Most joined him, singing from their hearts. A flickering fireplace with battery powered logs glowed beside a beautifully decorated tree.

Joe Garcia directed unseen while Kate helped coordinate live action.

ACT 1 ~ Carpenters scattered around the stage attempting to build meaningful projects out of wood: a treasure chest, bed, ladder, log cabin, raft, cross. Family members discussed, "Which is more essential?" The actors interacted, giving convincing arguments for their ventures. Several were former co-workers of Jake.

Party horns and confetti added to the frivolity.

"There's absolutely no reason to build a cross!" Grandpa Clark said gruffly.

ACT II ~ "Can you imagine Christmas without a nativity scene?" Holly asked Adam. "I always assumed placing a newborn in the manger represented a symbolic family unit—important for bonding over the holidays."

"Christmas seems more cheerful with a child," Lisa agreed.

"When Granny died, I looked at a basket of her old cards while I was grieving. After years of wondering, it began to make sense to me. The baby Jesus suddenly acquired new significance," Holly said.

She passed Christmas cards around the circle. Some were read.

"A sovereign Almighty knew dark hearts would reject forming a relationship with anyone but an innocent baby," she said.

"Only a simple manger would suffice. Suspicious, critical, evil natures would surely have revolted had Jesus been privy to a palace with pretentious provisions," Adam said. He began to sing. "Away in a manger ..."

ACT III ~ The third act included a vocal performance by Jake and Lisa. It started with a dark stage; one single light on the couple.

"Remember at the beginning of our courtship Jake, when I learned about a redeemer who died for me? Was that just an intellectual decision? I obviously was more concerned about spending time with you, than him."

"Perhaps you had an imaginary devotion to a supreme being you knew nothing about?"

Lisa began singing. "How do you act in secret when no one but God can see? When afternoon comes, how much time do you spend on your knees? If He is so important ... why did I spend no time ... I must have assumed the relationship was all about me."

Jake took the microphone. "We're living in uncertain times ... unaware how fragile life can be ... one glimpse of a carpenter wasn't enough to keep me on my knees," he sang. "Selfishness and pride ... took us on a thrilling roller coaster ride ..."

Lisa joined in. "Turn around; you've gone too far ... He listens when we cry out."

Together they sang, "Is your burden heavy as you bear it all alone ... Does the road seem weary with its trials and despair ..."

The light dimmed.

"When dark nights overcome your focus; just look up!" they sang together, as lights came on slowly. "You don't have to wonder why; a sunrise will break through ..."

Shimmers of white lights over the audience resembled snowflakes—while the falling laser light rays on stage increased the intensity. Lisa was dressed in a sapphire velvet gown embedded with rhinestones that sparkled like stars. Jake's sapphire tux matched his wife—minus the bling.

"Come sing with me ..." Lisa sang.

"We were made unique by an awesome creator ... for moments of destiny we never imagined," they sang. "We don't have to wonder why. Just look up!"

"Your song fills my heart with joy many don't know ... From within you gave a new sense of hope," Lisa sang.

"Only a Savior could remove shame from the night ... provide correction, direction, and then give delight," Jake added.

"We don't have to wonder why. Just look up!"

Jake stopped singing to make a comment. "I need to publicly apologize to several former co-workers—thanks for giving me this chance to share—and I ask you to consider my story. Only when we spend time alone with God can He reveal unbecoming character traits and make changes in our thought process."

"I would love to tell you what I think of Jesus ..." he began singing. "I will tell you how He changed my life completely ..."

Lisa joined in on the chorus.

They ended by singing, "It only takes a spark, to get a fire going ..." as family members took their original places.

ACT IV ~ The final family scene had family members passing a candle around the circle, lighting their own.

Adam sang, "The Lord loaned us an angel to come live with us below; and when He said, I want her back, we had to let her go ..."

When his father finished, Jake thanked God for the precious two-year-old who deeply impacted many lives. He continued. "Another sweet baby with adoring parents and few followers came to this earth and also died much too early. Jesus is proudly portrayed in a manger every Christmas, though few realize the significance of his birth. Angela is celebrating with Him right now."

"How did a tiny little baby get to be in charge? He offered His life on a cross so we could rejoice someday."

Candy canes were passed in baskets with big red bows as everyone sat speechless. Attached was a tiny note that told the Christmas Story. "These sugary treats are mementos of the stripes He bore and the blood He shed because He loves us very much. The J symbolizes that only one person was perfect enough to offer this gift."

"Don't ignore Him like I did—your life will be meaningless on earth, and you won't make it to heaven without His gift of redemption. My prayer is that you will come to know Him and develop an intimate relationship over the coming years. Your life will be as dramatically changed as Lisa and mine have."

"Studies show that attending church and spiritual involvement impact brain structure and enhances our well-being," Lisa said. "We hope this evening not only entertained but opened a window into your soul."

"As you begin another New Year, a clean heart is a great beginning! Start the cleaning out process right now in your own heart."

"Thanks for coming!"

"We'll stay for a few minutes, if you want to talk or have questions," Jake said.

A rush of activity followed with Phil Davis and several church members talking to the guests. Several kneeled by chairs. Adam listened with great interest to his father; as Holly described her relationship to a wonderful savior with his brother David.

Brianna sobbed in the back, eventually making her way forward while clinging to five-year-old daughter Meredith. Paul Garcia greeted them at the front. A cameraman and two stage helpers joined the group. Tears flowed as Jake and Lisa sat down to talk with them privately.

"If I knew then what I know now, I'd have done lots of things much differently."

"Everybody says that," Joe said.

"But I mean it! Time won't wait anymore," Jake said.

He talked about the importance of breaking news all of them had witnessed and how one incident can impact a life forever. "Eternity is at stake. Wise men sought baby Jesus and sensible people still seek Him today. How smart are you really? How long will you ignore and reject Him? Why? It's not a game of chance we're playing. We all make choices and this is the most important one you'll ever make."

Jake had the privilege of praying with several friends he previously had carelessly disregarded—watching the biggest miracle of all take place.

On Sunday afternoon, Mike Hintz and Paul Esse sat through the performance.

Time would tell.

Chapter 22
Memories

ADAM WAS SOUND ASLEEP as he dreamed about his beloved home.

The salty air pierced his nostrils wading in the California surf. His thoughts were far away and he begged God for words to say. His brother Josh was receptive to hearing about spiritual things but David closed up tight with any mention of God. A smelly fish floated up on the sand and he stepped over it.

What better way to love people than to effectively listen to their plight.

Josh's bitter divorce resulted in chaos arranging visits with his children, so he hadn't seen them recently. "That's not the worst of my woes. My job is eating me alive! How I get up and go every morning is a miracle. You'd think the fires would burn themselves out but they just keep smoldering and relight into bigger bonfires."

"Sounds like women I know," David said, joining in. "They look so sweet in the beginning—then play us for fools. I'm ready to dump Sally if she doesn't change her ways. She's starting to annoy me."

"So how did you figure it out Adam? I know you were miserable for a while."

"You can learn more about human nature by reading the Bible than by living in New York City," Adam said. The tone of the conversation changed as Josh leaned closer, carefully listening to his words. He was able to tell about frustrations, his brush with death, and answers that are so obvious most people miss them.

"God not only desires for us to know him but to believe him," Adam quoted from Isaiah 43:10.

He stretched, rubbed his eyes, and reached for his wife …

Holly woke earlier and was fixing a special breakfast. Jake and Lisa were coming to celebrate Angela's 16th birthday—before Grandpa Clark and Uncle David headed back to California. Cinnamon rolls piled high on a tray looked like a birthday cake. Sixteen candles were scattered on the top.

Her brief life was responsible for two more family member's names being written in the Book of Life. The entire family had much to be thankful … celebrating Angie was just one part.

The weekend had been a huge success!

Holly remembered back to Granny's legacy.

She loved Grandma Armstrong dearly—and was inspired by her character and example. Granny cheered her when she was discouraged. If Holly had a problem or decision to make, her grandma said, "I'll pray for you." Granny taught her about life using positive words. Those lessons and examples influenced her granddaughter, who was unaware of their significance at the time.

"One of these days I'm going to take a wonderful vacation," Granny once said. Everyone laughed and thought she was teasing but Granny smiled and replied, "My best friend wants to spend more time with me."

She knew Him personally! Holly thought, rejoicing.

Granny's voice echoed in her ear.

> "Always leave the porch light on!" Granny used to say.
> "Twill light the path if one goes by … and welcome those who stay."

"Halleluiah!" Holly said clapping her hands. "I know what the saying means." She determined to live like Granny—full of life but with an emphasis on spiritual truths.

Holly pulled out her sewing basket.

At Christmas time, Granny strung popcorn and cranberries on trees out back. She also hung chunks of fruit and nuts. "We can't forget the birds and squirrels. It's a special holiday for everyone," she said. Sometimes Holly and her cousins helped thread the treats. Birds seemed to notice the love and flocked to Granny's yard. These acts of kindness touched Holly and made her feel valuable.

"I'm fortunate to have met Granny," Lisa said. "Knowing her enables me to share personal details with my children ... about their great, great-grandmother. That's pretty awesome! I had no idea how powerful it was when I was a child. She left a priceless heritage for her granddaughter—and all of us who have come after her."

"Let's jump rope outside and celebrate Granny when we finish decorating for the birds," Jake said.

"Hooray!" Alex said; Pampa was in agreement.

*   *   *

With plans for a Christmas wedding taking shape in the Dominican Republic, the entire family flew south to join Abby and Ben for an informal ceremony on a secluded beach. Everyone brought two cans of meat, a can of fruit, a cake mix, wet wipes, and specific paper products.

They slept in a local church on mats.

Jake spotted a tarantula the first evening. "He won't hurt you! He just wants to scare you with his beady eyes," he told Lisa who snuggled closer. He caught the spider in a jar the second day ... at his wife's insistence.

A fishing contest, with nets, provided food for the hungry tourists. Alex was excited to catch one while Betsy preferred talking with Mimi and Aunt Abby back at the mission headquarters.

For Abby's 13th birthday, she had received a pine box—with little hearts carved on the front—filled with art supplies. She also received a Bible with *Abigail Susan Clark* inscribed in gold, on the cover. Inside was a note. "Delight yourself in the Lord and He will give you the desires of your heart." (Psalm 37:4 NIV)

Abby showed these to Betsy. She also shared a note her mother had written when she went to camp.

Dear Precious Abby,

I miss you already! The house is lonely with you gone and I can't wait for you to return. I have a special place saved just for you. As I pass your picture on the wall, I think of the treasure God gave me when my sweet baby Abby was born. You give me great joy—even if I don't express it. No matter how far away you are, I'll keep memories of you close to my heart! I love you more than you will ever know.

♥ *Mom*

"Remember the first boy you kissed down by the lake?" Holly asked her daughter. "You were excited for me to meet him and give my approval."

"I kiss a cuter boy now," Abby said smiling.

"My father won't let me kiss boys anymore," Betsy said very seriously.

"Someday you'll be glad you waited."

"There won't be any boys left."

"Sure there will. Just look at handsome Ben. We didn't meet until we were over thirty. Some of my friends back home married early and are already divorced. They're miserable about their bad choices."

"Spend time doing something more beneficial than looking for a boyfriend," her grandmother suggested.

"I learned about stars from my mom," Aunt Abby said to Betsy.

"Will you show me tonight?"

"Sure." Aunt Abby promised.

"And will you teach me to paint?" Betsy asked her grandmother, changing topics in the conversation.

"Of course—I didn't know you were interested," Mimi said. Getting out her art supplies was a special privilege for Holly. "Do you know why the sky is blue?" she asked her granddaughter.

Abby smiled.

"The earth's atmosphere absorbs color and the sun's rays scatter it. Blue spreads out the easiest," Holly answered. "And rainbows are made when drops of water in the air act like prisms and separate into colors—instead of just blue."

"Is red on the outside or inside?" Betsy asked.

"Red is on the outside and violet on the inside. If a second rainbow forms above the first, the colors are reversed," Holly explained. "We can even make our own rainbows when we get back home."

"How can we do that?"

"It's a surprise that I'll save for my precious granddaughter's birthday in January."

"I love doing stuff with you," Betsy said.

Abby agreed.

After a gorgeous sunset, Aunt Abby said to her niece, "Look over there. Do you see the hunter holding a bow? That is Orion."

"Wow," Betsy said.

"Do you see his right hand above his head? That is Betelgeuse—it's easy to spot because it is red," Abby explained.

"You're a real astronomer!" Lisa said, quite impressed.

Ben was also impressed.

He lit a bonfire on the beach where they talked long into the night.

An afternoon Christmas Eve ceremony brought natives, missionaries, and family members together. Ben's family arrived from Maine. His father was a minister who performed the rituals. Dress code required no sleeveless shirts. The females wore culottes or skirts. Men wore white shirts with ties and long pants.

Accompanied by her father, Abby looked radiant in a long ruffled sundress with short sleeves; a flowered wreath on her long golden hair reflected joy on her face. Her white sandals stepped over yellow rose petals—dropped by Lisa in a yellow sundress with a short white jacket who preceded her down the path.

In front of garland posts, Adam and Holly kissed their daughter's checks simultaneously just before Ben reached for her hand.

"Benjamin and Abigail ... Start measuring success by small victories in secret choices you make. Smile instead of frowning when a situation becomes frustrating. Forgive an offense while a breeze is still blowing through the window. Give your spouse a free get-out-of–jail-card rather than jump to conclusions over an escalating issue. No matter what the circumstance, respond with optimism instead of despair. These simple keys will result in our celebrating together on your 25th anniversary ... twenty-five years from today."

After hearing Ben and Abby make promises to each other, before God and witnesses, Jake and Lisa sang *To God be the Glory* and Adam sang *Household of Faith*.

The ocean sparkled.

An informal reception offered savory meat stew followed by delicious yellow wedding cake, covered with tropical fruit—all served in paper bowls and on small paper plates decorated with festive flowers—with clear plastic utensils. A mango, pineapple, pear juice concocted by Ben was the wedding drink.

"A unique feast, if I've ever tasted one," Jake said.

The couple enjoyed a special blessing prayer before leaving.

"May your New Year be filled with joy and laughter," Ben said. "We ought to be the most joyful people on earth, celebrating every day."

Colorful trays with small pieces of wood wrapped in exquisite foil tied with gorgeous metallic ribbon—never to be unwrapped but set aside in a visible spot—were presented to guests as mementos of the occasion. "The beauty of this *permanent present* should spark the interest of your friends," Abby explained. "Out of curiosity, they will want to know who it's for and ask questions. You can talk about God's gift to us; or your gift to God; or you can come up with a million other newsworthy things to talk about."

"I love it!" Betsy said. "I want to have a good life like Aunt Abby."

"I want to be like my father," Alex said proudly.

Jake winked at him.

Dancing on the beach continued until sunset.

Layers of pink, mauve, violet, and sapphire twirled in the sky illuminating the clouds. Mixed in were streaks of lingering sun glittering like gold, spreading across the horizon. A glorious sunset, hearts full of love, and memories to last a lifetime filled their beings.

"*Many, O LORD my God, are the wonders you have done. The things you planned for us no one can recount to you; were I to speak and tell of them, they would be too many to declare,*" Adam quoted from Psalms 40:5 to the remaining wedding guests who celebrated Christmas Eve together.

He broke into a much loved song.

"Oh Lord my God, when I in awesome wonder … consider all the worlds thy hands have made … I see the stars … thy power throughout the universe displayed ... Then sings my soul, my savior God to thee ... How great though art!"

Others joined him.

"I almost can't contain it all," Jake said, his spirit bursting with joy.

"You're a living mystery as a believer" Adam said. "He wants to use you to the maximum of your potential—to bring Himself glory. It's not about us at all, though it involves our cooperation. When we come to know Him personally, it's the beginning of a brand new life, one we never dreamed possible. Believers begin a walk of faith that takes us lots of different places and into sometimes difficult situations—but it's the most exciting life we can live."

"Life wouldn't make sense if God didn't exist," Lisa said.

"That's so true," Jake said. "Jesus came to earth during a time when relationships were significant. Men walked together on journeys. Women gathered around wells daily to get water. Peter was fishing with his brother when he met the carpenter."

"Interesting group Jesus called to be his disciples—fishermen, a tax collector, ordinary men who dramatically impacted the world," Adam said.

"I learned about spiritual things from my grandmother who likened life to seeds in a garden," Holly said.

Adam's face brightened. "Long ago people were smarter because they learned from cherished family members and valued experiences of kinfolk instead of struggling through difficulties alone. When was the last time someone asked their mother or grandmother for critical advice? It's much easier to ask a co-worker or Google an answer. In the process, they under-value those they should cherish most and end up making foolish decisions."

"Wish I'd listened to both of my parents more—as a child and an adult," Jake said.

"I value my mother-in-law's insight," Lisa said about Holly. "Guess I'm rare. Unfortunately, I failed to glean more when it could have made a huge difference in my days. Thanks for always being there for me, though. You've taught me a lot."

Granny's voice echoed in Holly's ear.

"Always leave the porch light on! Granny used to say. Twill light the path if one goes by ... and welcome those who stay." Adam winked at Holly as he reached for her hand. They had the rest of their lives to enjoy each other and impact others.

No one would forget that celebration around a fire, on the beach of a tropical island. What a Christmas to remember!

They lingered past midnight watching stars.

"It's amazing how He clothed the sky with majesty—yet performed a bigger miracle deep in my heart," Jake said.

Leaving everything from their suitcases behind in the Dominican Republic—except for basic clothes on their bodies and a precious memento from the wedding celebration—Abby's family returned home. The abandoned items would be used to help people Ben and Abby interacted with on the island. Monetary wedding gifts were placed in a fund for their ministry.

*   *   *

Holly carefully placed photos into an album—lingering over each pose.

The past filled with adventure, a new focus on the present, with hope for an inevitable future and whatever that might include, all remained in God's hands.

"Live every day as if it is your last. One day you'll be right," Adam said.

"It's ironic how some of the bleakest moments we encounter actually turn into the most cherished and brilliantly colored tapestries hanging on our walls," Lisa said. "Looking back, we would never part with any of them! Too bad we missed extra joy from the beginning—if we had just been more thankful."

"You are living proof God can turn the most painful experiences into examples of glorious hope and joy," Holly said to her daughter-in-law. "I'm eager to watch as you continue writing masterpieces but first let me get my dancing shoes on. The world is going to be dazzled by His plans for you."

Lisa and Jake decided to help their children make a book of memories for the best grandmother ever. It included: "My first memory of grandmother … something important Grandma taught me … I'm most like my grandma in the way I … A special time I spent with Grandma … The thing I like most about my grandma … One thing Grandma told me about her life that was special" … with a note to Mimi telling her what she meant personally to each of her grandchildren. Pictures revealed special views about poignant moments.

The memory book included a special thank-you from Holly's first grandchild, Angela Marie Clark—and a note from Jesus about how much fun they were having together.

Chapter 23
Lighthouse

A QUAINT STONE PATH led solemnly past wild rose bushes, disheveled pines, and poison ivy to a rocky shoreline where the stately lighthouse hovered. Even from a distance, dirty windows desperately needed attention from a caretaker—the last vacated these premises years before in a search for a brighter future. His services were no longer necessary with a new GPS system in use.

Jake reached for Lisa's hand—only momentarily. His shoe stuck between dislodged stones, as prickly undergrowth pulled him down to their level. He landed with a plop on a damaged trivet where fencing formerly enhanced the lighthouse property.

Lisa helped him stand up.

He picked up the silver canister and trudged forward.

A gnarled welcome sign stood proudly at attention.

HIGHPOINT LIGHTHOUSE
Oceanview, California
1873

Broken steps to the entry door guarded the historic treasure. Jake noticed a frayed ladder still attached to the base, down by the rocky foundation. An antique rowboat with two oars securely in place knocked against a nearby pier.

"Wanna go for a ride?" he asked Lisa.

She chuckled.

A turtle crawled across the rotted bottom, happy to remain undisturbed in the sunshine.

Jake thought about Francie taking off in his dinghy, *the Intrepid*. At first it seemed a terrible thing and anger consumed him—but someone was watching out for his foolishness and had much better plans.

To think he almost lost Lisa brought him to tears.

"Let's sit here for a minute," Jake said, getting comfortable on a bench. He pulled Lisa closer as they watched waves lap at the rocky shore. A seagull flew overhead waiting for a fresh taste of seafood. Squirrels quarreled in the brush, darting after each other. A tiny forgotten garden in the corner held a glimpse of red.

"Is it a flower?" Lisa asked.

"I'm glad he's in heaven," Jake finally said. "This is just the remains Grandpa left for us to dispose of."

"Too bad your grandmother never knew the truth … and my parents … though we can never know for certain what happened between them and God on their deathbed. Time will tell."

"I didn't realize the significance of sharing my faith, or the graveness of not sharing. Sure wish I could re-do some things. I have a bunch of people I still need to reconnect with before it's too late. Funerals aren't the place to ask difficult questions—but come to think of it, maybe they are. You know what I mean," he said.

"We still have each other, two wonderful children, and an increasingly intimate relationship with our Savior. Those are the most important treasures for me."

"I live with guilt over the unnecessary pain I added to your life, Lise. I should have been a safe place for you to grieve, offering love and comfort. Instead, I destroyed trust and your emotional well-being. You missed so much you should have enjoyed."

"You're the one who needs to learn true forgiveness!"

She ticked him and brushed his tears away. "If you can catch me before I get to that rowboat, you can chose the next cruise we'll take. Otherwise, I'm going to start paddling."

"You're not going anywhere," he said pulling her closer, before she could get two feet away. "We have a ceremony to perform."

They stood on a cliff his Grandpa Clark loved to watch the ocean from and scattered his ashes into the sea. "He's with you now Jesus, and celebrating with our precious Angela."

"Have fun, together!" Lisa said.

Final glimpses of the top of the isolated lighthouse—with it beacon that offered hope to numerous vessels traveling in the darkness—would be their focus for the future. It pointed to heaven. Obviously, the light inside didn't originate from the novel structure. Another source provided its powerful illumination when the electricity was switched on.

"Notice the rocky foundation," Lisa said. "Even a lighthouse can be stable on solid but precarious ground. Imagine what would have happened during storms if this had been built on a sandy beach?"

"See the different levels all the way to the top?" Jake said. "Each has a window but you sure don't see much from the bottom. As you move higher, the view gets better and better."

"We just need to keep the windows clean so hope can shine out."

$*$ $*$ $*$

The stunning stained glass windows in the lobby of Grace Fellowship captured many eyes, and conversations—sunshine radiating through rich hues with extraordinary delight. A twist of blue and green sparkled from the corner. *Where did that little lamb come from?* Lisa asked one day, after enjoying the colorful masterpiece for years.

She'd never noticed him before.

Just like other significant truths that lay secret in her Bible during their earliest years of marriage.

"Is your life wrapped up like a big present—yourself!!!?" Rev. Davis asked that same Sunday. "Are me, myself, and I your favorite friends? We're not being dishonest or unethical when we think about ourselves with no need for God's help. It comes naturally. We're important and need to consider what we say, do, how we respond to personal circumstances. But that's not where it should end. What do you refuse to let go of—have a death grip on? What we hold tightly, we sometimes lose. What becomes more significant than the Almighty God is an idol. Brokenness is sometimes necessary to remove those idols."

Speaking to the congregation offered an opportunity to humbly look at the past and remember the pain Jake and Lisa once considered too terrible to discuss with anyone. "Changed lives bring new challenges but sharing is essential for every believer," Jake told the minister. He agreed to let them tell their story.

"Charming Jake and dependable Lisa wanted to inspire the world," Pastor Phil Davis said in his greeting. "But in a shocking twist, they lost precious Angela and experienced unimaginable heartbreak … before sovereign circumstances transformed their willing hearts into a lighthouse of hope."

The churchgoers listened intently.

Jake placed his mother's fancy gold-gilded mirror with filigreed ribbon wrapped around the edges, a red bow in the corner—representing a present—on an easel beside the couple as they took their places on the platform.

Lisa's emerald dress represented growth that had taken place in her life over the past fifteen years. Her eyes sparkled as she tenderly clung to her husband's arm.

He kissed her on the lips.

"Every time we look at our own image, we should see how God looks at us—a delightful gift," Jake said. "Psalm 139:16 says, *You saw me before I was born. Every day of my life was recorded in your book. Every moment was laid out before a single day had passed.*"

Jake continued. "Meeting Jesus personally is the first step in our quest for eternal security. Learning to walk intimately with our Savior is more difficult. Unfortunately, Lisa and I held on to hurts—refusing to let go of our painful tragedy—and failed to cling to the only one who could make a difference. We both made mistakes but dark always precedes dawn in a glorious sunrise."

"Ephesians 3: 20 says, *Now all glory to God, who is able, through his mighty power at work within us, to accomplish infinitely more than we might ask or think.*"

Lisa leaned forward to speak. "We had so much sorrow for one brief moment that we almost drowned in our personal oceans," Lisa said. "Finally our pain has changed into a reason to celebrate—and to think God was there every minute, first weeping and now cheering! Most people are guided by feelings but that's like a ship sailing against the wind. We face obstacles, trials, and temptations but God wants us to persevere in overcoming our hardships. Biblical principles do nothing unless you apply them to your daily living. Transforming us into His image involves inopportune situations and unlikely people to do unique things—He works in ways we never expected."

Jake asked, "Who looks to you for encouragement?"

"Our relatives, friends, and acquaintances are seeking a thrilling new flavor in their lives," he said. "How can we be salt and light for them? Don't let the world squeeze you into its mold. Connect with those He brings into your path. We can't do it alone and shouldn't live isolated lives. Lisa heard about Samaritan's Purse pursuing a powerful ministry around the world. No doubt you've heard about their shoeboxes."

"Nothing my meager contribution can do," she said.

"So I told her the story of the guy making a difference for one starfish on the beach. Made a difference to that one!"

Jake offered a challenge.

"We should all be mentoring in some way: as creators, strategizers, problem-solvers, analyzers, organizers, motivators, mobilizers, managers, specializers, inspectors, evaluators, and relators—people who love others. Every believer should be involved in a local church within six months. What's on your bucket list? Is there something more He wants you to do? How can you think outside the box? Do you give with all your heart? What do you have to lose? Get off the couch and out of your comfort zone. When someone says, 'I don't have time for that!' they're really saying, 'That's not high enough on my to-do list.' You need to rethink your priorities."

"We work best on teams. Teammates are an invaluable commodity and enhance our power. When you give your energy, enthusiasm, and dedication to church ministries, imagine what might happen to our church?"

"A bunch of guys named Bill reached pinnacles of success over the past century. Regardless of your name, what legacy are you leaving? Who will win trophies for hustle, heart, teamwork awards at the spring banquet?"

Lisa said. "Our beautiful *Welcome Friends* tapestry in the foyer extends hope to those who read the motto. My desire is to make that more of a reality for everyone who comes into our church."

She continued sharing from her heart.

"God doesn't exist to make me look important but I exist to make a big deal of Him. We'll give an account of what we've done on earth someday. Few females actually do much personal interacting. We attend events like Christmas Coffees, or a Mother's Day Tea, but do we care about others in tangible ways? The world uses people and loves things; we need to do the opposite. God met our personal needs for a deep relationship and we need to offer something to others who yearn for a personal connection."

"Hospitality is essential in godly homes," Jake said, "so Lisa and I are beginning a new focus of monthly *Tables of Eight*. Anyone who wants to be involved can sign up. It will involve minimal preparation, potluck style—one entrée, one side, one dessert—with eight adults assigned to each specific group per quarter. We're rotate homes. Hopefully, you'll connect personally with four small groups each year."

"If we'd been involved in such a venture fifteen years ago," Lisa said, "I doubt we could have concealed our brokenness and likely would never have strayed so far away from God. Compassion and caring should begin in homes of believers—where transparency can uncover concerns and prayer can permeate the circumstances we face. Angela will be honored to have this ministry take place in her memory."

"What has happened in your circumstances recently?" Jake asked. "There's no problem too big, no relationship so broken, no need too great for our great mediator to solve. Reach out to Him! Your children are watching everything you do."

"Dad, can I talk to you?" Betsy said after lunch.

"Do you want to go somewhere alone?"

They went to a nearby park with a picturesque lookout. The sun was high in the sky.

"My friends had a party last week and someone brought alcohol. It turned into a mess, with the police called after a neighbor found a teenager tripping over his grass. Supposedly the parents were home but unaware what was happening downstairs. The dad swore he checked several times. Anyway, accusations were made and now everyone who went is taking sides. It's a mess. I'm glad I was sick and couldn't go."

"These situations occur often in life," Jake said. "We're foolish when we sit by passively and wonder what went wrong."

"I don't want to screw up my life like you did, Dad."

"That would be a bigger tragedy than you can imagine, Betsy."

"What should I do to make sure it doesn't happen?"

"Great question. Wish I'd been as smart as you when I was a teenager." Jake explained how fragile life is, as best as he could, and shared from his heart about some of his personal foolish mistakes. "Have you seen a snake handler who believes he's exempt from being effected by poisonous reptiles? He charms observers with his prowess but he doesn't fool the snake. Except maybe the baby rattlesnake that just slipped out of his cage. Oops! Where'd he go?"

"I would run," Betsy said.

"That should bring me to my knees."

Jake explained the truth he ignored in his quest for happiness. "Spending time with Jesus is the only answer. It sounds simple but what a difference it makes for the future."

"Dad, what if I move down with Abby when I graduate from high school? I would like to help make a good life for the children that no one cares about. You'll always have Alex up here."

"Choices are significant but talk to Him about His purpose for creating you. Keep your dreams alive until He gives you something better. He can't replace what we grasp in our arms until we're willing to give that up for His best. You're a really special girl, Betsy. I know we'll be proud of you if you please the only one who matters. Right now, I believe He plans to use you with a bunch of foolish teenagers. You can help them discover destinies they've never considered. While you're at it, inspire them to climb to new heights."

"Thanks, Dad. I'm glad you're back into our lives! We really need you."

"Let's have a real party next week to celebrate your 15th birthday. We can have a shindig over at Pampa and Mimi's. I'll even teach your friends to line dance in the barn. We'll end with a campfire and talk about eternity."

Betsy couldn't wait to get home and start inviting friends.

Lisa found the treasured name plate, with *Jake and Lisa Clark* etched on wood, and mounted it to the front door before Jake returned. It offered a cheerful welcome, unfolding a magnificent story. At times it had brought intense pain, hidden in the bottom of Jake's empty drawer.

Other days, she gleaned strength remembering her sacred wedding promise and the possibility of eventually reclaiming a relationship God would never allow to be sabotaged.

Jake rushed in with a huge smile.

"I remember the day when we heard the knock on our door," he said. "There was no sender's name on the box."

"You were pulling flaps open so fast, the $100's had nowhere to go but jump out."

"The most important surprise was on the bottom." Jake said.

"I didn't think you even noticed."

"Oh, but I did! It pierced my heart over and over the following year—how things were supposed to be. Why do you think I ran?"

"Who do you think it was from?"

"Dad told me when he came up to Seattle to confront me. They believed in us and trusted God to do mighty things in our marriage, in spite of my foolishness. They never stopped pleading with Him for a miracle."

"That's so sweet! I didn't know."

"Our home has been impacted by actions of my godly parents," Jake said. "We need to do the same for our children, and for others God brings into our lives. Angela's tragedy opened the windows of heaven for us."

"Hey Jake, I forgot to show you these new cards I made for guests." She reached for an imprinted business card from a silver holder on the foyer table. "What do you think? It was your mother's idea."

Come to Me, all of you who are weary and burdened, and I will give you rest. Take up My yoke and learn from Me, because I am gentle and humble in heart, and you will find rest for yourselves. For My yoke is easy and My burden is light. Matt. 11:28-30

"Those words speak volumes," he said.

Running her fingers over the rim of a goblet at dinner, music played in Lisa's soul. She cupped her hand in a heart over her plate. What was that verse about finding fullness of joy in his presence?

"When it looked like we were gonna lose it all, who knew?" Jake said. "Walking away didn't make sense but that has become even more illogical now that I understand."

"Most men don't relate to heart things but use thinking and logic to explain everything. Never once does it enter your thoughts, 'How does this make me feel?' Women center on the feeling part—maybe not using their brain so much," she joked.

"In reality, you were the one using intellect most of the time, trying to protect me from not guarding my heart." He stretched his foot under the table to stroke her calf. "We can continue this conversation when the kids are asleep."

He winked.

Jake spent quality time in the back yard playing soccer with his energetic son Alex; while Lisa baked assorted treats and cleaned the kitchen with help from their beautiful daughter Betsy. The house was filled with enticing aromas—which joined the sounds of grateful hearts laughing and singing.

They had been blessed beyond measure despite the wasted years but even what locusts had eaten could be reclaimed by a mighty Savior.

As moonlight settled over the house, flickering shadows in the window mimicked the shimmering red candles burning on the dresser. Jake pressed his lips against Lisa's as he pulled her closer. His hand stroked her chestnut hair, moving slowly to caress her neck. Giving her shivers, his hands swayed back and forth on her back—hesitating from time to time as they moved slowly to her waist. They leaned back on the bed.

"Wait!" he said, sitting up abruptly.

He reached under the bed for a bottle of *Simple Pleasures* Peppermint Lotion he bought at the store. "Building a strong marriage is my first act of worship from now on," he said. "I can never please God without cherishing the best gift He's ever given me. And I don't want my treasured wife to spend another day wondering about my love. You're the only female I want, Lise. You're the only woman I've ever needed … and God has graciously given you back to me. I'll spend the rest of my life taking care of you. Only then can we both serve Him effectively."

Jake opened the lotion and tenderly smoothed it over his wife's feet. His hands moved up her calves, then thighs, before moistening a trembling torso with her favorite scent.

"This takes the grand prize for a reason to celebrate!!!" Lisa said smiling.

Reading Group Guide

Discussion questions

1. What makes you feel loved? How do you demonstrate love to others? What happens when someone inflicts pain on you or turns against you?

2. What inspires you and gives you hope? Do you have a special place to reflect on the good things in your life?

3. Our lives are filled with people. Which individuals offer love, humor, and support to you? Who needs your encouragement?

4. What painful memories are you trying to repress? Why? Is it true time heals all wounds?

5. How can pursuing our goals prevent us from accomplishing meaningful interactions with those we care about most? Can both be done simultaneously? When you're fifty years old what will matter in your life? When you're eighty-five?

6. Why did Jesus come to the earth as a baby? What did growing up as a human include for this carpenter's son? What would be the benefits of knowing Him now ~ versus having known Him personally while He was on earth?

7. What do atheists offer in terms of hope? They are quick to point out faults in religion—but what solutions do they suggest, to attain meaningful change in a person's life?

8. What does the following quote mean? "Always leave the porch light on!" Granny used to say. "Twill light the path if one goes by and welcome those who stay."

9. Is the individual you see in a mirror, the same person your Creator sees? He loves you too much to allow you to stay exactly as you are right now. What does Jeremiah 29:11 mean to you?

10. Have you ever considered making a radical change in your thinking? Why? How does the dictionary define redemption? Transformation?

About The Author

A TAYLOR UNIVERSITY GRADUATE, Cindy Jean Wilson married her sweetheart and birthed four children—who she writes occasional "Sugar Cookies" for—with nine precious grandchildren. An enthusiastic storyteller, oil painter, and scuba diver, she enjoys watching majestic sunrises and sunsets as the heavens display the glory of an awesome Creator. Seeing His masterpieces in a darkened robe of space can never compare to Jesus satisfying the deepest longings of her heart. Her experiences include owning a Bed & Breakfast, wedding coordinator, teacher for Gifted & Talented (IA) & Soaring High (TX), and a devotional writer at saworship.com. She lives with her husband in the Washington DC area. Her first inspirational novel, Here's An Apple Sweet Adam, is available from WestBow Press.

"Once in a while I sneak away to a secluded cottage in the woods, where serenity in nature soothes my spirit, as stories crowd my head and burst on paper when I write. Singing birds, frisky squirrel, curious fox, leaping deer, and moments with my charming husband - enable extrovert tendencies to flourish. My current passion is painting pictures with words."

Here's An Apple, Sweet Adam is the intriguing story about Jake Clark's parents. They are an ambitious couple who dives into marriage, eager to attain happiness at any cost. This charming duo expends energy chasing idealistic dreams only to encounter disillusionment. Innovative Holly craves unattainable goals and entices her husband with an offer—unaware insurmountable personal problems and dreaded failure will result. Spectacular glimpses of majestic creation offer clues but hopelessness steals contentment they feel entitled. As the once-storybook romance sours, their promising relationship disintegrates. After Adam suffers life-threatening injuries, desperation brings them face-to-face with the Creator. Holly discovers answers that satisfy and shares her dramatic change-of-heart with receptive family and friends. Finally at peace, the Clark family pursues joy and meaning they never believed possible.